Shades of Witches

Witches of New York
Book 5

KIM RICHARDSON

KR PUBLISHING

This book is a work of fiction. Any references to historical events, real people, or real locales are used fictitiously. Other names, characters, places, and incidents are the product of the author's imagination, and any resemblance to actual events, locales, or persons, living or dead, is entirely coincidental.

Shades of Witches, Witches of New York, Book Five
Copyright © 2023 by Kim Richardson
Cover designer: Karen Dimmick/ ArcaneCovers.com
All rights reserved, including the right of reproduction
in whole or in any form.

www.kimrichardsonbooks.com

Shades of Witches

Witches of New York
Book 5

KIM RICHARDSON

KR PUBLISHING

CHAPTER 1

"Can I help you?"

"Huh?" I looked up, way up, into the face of an extraordinary woman. She was the tallest, largest woman I'd ever seen. Well, if you counted Catelyn in her giantess form, she was a close second. This woman looked like she might have some giantess ancestry in her as well. She had to be at least seven feet tall, if not taller.

Her long, black hair hovered at her waist, tied into a braid. She wore black cargo pants tucked into boots and a black shirt. Something about her hinted at an Asian heritage, although I couldn't be sure.

"Wow. You're big—I mean, large—sorry, I meant to say that you're not what I was expecting." By her terrifying frown, I gathered she didn't appreciate my verbal diarrhea. But in my defense, she did kind of throw me off for a moment.

I'd been so deep in thought on my way here, reflecting on my meeting with Freida only half an hour ago, that when this generous female opened the door, I had to blink a few times to ensure I wasn't hallucinating. I barely remembered getting into a cab and riding all the way here. Freida's appearance was still fresh as I replayed the events in my head. Disturbingly fresh.

The vampiress had been waiting for us as if she knew Shay attended Fantasia Academy. Or maybe she just wanted me to see her, for me to know that she knew about Shay and where to find her. Either way, the vampiress knew Shay went to that school. Although she might not be able to get in, she could still grab Shay the moment she stepped out.

Fear slid into the corners of my mind at how she'd been staring at me, like I wasn't a threat, like I was an easy obstacle to remove so she could get her bloodsucking hands on my little sister.

She knew I was a Starlight witch. Good for her. And I knew she was a bloodsucking leech. Whoop-dee freaking-doo.

I was going to need help retrieving my little sister from school today. A giant's help. With Valen accompanying me, I'd feel much better. Safer since my starlights wouldn't be of much help. Still, it meant that from now on, Shay couldn't go anywhere without me or Valen, preferably both. If Freida knew Shay went to that school, I was certain she knew where we lived.

The thought of grabbing my little sister and running away north hit me again. It looked like now was the time for us to run.

But if we did, I might not be able to find the cure for the Mark of Death curse for Shay. My gut told me I would find the cure for the curse here in the city, not out in the wilderness. What if I took Shay up north, only to discover that she got weaker, and Valen's healing magic stopped helping her? What if taking her away from the vampiress inadvertently made her worse? I didn't know if I could risk my sister's life on such a chance.

I needed to talk to Valen. But first, I needed to speak with this coven of sorceresses.

The woman crossed her larger-than-life arms over her chest. Her eyes wrinkled in displeasure. "What do you want?" Her voice was rough, deep, and manly. I wasn't sure if she was doing that on purpose to make herself even more frightening, but it worked. She stood there before the doors to the building like a doorman, or rather, doorwoman, looking like she was ready to pound the heads of intruders or the unwelcomed. Me.

Please don't pound my head. "Right. I'm here to see the coven. Ladies of the Light. They're expecting me."

Elsa had pulled some strings and managed to get me a meeting with them. Through, with who, I didn't know. And I didn't have the name of any of the sorceresses, just the name of the coven and the address. I blinked and looked past the doorwoman to the stone chapel behind her.

The chapel was small, but its steeple towered over the trees in the center of the block, glinting in the sunlight with a white stone façade. Four columns supported an imposing portico, which served as the main entrance and was shielded by a line of seven-foot cedar trees that kept it out of sight from humans.

Elsa had told me that the coven had bought the chapel in the 1900s and converted it to their needs, whatever that meant. It was pretty, but I wasn't here to admire the view or discuss the architecture.

When the doorwoman didn't let me through, I added, "I'm Leana Fairchild. The Starlight witch. You can tell them I'm here."

The doorwoman's dark eyes flickered with interest at the mention of my name. "You're the Starlight witch?"

"That's what I said."

"This way." She turned around and walked into the chapel.

Okay then.

I followed the doorwoman inside, and my body immediately filled with a strange sensation. I couldn't help but inhale deeply, feeling the electric-charged air cling to me. The energy in the room seemed to build around me as I crossed the thresh-old, t... toe.

... wards. No doubt to fry curious ... doorwoman was indisposed.

... through a short entrance lit with ... s that lined the walls, illuminating everything in a bright yellow glow. The light reminded me of Shay when she'd turned on her sun magic and stood there in her dazzling glory for all to see. I shook my head, trying to get rid of the thoughts of the vampiress. I needed to focus on getting Shay the cure or counter-curse. It was why I was here.

Pushing down my thoughts, I followed the doorwoman up a small set of steps leading to another hallway. My shoes clonked loudly as I made my way up. Every ten feet, the lights flickered on, sending yellow beams reflecting on the stone walls.

At the end of the hallway stood a door. Not just any door. Golden sigils and runes were etched all around the doorframe. The markings pulsed and thrummed along with the massive energy rippling from them.

This had to be it. The coven was behind that door. Why else would it be so heavily guarded by magical wards and energies?

I felt like I was staring at a high-voltage power outlet that would cook you like a fried chicken if you got too close.

The doorwoman gestured toward the door. "In."

I raised a brow. "Not much for small talk, huh? But I'm guessing you're more muscle than brains. Right?"

A glimmer of annoyance crossed her face. She waved her hand at the door like I hadn't understood her the first time. "You need to go through the door."

"I got that." I wasn't an idiot. The door was decorated with powerful sigils for a reason. "What happens when I open the door?"

The doorwoman stared blandly at me. "If you are who you say you are, there shouldn't be a problem."

I like how she purposely avoided my question. "And if I'm not? What happens then?"

She blinked. "You will die."

"Nice." So this was some sort of test. A truth test or magical test of sorts. If I was the Starlight witch, then technically, I should live. If not…

"Only those with magic in their blood can enter and speak to the Ladies of the Light. If you're not who you say you are… then…"

"I'll be a fried chicken."

I stared at the door. I didn't know why, but I was suddenly really nervous. My armpits were damp with stress sweat. And for a moment, I doubted my abilities as a witch. It was daylight. What if the wards didn't recognize my starlight magic? What if I wasn't "witch" enough to pass through those doors?

No. I came here to see the coven, and the coven I would see.

Determined, I sucked in a breath, stepped up to the door, and turned the handle.

The door lit up in bright yellow-and-white hues. I could feel the magical power of the protective wards quivering as they moved through me. I felt a sudden rush of energy exit my body as the wards locked into place.

The wall shook, and then the heavy door opened silently, revealing another room beyond it.

I reached out and patted myself down to reassure myself that I was indeed still alive. I was. It seemed I'd passed this test.

Drawing in a deep breath, I walked through.

I entered a room that must have been the hub of the chapel at some point with its towering ceilings and elaborate stained-glass windows. Being that the chapel was small, it was a short walk—stressful but brief. I crossed the room, and where the altar would have been stood a half-moon desk made of gleaming hardwood.

Around the desk sat twelve females, the sorceresses.

They wore matching white robes, but that's where the similarities ended. Their hair was a mix of colors and styles, some cascading down their shoulders, while others were bald as eggs. Some held themselves with otherworldly poise and hidden strength, like older people with a secret youthful vigor and power. A couple looked to be my age, and others were frail and bent. But I knew that was a ruse. They were still as sharp and powerful as they came.

The sorceresses' eyes fixed on me as I neared. My skin tingled as I approached, like I was rubbing against static electricity, but I felt no pain. I cast a quick glance around them as I kept walking, not settling on any of them. I thought about stopping. Maybe I needed them to invite me closer. But I'd come this far and passed their stupid test, so I decided to keep going. I walked up to the desk and stopped.

Again, they just ogled me without a single word. The silence was making me uncomfortable, but more restless than anything.

"Hi," I said, my voice echoing through the room.

Looked like I was going to be doing the talking. I had no problem with that. "I'm here because I need your help." Might as well cut to the chase.

"Leana Fairchild, the Starlight witch," said one of the sorceresses. Her long, blonde hair gleamed like it was under the sun, which it wasn't, and her voice was aged, unlike the face of a thirtysomething woman staring at me. She reminded me of Galadriel from *The Lord of the Rings* movies. She looked like an elf. I had to refrain from angling my head to see if she had pointy ears.

"Yes. That's me," I said instead. "Listen. I'm here because—"

"I am Cassia," said the same sorceress. "It's been a long time since we've seen another Starlight witch." Her light eyes widened in delight and... was that curiosity?

I narrowed my eyes. Her tone was friendly enough, yet I could detect some ulterior motive behind her words. A stirring of unease pulled through me.

"You knew another Starlight witch?" I had to admit that piqued my curiosity. I'd only heard about others like me. I'd never met one. Not if you didn't count Shay, who is *technically* a Starlight witch since she can harness the sun's power, which is a star. And *my* starlights *loved* her.

"Over a hundred years," said another sorceress with coffee-colored skin whose hair was cut so sort, she looked bald. Light from the room reflected off her scalp. "Her name was Odessa Devereux."

By the gloomy tone in her voice, I gathered that she didn't live to the ripe old age of one hundred and one. "What happened to her?"

"She was murdered by a cabal of Dark wizards," answered Cassia. "They were trying to tap into her starlight power and use it for their own gain."

"Doesn't work like that." It angered me to know that some fools, even back then, thought they could steal the power of a Starlight witch. And it was still happening.

"Yes. We know." Cassia shared a look with her coven. They were silent, staring at each other, and I had the feeling they were communicating telepathically. Could sorceresses do that?

"Which stars do you draw your powers from?" asked another sorceress, who looked as old as Auria had before she'd gone under her magical knife and ended up looking younger than me.

I felt pressure in my head behind my eyes. I opened my mouth to tell them, and then at the last minute, I withdrew. Weird. I'd never be so candid with strangers, especially strangers who were all looking at me like they couldn't wait to cut open my head to see what made me tick. This felt... felt like they'd used a persuasion spell on me. To *make* me communicate what they wanted. When I reached out to my starlights, what little I could, I felt a slight tingle of magic inside me that wasn't my own. Foreign. The sorceresses'. Yup. They'd just tried to manipulate me. My head throbbed from the pressure like I was suffering from a sinus headache. But I hadn't told them anything. I resisted.

Cassia's eyebrow lifted, seemingly sensing that I'd broken whatever coaxing spell they'd tried on me. She looked... she looked impressed. The others looked at me with even more interest than before, like I'd just grown a third arm, and they were watching me clap.

It ticked me off. I found it rude. They were trying to force me to tell them my secrets about my magic. This alone would have enraged me, but I was in a time crunch. Plus, I was in a room with twelve mighty magical practitioners. The odds were most definitely against me. I also needed their help. If I gave them the finger, I doubted they would offer their assistance.

"Be on your guard," Elsa had said to me over the phone on my way here. "Sorceresses don't think like we do. We're nothing to them. Don't consent to anything you don't want to do. Just remember who they are and what we mean to them."

We were objects of curiosity, it appeared. I'd admit, this group of females had gone too far to spell me like that. But I had to remind myself *why* I was here in the first place. It wasn't about me.

This is for Shay. For my sister.

I smoothed out my anger as best as I could, cleared my throat, and said, "Do you know the sorceress Auria?"

At that, I had all their attention on me again. Good.

"Yes, we do," answered the dark-skinned sorceress. "Auria is a troubled soul. She was once part of our coven long ago. But she became obsessed with the forbidden, so we had to sever our bond."

"She'd lost her mind," said another sorceress, the only one with red hair. "She wasn't Auria anymore. Not after…" She clamped her mouth shut like she'd said too much.

"She was warned, Mave," said another sorceress, her eyes hidden in the folds of her wrinkles. "We did all we could. And she chose the forbidden over her own coven. She was lost to us."

Again, the coven lapsed into another bout of silence, all gazing into each other's eyes with their brows twitching and their expressions shifting like they were having a telepathic argument. I stood there feeling like an idiot as things became awkward.

Finally, Cassia folded her hands on the desk. "If you're here to seek her out, I'm afraid she won't help you. Auria hasn't been part of this coven for years."

"Oh. I know she won't." I clasped my hands in front of me and said, "She's dead."

A gasp rippled through the assembled sorceresses. Some leaned back in their chairs, their expressions sour like I'd just passed gas. It happens when I'm nervous.

"Preposterous," cried the sorceress named Mave, her eyes on me. Her pale skin flashed red on her cheeks. "That is absurd. You insult us with your claims, Starlight witch. Auria isn't an ordinary witch. She is a *sorceress*. And a mighty one at that. She wields powerful magics that could level mountains and topple fortresses. Her arcane knowledge is unsurpassed. Her power is undeniable."

Here we go. She'd said it like Auria was some kind of indestructible goddess. "Yes. I know she was a sorceress. But she's still dead. So unless she can return from the dead, your old pal Auria is gone."

"How do you know this?" asked the bald sorceress.

Hmmm. This was the part where I wasn't sure they'd be happy. I still needed them to help me with the curse. The last thing I needed was to anger them because I'd killed one of their own. I didn't sense their love for Auria, but that didn't mean they wouldn't turn on me.

Resolute, I said, "I killed her."

The coven exploded in a cacophony of suspicion. Then the expected outcries followed, ending in a weird silent treatment as they presumably had a joined freakout moment inside their own minds.

This was most definitely the strangest thing I'd ever witnessed in my life. And I'd had my share of weird.

The only one who didn't look surprised was Cassia. She regarded me for a moment. "How did she... die?"

"I'm assuming because of this." I pulled out the pendant with the blue stone I'd pulled off Auria's neck. Elsa had dropped it off last night after our phone call, thinking it might come in handy if I were to meet with the coven.

I held out my hand. When Cassia gestured for me to come forward, I stepped closer, dropped the pendant in her hand, and took a step back. "I don't know what it is, but it made her younger. She killed a few witches, took their powers, and made herself young again. You can check with the Gray Council. They should have everything you need to verify my story."

Cassia rolled the stone in her hands, her eyes closed. "Auria tried to kill me. I didn't want to kill her. I needed her. But she left me no other choice." No one said a word, so I kept going. "She was powerful, a formidable opponent. And she might have killed me, too, but when I ripped that pendant off… she…"

"Became old and frail." Cassia opened her eyes. "I can feel an echo of Auria's essence in the stone. Yes, I believe you. She is dead."

A murmur traveled along the other sorceresses. She passed it on to the bald sorceress next to her, who widened her eyes appreciatively like she'd never held one or hadn't in a very long time. "This is a Neidr stone. They are extremely rare and extremely dangerous. It can store power."

"I got that."

Cassia fixed her gaze on me. "And you say Auria attacked you? I know her well enough to know she wouldn't do such a thing without a good reason."

"Yes, well…" I exhaled, thinking of how to explain it all. "She was angry because I stole her book of curses a few months ago." At their collective frowns,

I added, "To rid the curse she put on my friend Jimmy, which turned him into a wooden toy dog." I tried to gauge their reactions to see if they knew what I had done, but all I got back was a set of blank faces.

"Well, she wanted revenge and cursed my little eleven-year-old sister. She cursed her with the Mark of Death." I looked into their faces, and still their expressions showed nothing. "So, I'm here to ask for your help to rid her of the curse."

At that, the group of sorceresses gazed at each other and had another one of those telepathic chats.

I stood there feeling my blood pressure rise until Cassia broke the silence. "I'm sorry, Starlight witch, but we cannot help you."

My jaw dropped open. Anger and frustration filled me, and I curled my fingers into fists to keep them from shaking. "You *can't*, or you *won't*?"

The bald sorceress looked at Cassia before replying, "We do not have dealings with witches and the other paranormal races. We are a private coven. We don't involve ourselves in matters with the other communities."

"So you're just going to let a little girl die because you don't *want* to get involved?" I seethed, fury pounding me.

"Even if we wanted to help," said Cassia. "Auria's curses were legend. The Mark of Death is, well... simply put... it cannot be undone."

"Bull," I told them. I knew they were holding back. I could see it in their eyes, even though they tried to hide it. They knew how to remove it, but they wouldn't tell me because of some misplaced loyalty to Auria. She was a sorceress, whereas I was just a mere witch, a lesser magical practitioner to them. I was nothing.

"Licasta, please escort the Starlight witch out," said the bald sorceress.

I flinched, seeing the mammoth-sized woman beside me and not having heard her approach.

With a last hateful glance their way, I spun around and marched out, my steps hurried. I needed to get the hell out of here before I did something stupid. The fact that they had kept the pendant wasn't lost on me either.

It couldn't have gone more wrong if I'd tried. The coven refused to help me.

I'd failed Shay.

But it wasn't over yet. It was time to make that celestial phone call to Matiel, my dearest angel father.

CHAPTER 2

"They *refused*?" Jade stood in the living room of my apartment back on the thirteenth floor, looking like a long-lost eighties' band member with her pink headband, leather pants, and her crimped blonde hair that stuck out of her scalp like a star.

"They did." I gripped my coffee mug and leaned on the kitchen counter. My fingers shook, still pulsing with rage and a feeling of insignificance. The coven had made me feel like my presence as a witch didn't matter, like the death of a young girl due to a curse from one of their own was inconsequential. I hadn't felt that low since Martin's comments about me not being a real woman because I couldn't have children.

"Sorceresses are a different breed altogether," said Elsa, leaning on the counter beside me. "They care nothing for others. Still, I thought they would have helped in some way. After all, Auria, as you say, had been one of them at some point."

"Yeah. Seems that even if she was a vile, evil bitch, they're still protecting her. Even in death."

"Because she was a sorceress," guessed Jade.

"Exactly."

Ecstatic screams filled the air, and I glanced up to see two young girls in matching silver princess dresses running into the apartment. The smell of animals and grass wafted in with them, making my skin tingle with energy, the scent of werehorses.

"Guys. This is *not* funny." Julian stumbled in after them. Blue and purple eyeshadow covered his eyelids and eyebrows. Bright red blush marked his cheeks and matched his red lipstick. "How do you take this crap off?"

The twins howled in laughter, skipping around the living room couch as Julian paced behind them, trying to catch them. After another volley of giggles, the twins galloped out. They were surprisingly fast. That's the werehorses in them.

I laughed. "I like that shade of lipstick on you."

Julian pointed a finger at us. "Don't even start." He rushed out as we heard him call out, "Girls! Wait! It won't come off with soap!"

Elsa laughed. "Boy, does he have his hands full."

My smile faded as I thought of Shay. I gripped my mug tighter until I feared it might break.

"We'll figure this out, Leana," comforted Elsa, and she squeezed my shoulder. "They're not the only sorceress coven in this country. There are others."

I didn't want to disappoint her by telling her I seriously doubted any coven would offer their help.

"Something happened this morning when I took Shay to school," I said instead.

Both witches went still.

"Freida was there. She was waiting just outside the school, next to her vamp entourage."

"Are you sure it was her?" asked Elsa.

"Oh, I'm sure," I replied, remembering the vampiress's expression. "Then Shay decided to tell me that she could do her magic all along. She gave me a demonstration."

"In front of Freida?" added Jade, her eyes as wide as her hair. "But why would Shay lie about that?"

"After all those mornings of training?" Elsa shook her head.

"Long story. The short version is that she wanted us to hang out." It was cute, and I wouldn't have been upset under any other circumstances. But now that Freida had seen Shay's magic with her own eyes, that was a problem. "Freida can't enter the school, so that's good. But if you don't mind, I'd like you to come with me when I pick her up later today."

"Not a problem," said Elsa. "We won't let that vampire near our Shay."

I smiled at her usage of the word *our*. "Thanks." I tilted my head back, downed the rest of my coffee, and set my empty mug in the kitchen sink.

Elsa eyed me. "What's that on your face?"

"What?"

"The look that says you're conjuring up a plan."

Jade laughed. "You do have that face."

I smiled, made my way toward the apartment door, and closed it. "As a matter of fact, I do."

"A plan that requires you to close the door?" Jade looked at Elsa, her eyebrows high on her head. "I like those kinds of plans."

"I don't want anyone walking in while I discuss it." I crossed the living room, moved to my desk, and hoisted an old brown leather tome. "I picked this up on my way back from the Gray Council archives on my way here. It's got everything I need. But I will need your help."

Elsa joined me at my desk. "Everything you need for what? What is this plan you're scheming in that big brain of yours?" Concern flashed in her eyes.

"It has something to do with Shay. Doesn't it?" Jade came over. Her coffee mug cupped between her hands.

"It does." I looked between my friends. "I'm going to call Matiel, my father."

Jade sucked in a breath through her teeth. "Wait!" She rushed over to the kitchen, tossed her mug in the sink, and rushed back. "Okay. I'm ready."

Elsa shook her head. "This isn't a race, Jade." She gave me a pointed look. "And you know how to do this?"

I shrugged. "Of course not. But it's all in this big baby," I said, tapping the book. And it'll work. I know it will.

"And they let you borrow this book?" Elsa gave me a suspicious look. "From what I know of the Gray Council archives, they don't let just anyone take out books or pictures of important tomes. Especially one that has the recipe to summon angels. That was in the restricted section. Wasn't it?"

"Hmmm?"

Elsa quirked her head at me, narrowing her eyes. "They don't want those types of books to fall in the hands of some idiots and get themselves killed by the wrath of angels."

I nodded. "It's why I stole it."

Elsa let out a howl while Jade smacked her forehand with an open palm. "Leana. You didn't?"

"Oh, I did. And I'd do it again in a heartbeat."

The older witch rubbed her locket with both hands. "If they find out… you'll be banned for life."

"If it works," I said, "they can ban me all they want. I don't care about that. All I care about is finding a way to help Shay. Nothing else matters. Nothing."

Elsa nodded, her eyebrows furrowed in contemplation. "You're right. You're absolutely right. And if those old, wrinkled scholastic fools think they can stop you from succeeding, they'll have me to answer to."

"Have you told Valen yet?" asked Jade.

"Not yet. I haven't had the time. I'll call him when we're done." Besides, I needed witches with me, not a giant.

"I don't see a problem with summoning an angel," said Jade, her lips pursed in thought. "I mean, he *is* your father. But why do you want to speak to him?"

I moved to a clear spot in the living room. "Because he must know how to cure Shay. I mean, he's an angel. They can do that sort of thing, right?" Or at least I hoped they could.

"Excellent thinking, Leana," encouraged Elsa. "Of course, we will help you."

I let out a breath, along with some tension. "Thank you. And if it works, I'll have a means to talk to him when I want. When Shay wants." I thought it crucial that we somehow open the lines of communication with him. Especially at a time like this, when Shay needed him. I still thought it strange that he hadn't shown up yet.

"Have you ever summoned another being before?" Jade watched me, her fingers twitching nervously at her sides.

I swallowed. "No. Have you?"

Jade shook her head, a nervous smile forming on her lips. "No."

"The only thing I've summoned lately is heartburn," said Elsa, rubbing her chest.

"Told you, you put too much cayenne peppers in your chili," noted Jade, who was rewarded by a scowl from Elsa.

I rubbed my eyes. "This should be interesting."

"Wait." Jade pulled out her cell, swiped her fingers over the screen, and then held it up, aimed at me. She caught my confused expression and said, "In case we need to go over it again, in case something goes wrong, you know. It's important that we record this session."

"Okay." I was hoping nothing would go wrong, but I understood her logic.

My life had quickly gone from bad to worse in a matter of weeks. Not only had I nearly been killed in the hands of my giantess friend, Catelyn, attacked by a chain-smoking witch named Clive, and then almost obliterated by the evil sorceress Auria, Freida wanted my sister. To bend her to her will. To use her magic.

My dream of a simple witch life with Shay and Valen, with a few paranormal cases thrown in and the steady Twilight Hotel paychecks, had vanished.

Everything was different now. There was no going back.

"So, what's first?" Elsa propped her hands on her hips and tapped her foot.

I glanced down at the book and reread the first paragraph. The Latin on the pages had faded significantly since it was written, making it difficult to distinguish the words. I needed to be able to read the spell correctly: too many tales of witches attempting to summon demons and other beasts came to mind, each ending with the witch's sudden disappearance.

"I need to draw a seven-point star," I said, my eyes flicking over the inscription. "Where my father will appear. And then, inside each point, I have to draw one of the seven archangel sigils, whatever those are." This was out of my league. I had no knowledge of angels and archangels. I pulled out the chalk I'd also stolen from the archives' blackboard stations. Never said I was perfect. "But it'll be hard drawing on the carpet. Maybe we should do this somewhere else." Maybe I should have thought this through. This was a disaster.

"I'll do it." Jade angled her phone against a pile of books on my desk so she could get a clear view of the living room. Next, she took the chalk from me and knelt. "The carpet pile is really low. It's practically sandpaper. Shouldn't be a problem."

My heart slammed against my rib cage as I watched her finish drawing the star with my chalk. She did an excellent job of it too. An actual white star on the green carpet.

I lowered the book to the floor next to her. "These are the sigils." I pointed. I figured while she was down there, she might as well continue.

When Jade was done drawing the seven sigils with a strange accuracy, like drawing on carpets with chalk was a common thing for her, she sat back on her heels. "Done. Next?"

My eyes flicked to the page. "Next… is you need to write the name Matiel in the center."

Elsa moved forward and snatched the chalk from Jade. "I'll do that. You have the penmanship of a five-year-old."

Jade made a face. "Thanks."

"We can't risk summoning a demon because your Ms look like Ws."

Jade rolled her eyes. "She's moody today. Must be all that red hair."

Elsa raised her chin proudly. "Every single strand is dipped in the blood of my enemies."

I let out a laugh. I was glad they were assisting me. I

needed their magic, not just with the chalk-drawing part. Without it, I couldn't summon Matiel, my angel father. My starlight magic wasn't strong enough during the day, and I was done waiting. I needed his help now.

Jade pushed herself up and stood next to me. "She's right. My writing's horrible."

I leaned over and watched Elsa meticulously write the name MATIEL in the middle of the star like a pro.

"There!" she said, satisfied with her oeuvre. "A work of art." She rolled to the side, leaned forward, positioned her feet, and pushed up, her knees popping. She handed me back the chalk. "Now what?"

"Now comes the fun part," I said.

"I thought that was the fun part," stated Jade. Her eyes were wide with curiosity as she pointed to the chalk star on the carpet.

I flashed her a smile. "Oh. It gets better." I walked over to the kitchen, grabbed the seven glasses of water I'd filled a few moments ago, and placed one above a sigil.

"I was wondering what those were for," said Elsa, watching me.

"Here, I thought she was just thirsty," commented Jade with a shrug.

Once that was done, I returned to the kitchen, grabbed the two large metal buckets I'd found in the maintenance closet on the thirteenth floor, and filled them with water.

"Okay, now I'm *really* curious," said Elsa, rubbing her locket.

When they were both filled, I set the first one carefully inside the seven-point star and the other one I placed about six feet from the star's outline.

Elsa bent forward, her necklace swinging. "What are you doing with all that water? I've never heard of a spell that needed this much water."

Jade looked at the other witch. "Have you ever summoned an angel?"

Elsa made a face. "No."

I straightened. "Water's the essential ingredient for this summoning. At least, that's what it says in the book. Water is needed to travel between planes and realms, to slip through the cracks into other dimensions."

Elsa propped her hands on her hips. "Well, I'm seriously intrigued. What's next?"

I stared at my friends and said, "Blood." They gave me a joint shocked expression. "I need blood. Otherwise, it won't work." I reached over to my desk where I'd laid a sharp kitchen knife I had doused in rubbing alcohol a few moments ago. Can't be too careful.

Jade shifted, her eyes on the knife in my hand and looking like she'd regretted her participation in this. "You need *our* blood? Is that why we're here?"

"Cauldron help us," said Elsa, clutching her locket like she was about to pray.

I nearly laughed at the panic in her voice. "No.

Mine. My blood. The blood of the summoner. Without it, the spell won't work."

I stared at the sharp blade. I wasn't exactly thrilled about slicing my palm, but I had to for the spell to work. And right now, conjuring Matiel was my only shot at healing Shay.

And I was going to do it.

I gritted my teeth and inhaled deeply before pressing the blade against the inside of my left palm, drawing out a long stream of dark crimson blood and hissing at the sting. Then quickly, I caught the dripping liquid in a bucket inside the seven-point star and released seven equal drops of blood, as instructed by the book. Then I repeated the process with the other bucket.

"That was really gross," said Jade with a smile on her face, as I bandaged my hand. "But kinda exciting." She showed me her palms. "If you need more, you can have my blood."

I laughed. "Thanks. But mine's enough." My heart raced. Taking a deep breath, I grabbed the thick book and placed it next to the bucket.

"You're both crazy," said Elsa. "It's no wonder I've never seen this spell performed by other witches. It's self-mutilation. Witches don't cut themselves."

To save little girls, they do. And I was pretty sure loads of Dark witches did, though I kept that conjecture to myself.

"Okay. I'm going to need your help. I need you to summon your magic while saying the incantation with me."

Elsa grabbed the book from me, her expression grave as she studied the spell. "It's a complicated spell, but nothing we can't handle with our magics combined. The three of us." She handed the book to Jade. "Besides. I wouldn't mind seeing your father again. He's very handsome," she added with a wink.

I sighed. "I just hope he can heal Shay."

"I'm sure he will," said Jade. "He's a freaking angel. Like you said, they have healing powers. Right?"

"That's what I'm thinking." I took a slow breath, willing my mind to focus. "Ready?"

"Ready," chorused the witches as Jade placed the book on my desk and came back to stand on my right while Elsa moved to my left.

I stepped into the bucket of water, which had a pink tint now that my blood was in it. I wiggled my toes, the warm water soothing as I positioned myself.

Then I took Elsa's hand with my left hand and Jade's with my right, and she closed the circle with Elsa's. We were all connected physically.

I bit down the fear that threatened to crawl into my mind. *This was going to work. It had to. And Matiel would heal Shay.*

"Do you remember all the words?"

"Yes," answered Elsa.

Jade giggled. "Can't wait to see the look on your father's face. You think he'll be happy to see you or pissed that he's trapped in that star?"

I pursed my lips. "Let's go with happy." No. He'd be pissed, but I had already worked that out. Once he heard what had happened to Shay, he wouldn't be furious with me. He'd be more worried about her.

I let out a breath. "Let's do this. Together now."

"We call upon the goddess and her sacred power," I chanted with the others as I reached to the power of the stars, which wasn't much. "To help us in this sacred hour. We summon the angel Matiel to be subject to my will. I invoke the angel Matiel in the space in front of me."

Nothing happened, and for a moment, I feared it wouldn't work. I wasn't sensing my friends' magic. Nothing. Just their warm fingers around my own. I must have done it wrong. I was an amateur. Maybe I'd misread one of the words.

But then I flinched at the sudden surge of my friends' magic, sending my skin rippling with goose bumps as magical energy poured into me, through our hands.

My hair lifted in a sudden wind, carrying the scent of wildflowers, earth, and pine needles—the scent of White magic. The air hummed with power, and I stared as a visible shimmer of blue, orange, and yellow rushed through me and the others.

I noted an underlying citrus aroma, like the smell of lemons and oranges—the essence of angels—or maybe that was the lemonade Elsa had been preparing for later.

An invisible force pulled at my chest, reaching down to my toes and causing panic to flood through me. When I glanced down, I saw the water around my ankles spinning into a frenzied whirlpool. I felt like my lungs were being squeezed. I couldn't breathe.

What the hell?

This was wrong, all wrong. Not only was I not breathing, but what if I hadn't summoned an angel? What if I'd conjured something else, like a demon? And it was pissed.

I let go of the witches, my hands going to my throat as I coughed desperately while trying to get some air into my lungs.

"Leana!" cried Jade. "What's the matter?"

"She can't breathe," shouted Elsa.

"Help her!" shouted Jade as my head started to spin from lack of air.

Elsa threw her hands in the air. "I don't know how!"

Jade rushed around me, and the next thing I knew, she'd wrapped her arms around my chest—and heaved.

Was she giving me the Heimlich maneuver? Yes. Yes, she was.

My body was thrust forward and up with more strength than I thought Jade had. Must be all those polymers from her hair spray giving her some uber power.

"What are you doing!" shouted Elsa. "She's not choking, you idiot!"

"You got a better idea?" cried Jade, though she never stopped crushing, squeezing my chest, right below my rib cage. I think she broke a rib. "She's turning blue!"

The water lapped around my feet, sending a chill through me that went deep into my core. I felt dizzy and light-headed, and I knew I was about to pass out at any moment.

"Move," snapped Elsa, and I felt a release around my middle as though she'd pulled Jade off me, but I still couldn't breathe. Damn. I was going to suffocate, and I hadn't even healed Shay.

The next thing I knew, I was lifted out of the bucket, more like pulled, and I fell to the floor, water from the bucket splashing on the carpet with me.

A wave of fiery agony coursed through me, feeling like my internal organs were igniting. I attempted to stand up and move my limp limbs, yet it seemed as if an immense weight was pinning me down, or like I was stuck in a concrete bed. My body wouldn't budge.

What the hell have I done?

Despite the loud humming in my ears, I heard Jade shouting at me, but I couldn't even open my mouth. A chill ran through me as a gust of wind glided against my skin. The force of the enchantment coursed through my veins like boiling water.

The sensation of being pulled faded and so did the pain as the feeling in my limbs returned. The pressure around my lungs faded, and I could breathe again. I downed gulps of delicious air as I wiped away the black spots clouding my vision and whirled around.

With a sudden shift in air pressure, the chalk-drawn, seven-point star burst into fire.

"Ah!" shouted Elsa, rushing over. She grabbed the other water bucket and doused the fire.

Gray smoke rose around a loud hissing sound, and the choking stink of burnt plastic permeated the air.

"Leana? Are you okay?"

I pushed to my knees, seeing Elsa and Jade staring down at me. "Yeah. Just peachy." My frustration rose as I stared at the now blackened seven-point star etched into the carpet. "Guess that means it didn't work."

No it didn't. But I had the strangest feeling that it *had* worked, and someone other than Matiel hadn't wanted me to reach him.

My line of communication with my angel father had been disconnected.

CHAPTER 3

"Stop fidgeting, or I'll have to use other means to keep you still," ordered Polly.

I slumped in my chair. "I feel fine. Seriously. No need for all this," I said, gesturing to the assortment of tonics and ointment jars she'd pulled out of her chef's coat and dropped on the kitchen table. That was a lot of stuff, and I had a feeling she had a special room in the hotel where she kept them all and practiced her healing skills.

Polly's eyes glared at me from under her white toque. "That's not what I heard. I heard you performed a spell way beyond your abilities, and it bit you in the ass."

It was my time to glare at Elsa and Jade, wondering which of them had blabbed. They conveniently avoided my eyes as they worked on fixing the carpet with some spells.

Since Valen was under strict orders from none other than the hotel healer, Polly, to use his healing abilities *only* on Shay, she was now my designated healer.

Yes, I was disappointed that it hadn't worked, but I was angrier that someone on the "other" side had sabotaged my—our—spell. Though I couldn't prove it, I had a gut feeling. And my gut was usually right.

And if I was right, what did that imply? Who wouldn't want me to reach our father? Was this the reason he hadn't reached out and visited us? Was he in trouble? I thought back to our conversation. He'd told me the Legion of Angels wouldn't be thrilled if they discovered he had fathered not one—but *two* children. What if they'd found out, and he was stripped of his wings or whatever it was called? Would we ever see him again?

My chest squeezed, and my nerves fluttered inside like I was harboring moths. Without my father's help, I'd have to think of something else to rid Shay of the curse. Auria had used something earthly, something here, to create that curse, which meant I had the chance to find it and use it to make a counter-curse.

I just didn't know what it was or where to start looking.

Polly released a few drops of liquid from one of her vials into a glass of water. The water began to stir by itself as magic pinged my senses. When the water stilled, she handed it to me. "Here. Drink this."

I took the glass and sniffed. Smelled like dirty sneakers. "Mmm. Smells delicious. What is it?"

Polly waved an impatient hand at me. "Never

mind what it is. Drink it. All of it." She crossed her arms over her ample chest, waiting for me to drink whatever concoction was in the glass.

Lovely. "Bottoms up." I tipped the drink to my lips and took a gulp. And then I gagged. "Tastes like dirty feet." Though, that was a strange comment since I'd never tasted feet, and dirty ones at that.

"Drink," commanded Polly, making Jade snort.

I shot her a scowl, and she turned around, smiling. "Okay. Okay. Keep your hat on." Grimacing and fighting down the urge to puke, I drank the rest.

"Well?" prompted Polly as she rolled her eyes over me like she was trying to see if I had any hidden injuries.

I placed the glass on the table. "Still tastes like dirty feet."

The healer narrowed her eyes at me. "It doesn't matter what it tastes like."

"Says the person who *didn't* drink it."

"What matters is that it works." Polly let out a breath. "How do you feel? Less nauseated and weak? Better? What?"

"Still nauseated from whatever you made me drink," I told her. "But I do feel like I have more energy. Less tired."

"Hmmm." Polly moved to the table and started to go through her stock.

"I feel great," I said quickly, realizing that she was looking for something else to make me drink. "Really. I don't need you anymore. All better."

Apparently, that was *not* the right thing to say,

judging by the flush of color on her cheeks and the anger dancing in her eyes.

Polly pointed a finger at my chest. "Listen here, young witch. I'm the healer, not you. And I'll decide when I think you're cured. Got it?"

I leaned back in my chair. She was kind of scary when she was mad. "I got it."

"Good." Polly returned to her stock and pulled out what looked like crushed nuts in a small jar.

I sighed and looked over at Jade and Elsa. "How's the carpet repair going?"

Elsa wiped her brow. "It's not. I don't understand it. We should have been able to do a quick repair charm. I've done them countless times. You can't imagine what repairs we've had to do over the years. The young spill things. The old… spill things."

Jade leaned back on her knees and laughed. "Good one."

"The point is," said Elsa, "I'm a true professional when it comes to repairs around here. And whatever did this"—she gestured to the black seven-point star burned into the carpet—"won't let me get my magic into it."

At her quizzical frown, I asked. "Why do you think that is?" What I really wanted to ask was how much Basil was going to charge me to replace the carpet if Elsa and Jade couldn't figure out a way to fix it.

Elsa's frown deepened until I could barely see her eyes. "Well, the only plausible explanation is… that fire wasn't earthbound. It was celestial fire."

"No shit." I blinked. "That makes sense."

"Of course it does," said Elsa as though I'd just insulted her intelligence. "And if I'm right, we can't do anything to repair the damage. I'm sorry, Leana. But it looks like we'll have to have the carpet replaced."

"I know." Since Valen had paid for Shay's school and most of the groceries, I could probably afford to replace the carpet.

"You shouldn't have been trying to summon an angel in the first place," scolded Polly. "See what you've done? You could have gotten yourself killed."

I scowled. "I was trying to communicate with my father. He might have been able to save Shay."

Polly's eyes rounded. "Okay. No need to take that tone with me. My job is to ensure the tenants and guests are safe and in good health. No need to try and kill me with that death stare."

Jade laughed. "She does that a lot."

My lips parted. "I do *not*."

"You do too," chorused Elsa and Jade.

"You probably don't realize when you do it," said Jade, pushing to her feet, her knees wet from the spilled bucket of water. "'Cause you can't see your face while you're doing it."

Guess not.

Polly grabbed my right hand and dumped what looked like crushed nuts into my palm. "Eat those."

I stared at the flaky brown crumbs. "Please tell me this isn't mice poop."

Polly sighed, clearly growing impatient with my

remarks. "It's not. It'll give you more strength and keep you hydrated. It's powerful. And you'll feel a kick. Like a sugar high."

I picked one up and smelled it. It didn't smell like anything. Or maybe the feet tonic from before messed up my nasal receptor cells. Probably a good thing.

I popped it into my mouth just as the door opened and Valen entered. He halted, taking in the people in the room, the atmosphere. His eyes traveled over to the prominent seven-point star scorched on the carpet and then to me sitting on the chair with Polly next to me.

And then his eyes darkened. "What happened?"

I opened my mouth to tell him but choked as some of those damn nuggets got stuck in my throat.

"*Now* you can perform the Heimlich maneuver," Elsa told Jade.

I blinked, and Polly was there with a glass of actual water this time. I took it and sipped some, feeling that clump dislodge in my throat, and swallowed. "Thanks," I wheezed, seeing Valen cross the room to me. From his glower, I knew he was worried about me. "I'm fine," I told him, feeling my senses rebound, followed by a boost of energy. Must be the "kick" Polly had suggested. Okay, so those little nuggets weren't so bad after all. "Just burned the carpet is all."

"What kind of summoning is that?" Valen's voice was even, but I could still sense the worry hidden there. "And why did it leave a mark?"

His voice sent tiny shivers down my spine. I loved that he was worried about me. "I tried summoning my father."

"You tried?" Valen came right up to me, searching my face and body like he was looking for marks and wounds, just as Polly had done.

"And failed. That there... that's the seven-point star that caught on fire."

Valen let out a long breath through his nose, his muscles popping along his neck under the collar of his jacket. "And that wasn't what you intended?"

"I was hoping he'd pop up in the middle of it."

"You must have done something wrong," said Polly as she began stuffing her coat with the supplies she'd brought with her.

Irritation surged, but I pressed it down. She had just helped me. And those magical tidbits—whatever they were—did make me feel better. More than better. Amazing.

"She—*we* didn't do it wrong." Elsa came to my defense. "We followed the instructions to a T. I—*we* think it was sabotage." She looked at me, and I knew we'd all come to the same conclusion that whoever had sabotaged it was an angel or group of angels.

"Sabotage?" asked Valen.

"Yes." Elsa flattened out her skirt, and two damp patches were visible where her knees had been.

"Someone on the other side made sure it wouldn't work," I told him. "It's the only thing that makes sense. It's why Elsa and Jade can't fix the burn marks. Because it was celestial fire."

Valen watched me, his gaze so intense that it nearly made me look away, but I didn't. "And you think it's the reason why they can't repair the carpet? Not something else?"

Elsa walked over to us. "My repair spells have *never* failed. Ever. What Leana says is true. That was celestial fire."

"And unfortunately, she'll have to replace the carpet," added Jade as she joined us.

"I'll take care of it. The carpet is the least of my worries."

"Why?" Valen's gaze was imposing. "Why did you need to summon your father?" His dark eyes roamed over my face. "I thought you went to speak to that coven of sorceresses."

I opened my mouth to tell him, but Polly cut me off.

"If there's nothing more, I have lunch to prepare downstairs," said the healer, her hands stuffed in her pockets.

I shook my head. "No. Thanks for your help."

Polly smiled. "Anytime." She pointed to my hand, where I still held some of those nuggets. "Don't forget to take those."

"I won't."

"Okay then. You seemed to be on the mend. I'll see you all later." And with that, Polly walked out of my apartment.

"We should go too," said Jade. "I need to change."

"Yes," agreed Elsa. "Lunch at After Dark?"

I smiled. "Sounds like a plan." Come to think of it. I was ravenous.

Once Jade and Elsa had disappeared through the door, Valen turned on me. "What happened with the coven?"

I sighed, remembering how snotty and unhelpful they'd been. "Not much. They refused to help."

Valen leaned forward, and I wrapped my thighs around his legs.

"Refused?"

I nodded. "They knew what Auria used. I'm sure of it. But because of some misplaced loyalty, they didn't want to give it up. Even though a little girl's life is in jeopardy. It was like they just wanted to have a look at me, the Starlight witch. Like a monkey at the zoo. They couldn't care less about helping. I think I hate them."

Valen laughed. It was such a lovely sound. "At least you tried."

"That's one strike. And now, with this." I gestured to the carpet. "That's strike two."

"And so you tried to summon your father because the coven wouldn't help."

"Yes. I'm telling you, Valen. I did everything right. Someone, an angel, doesn't want me to communicate with Matiel. Either that, or he's in some sort of trouble." I didn't need to add that stress to myself. My nerves were already stretched. I didn't need to worry about an angel father as well as my little sister. Besides, if I couldn't reach him, there was nothing I could do. He was on his own.

SHADES OF WITCHES

"Hmmm." Valen leaned forward and wrapped his big strong arms around me, and I leaned into him, enjoying his warmth, his comfort. "What if we try another coven? There's got to be more."

"I thought of that," I said, running my hands over his broad back. "They won't help. I have a feeling they'll be just as secretive and loyal as this stupid group. But if I were a sorceress, that'd be a different story. As a witch, I might as well be a doorknob."

Valen laughed again. "Maybe it's time I contact those Dark wizards."

I looked up at him. "I thought they were assassins? Mercenaries? You planning on assassinating that coven?" Not that I minded.

"They're skilled with poison, curses. They might have used this curse before. It's worth asking."

"It'll cost you."

"I don't care." He kissed the top of my head. "I'll sell the restaurant if I have to."

Moisture filled my eyes, and I needed a moment to be able to find my voice again. "I won't let that happen. I'm going to find a way to help Shay. I will."

Valen bent down and kissed me again. It wasn't a friendly kiss. It was more passionate, hungry, with a dangerous edge to it.

His magic flowed into me—not the healing part, the other part that had my nether regions pounding with desire. A growl escaped his throat as I pulled away.

"Valen..."

Deep concern appeared on his face. "What is it?"

I took a breath. "I saw Freida today. The vampiress."

Valen flinched as though I'd slapped him. "What happened?"

"Well," I exhaled. "She saw Shay. And by the way, your little squirt can do magic. She's been pretending she couldn't so we could hang out."

The giant shifted his weight. "I'm not surprised she'd pull something like that."

"I am." But it was hard to be upset at the memory of her face and how proud and happy she'd been to show me she could conjure her sun magic.

"What about the vampiress?" Tension was heavy in Valen's tone.

"Shay decided to demonstrate her powers in front of me. Freida and her crew were there, watching. She saw everything. Shay. Me. And she'd been waiting for us. She knew we'd be there. The precise time I'd take Shay to school. And then... then her voice sounded inside my head."

"What did she say?" demanded Valen, rage coloring his voice. Muscles shifted along his shoulders, his jaw, his fury barely controlled. I could sense he was trying hard to keep his cool and not transform into his giant self right here, making a mess of the apartment. Basil would surely fire me for that.

"I'll be seeing you, Starlight witch," I recited, wishing I could have pulled her long hair and slapped her face with it. Bet she would have hated that. "I know what she looks like now, but she also knows what I look like. And Shay."

Valen exhaled as he pushed away from me, and I felt the loss of his warm and muscular arms. I watched him as he paced the room, his emotions shifting faster than vampire speed. "Did she say anything else? Anything about Shay?"

"No. But she didn't need to. It was clear. We know this from Clive. And for what other reason would she present herself near Shay's school? She wasn't there for me. And Shay… she just showed the vampiress how easily she could summon her magic." If she'd been telling the truth and she'd been a dud, we could have worked with that. No power. No one would be looking for her. But I knew now this wasn't the case anymore.

Valen's face rippled like he was about to change, his anger cresting to a savage ruthlessness. But then he took a moment, visibly trying to calm himself. "She's going to try and take Shay."

"I won't let that happen."

"She'll be waiting for her after school."

"And I'll be there. You'll be there. Ready for anything."

Valen let out a growl, which wasn't a horny one this time. It was an *I'm going to pound in her face* one. "She's watching Shay. After Clive told the vampiress what we did to him, what we know, *she* knows she has limited time to grab Shay."

I jumped off my seat. "Is Arther still expecting us this weekend?"

"Yes."

Today was Wednesday. But I didn't care. "Can we

leave tonight?" Somewhere in a remote part of the forest up north was probably the safest place for Shay.

Valen's steady gaze fixed on mine. "We can."

"Good." My heart raced, knowing this was the right call. "We'll pack now. I'll pack all of Shay's things since I don't know how long we'll be." I knew this would be hard for her. She'd hate being pulled out of school, but she would understand. I hoped.

"Okay," I said, looking at my giant and seeing the agreement over his handsome face. "We'll grab Shay after school, and then we'll leave."

CHAPTER 4

The sun was long gone by the time Valen's Range Rover entered Woodcroft Forest. Brilliant stars blinked down at us. Glass-smooth lakes shone in silver hues from the moon. I bounced in my seat as the large SUV climbed onto a gravel path just off the road. Narrow and uneven, branches hit the windows and scratched Valen's luxurious SUV, but the giant didn't seem to notice. Or maybe he just didn't care. His priority—both our priorities—was to get Shay somewhere safe.

And the sooner we got there, the better for everyone.

Shay had been adamant about staying in New York, as I'd expected.

"I can defend myself." She'd stood her ground, looking determined in the back seat of the SUV after we'd picked her up from Fantasia Academy.

"Yes, I know that now."

"I'm not afraid of that vampire."

"*Vampiress*. And you should be. She's not just any vampire. She's old. And *old* with vampires doesn't mean wrinkles, memory loss, or dentures. It means power. More than you can imagine." And she can talk inside your head.

Shay crossed her arms over her chest. "I beat the other one. I can beat her too." She had that cute frown of hers again. It was tough to take her seriously when she looked like that.

I sighed, knowing she meant Darius. "He was just a Dark witch with twisted ideas who happened to sit on an important council. Nothing more. But Freida... she's something else. She can rip your mind apart just by looking at you. She can get inside your head and control you. Force you to do things for her, even when you don't want to. The power of compulsion."

Clive had blabbed to me when I'd tied him up and questioned him, that Freida would control Shay, and she would do as the vampiress commanded. I verified it this afternoon when I looked through the Merlin database, skipping out on lunch with Elsa and Jade as Valen and I waited to pick up Shay. I wanted her to be scared, to know just how dangerous this new foe was.

Shay stared at her fingers, her face twisted in a way that said she was thinking. "I read that you can block people from getting inside your head."

Damn, that kid was too clever. "Yes. I've heard of that. But not everyone can do it, and it takes months of practice. That's if it works."

"Can you teach me?"

I thought about it. It wasn't a bad idea, especially up north where Shay could concentrate without worrying about a vampiress jumping her. I'd never tried it myself, though I knew a few witch Merlins who'd trained themselves against mind intrusion, so I knew it could be done.

I looked at Valen for an indication of whether he thought that was a good idea, but the giant was staring ahead through the SUV's windshield.

"I guess we could try. I think it's a good skill for you to develop in the future."

Her eyes brightened. "So, we can stay?"

"No," came Valen's answer from the front driver's seat as he pulled out from the curb in front of the school and headed down the street.

His voice was rougher than it had ever been when he addressed Shay, and she was shocked by the look of surprise on her face. Me too, for that matter. But I knew why. He was afraid for her. He knew she'd fight us if we didn't show her we were serious and meant business. I knew it had upset Valen to talk to Shay with such aggression, but he had to. And it had worked.

Shay hadn't said another word for the remainder of our drive and all three stops we took along the way. She kept to herself the entire time.

Before Valen and I had left, I'd stopped by to talk to the gang, to tell them we were going north to Arther's compound or pack or whatever it was called.

"How long will you be there?" Elsa had asked, concern high in her expression.

"I don't know. Two weeks? A month? Freida won't give up looking for Shay. Not after she saw how easily my sister could conjure that sun magic. We have to sit tight for a while and figure out our next move."

"But what about school?" Jade's shoulders slumped, and she looked sad at the loss of Shay.

"Valen took care of it," I told them. "He told the head of faculty that it was an emergency, having to do with Shay's curse. They already know all about Auria, so they were very understanding. They said they'd have everything ready for her when she returned." Which I thought was a miracle. Guess they could see the potential in that girl the way I did.

"It's not forever," I said, seeing how distraught they were. "Just for a while. And it'll be nice to see Catelyn again. I have to talk to her."

"Give her my love," said Elsa, her eyes brimming with tears.

I nodded. "I'll call you. And tell Julian, okay?" After that, I'd left both witches looking like I'd just told them I had an incurable disease. A part of me wanted to stay and comfort them, but I needed to get to Fantasia Academy.

At first, when we'd arrived at the school, Valen and I had been prepared to fight off a swarm of vampires, or whatever you call a group of them. But when we'd reached the school an hour early, Freida and her vamp minions were nowhere to be found.

"Maybe she planned on taking Shay back at the hotel or the restaurant," Valen had commented. "The school's too heavily protected. She didn't want to risk it."

"I think you're right."

Fast-forward to five hours later, Shay was alive, away from Freida's grip, and sleeping soundlessly. She had been for the past two hours. Her backpack was squished against her window, and she used it like a pillow.

Running away north wasn't ideal. But we were out of options. I knew Shay was angry, but she'd realize we didn't have a choice. Coming here would keep her safe until we figured out what to do next.

I was still unsure whether to tell her about our father and how trying to summon him had resulted in me purchasing a new carpet. I'd promised Elsa that I would wire her the amount to cover the new rug once she'd notified Basil. I was glad I didn't have to witness that.

It was daunting I couldn't reach Matiel. It was clear the celestial crowd didn't want me to. If Shay lost her father, well, I tried not to think about that right now. She'd been through enough, and losing him would devastate her.

I stared out the window. It was pitch black. Even the moon's light couldn't penetrate through the density of the forest. The only light came from the high beams of Valen's SUV lighting up the dirt road ahead.

I reached out and pressed the window power

button to lower it. Cool air slapped my face, and I closed my eyes for a moment, letting the smell of nature, deep forest, pine needles, leaves, and earth soothe me.

"You okay?"

I opened my eyes, turned around, and found Valen's gaze on me, his face cast in shadow. "Yeah." I was happy he cared how I felt. It was such a change from Martin, who cared more about a stain on his shirt than his wife. I was still getting used to someone else being concerned about me. "I'm happy we did this. Yes. This was a good idea."

"You're just full of good ideas."

"I'd love to take credit for it, but you were the one who mentioned coming here."

Valen made a sound of approval in his throat. "But you wanted to come tonight. It was smart. If the vampiress planned to take Shay back at the hotel or the restaurant... she's in for a surprise."

"Too bad we're not there to see her face." Valen was right. Taking Shay away from the city tonight was a good decision. "Are there kids here? Kids Shay's age?"

"Probably. I know there are many families. I'm sure some have kids her age."

"Good. At least she can make friends while we're here."

"This is it," said Valen, and I leaned forward in my seat to get a better look.

The Range Rover descended a hill, and the end of the winding dirt road opened up to a large campground the size of a football field. It was still hard to see, given the trees spread out sporadically inside the compound, but some light fixtures were hanging from trees. I couldn't see any power lines, so I figured either a generator powered most of what was here or they used solar. This place was off the grid, so I was positive that's how the paranormals lived here.

As I surveyed the area, I estimated at least fifty log cabins scattered across the expanse. They all sported tall trees and shrubs as neighbors, obviously meant to be family homes. In the center of them sat a much larger building, likely an inn or hotel.

As we drove past, a few paranormals standing outside one of the first cabins noticed us and stopped their conversation to stare. Their expressions were curious, not shocked, as though they'd been expecting us. It was half past eight at night, and the compound was buzzing with life. They were werewolves. They thrived at night. But from what I remembered, it was a sanctuary for all paranormals, so it wasn't just werewolves. Shifters, witches, and many different other races were here.

A group ran toward the SUV and stopped just at the road's edge. Kids. Kids Shay's age. Their eyes were wide as they tried to see into the vehicle, but at night and with the tinted windows, they only saw me and possibly Valen. But I had a feeling they were trying to get a glimpse of someone else.

I turned around and nudged Shay's knee. "Shay? Shay, wake up. We're here." I didn't want her to miss our arrival.

Shay stirred and blinked a few times until she remembered where she was. "We're here?"

"Yes. Look."

Shay tugged her backpack down from the window and lowered it, peering out in time to see that same group of kids ogling the SUV on the right. One of the girls, with a high ponytail and round face about Shay's age, waved.

A pang touched my heart. That little girl was a stranger and waved at us, at Shay. And when Shay waved back, well, god help me, I got all choked up.

Thank goodness I can control my emotions—when I'm not battling a delusional sorceress and a chain-smoking witch.

After a few minutes of driving at a plodding pace, and letting Shay and me get a good look around, Valen pulled the Range Rover into a parking lot of one of the more significant buildings. The one-floor structure was longer and deeper than the ones I'd seen so far.

"This is Arther's place," said Valen as he killed the engine.

It seemed the pack leader got the largest house. Made sense.

Sure enough, the same Viking-like werewolf with an impressively muscular build, golden hair, and mesmerizing blue eyes that could hypnotize most warm-blooded females, stepped out and sauntered over to the SUV.

Valen climbed out first. Shay and I followed and made our way to stand next to the giant.

I was struck by how quiet it was. Distant murmurs of the paranormals were drowned by the deep squelching of *crawk crawk crawk* of tree frogs, crickets, and all the other night creatures that dwelled in the forest. It was the complete opposite of New York City's familiar loud bustle of humanity.

The air was thick with woodsmoke as it floated from the chimneys of some of the cabins. The smell was a joyous contrast to the exhaust I'd grown accustomed to in my life.

My eyes traveled over the alpha male. Arther wore dark jeans and a shirt under a black leather jacket spread over his broad shoulders. His hands were large and robust with scars marring his knuckles. His four-day-old stubble was dark, except for just enough silver peppered through it to announce a man in his late forties and in his physical and mental prime. His handsome features played with the shadows, making him look more rugged and rough, like Valen. His light eyes projected strength and competence like he was accustomed to giving orders.

As the men shook their hands, I looked at Shay, wondering if she was nervous. But my little sister was staring over at the spot where the cluster of kids was still standing. And, of course, they were staring at us.

"Leana."

I pulled my attention to the sound of my name and found Arther watching me.

"It's nice to see you again," said the werewolf pack leader. He flashed me one of those million—no, *billion-dollar* smiles, and I glanced around, expecting to see a group of females throw themselves at that dazzling grin. Nope. Just us.

"It's nice to see you too," I added with a smile of my own. "This is Shay, my sister."

At that, Shay turned around. Her lips pressed tightly in an embarrassed kind of way. She was not making eye contact with Arther.

"Hi, Shay," said the pack leader. "It's nice to meet you." He glanced over her to the group of cheerful kids. "That's my niece, Eve, and her friends. I told her you were coming. She's about your age. She's very excited to meet you."

Shay shrugged her response.

"She's going to show you around tomorrow, if that's okay with you."

Another shrug.

"I know you can't see much at night, but it's nice during the day." Arther pointed to a building in the distance. "This is where the kids are taught. You might consider Shay attending some of the classes, depending on how long you stay."

"Yes, thank you." I looked at Shay, but she was staring down at her sneakers.

Arther looked at me. "The community is anxious to meet you all. But I told them to leave you alone for the night. You've come a long way. You need to rest."

By the way, he was eyeing me and speaking to me directly. I realized he was implying that *I* was tired—me and Shay. Not Valen, the uber-strong, resilient giant. But just us females.

On another night, his comment might have ticked me off, and I would have told him to shove it. I *wasn't* tired, and I *didn't* need rest. But Shay did.

I'd noticed since she was cursed that she tired much faster and easier than before. She'd go to bed earlier than she used to, and I'd had difficulty waking her up this morning for school. I'd have to keep my eye on that. I wouldn't want her to exert herself.

I made a mental note to ask Arther if they had a healer here. They must if it was as well-equipped and self-sufficient as Valen led me to believe. They had to have someone equivalent to a doctor, and I would need to make my presence known to them.

"Thank you," I said to the pack leader instead. "That was very thoughtful." And it was, once my temper calmed down.

Arther gave me another of his panty-melting smiles. "I have your cabin ready," said the pack leader. "You go in, settle for the night, and I'll give you the tour tomorrow. Don't worry. This place is highly protected. You didn't know it, but you passed several guards on your way in. All heavily armed. They could have taken you down an hour ago."

"Good to know." Damn. That was scary. But also reassuring to know that we were safe here.

"Come." Arther gestured. "Your cabin is right next to mine."

Good again. If we were next to the pack leader, we'd be even better protected, being so close.

"I'll get our bags," said Valen as he opened the

trunk of his SUV, grabbed all three carry-ons we'd brought with us, and tossed them over his shoulder. "You're gonna love it here," he said as he pushed the trunk's automatic button. It closed with a soft click.

I gave him a smile. "I think so too."

As we started to follow the pack leader, I leaned in and whispered in Valen's ear. "Does Arther have a wife? Or a mate? Girlfriend?"

"Why? Are you offering yourself?" asked the giant with a toothy grin.

When Arther angled his head slightly, I knew he'd heard me. Damn that werewolf super hearing.

My face went on instant flush. I could even feel my ears burning. I had no idea why I asked that, but I was glad my mortified face was covered by darkness. "No. I mean… he's a pack leader. He's… you know… easy on the eyes." I was blabbing. I did that when I was nervous. "I just thought we'd meet his other half." Damn. I sounded like an idiot.

"I haven't met the right woman yet," answered Arther, amusement high in his voice.

Might as well throw myself in one of those lakes and drown in humiliation. I was only asking because I thought it strange that a pack leader that good-looking and in his prime was single. But, like he said, it was hard to find the right person. I knew all about being married to the wrong guy. Maybe he'd been married before. I didn't know his history, and it wasn't any of my business either.

I looked over at Shay to see if she'd noticed my

mortification, but she was slowly shuffling her legs forward and still staring off at that group of kids.

I halted, seeing a woman step into a pool of light. The moon's illumination and the light coming off a nearby home were enough to catch her details. She was almost as tall as me, with a voluptuous build that I lacked. Her light brown hair was done up in a French braid, highlighting her high cheekbones and plump lips. She had gorgeous hazel eyes, though it was too dark at the moment to see them, and most of her face was cast in shadow. But I could see well enough to recognize her.

Catelyn.

I raised my hand and waved. "Catelyn. Hi."

The giantess cut me a look like she loathed the very soil I walked on. More like she wanted to shove my face in said soil and hoped I choked to death in it. And then she spun around and walked in the opposite direction from me.

I sighed. "Ah. That went well."

CHAPTER 5

I woke up the following morning somewhere bright and warm. I blinked at the sun shining through the window. The room smelled of wood and uncertainties. As sleep lifted from my foggy brain, I realized I was in one of those cottages.

I sat up and glanced around. The room looked much brighter and cozier now that I saw it in daylight. The wood paneling and heavy wood furniture were perfect for a cottage at the lake. I liked it.

Seeing the empty and cold other side of the bed, and hearing the soft murmurs of chatter coming out through the bedroom door, I knew Valen and Shay were up. I grabbed my phone from the night table. The screen read seven twenty-two. A bit early for me, but we were somewhere different, and I had a feeling Shay wanted to explore.

Swinging my legs off the bed, I headed for the connecting bathroom. After I brushed my teeth, showered, and pulled on some clean clothes, I yanked open the door and walked out.

The one-floor, two-bedroom, two-bath cottage had the kitchen, dining room, and living room arranged in an open-concept style with lots of windows looking out into the wilderness beyond. I could see tall pines and spruce trees surrounding it, creating a sense of seclusion, and making it difficult to even see Arther's nearby home.

Valen and Shay sat on a couch with a green-and-orange floral print, huddled over what looked like a map spread out before them on the wood coffee table.

"What's that?" I walked over to them, and the aroma of fresh coffee alerted my senses.

The giant smiled at me. "Map of the compound. I want Shay to familiarize herself with the place in case she wants to go exploring."

"I should too," I said, moving closer. Forests weren't my forte. I wasn't a were or a shifter, and I couldn't rely on my innate sense of direction if I got lost.

"It's huge," said Shay, her eyes round and twinkling with excitement. "There's even a training dojo. That's where the kids go to learn how to fight."

I pulled out my phone and snapped a picture of the map. "How you feeling today?" I didn't think Shay should be anywhere near a dojo. Not in her condition.

She lost some of her smile. "I feel fine. Better. I think it's the fresh air." She gave me a sly grin. I knew she was playing me because she wanted to train with the other kids.

I could play this game too. "Well, since you're feeling better, I think we should start training you on how to block your mind from unwanted guests." I matched her smile. I was prepared for her to object and fight me on this.

"About that," said Valen. "I've spoken to Arther, and a vampire here can help. He's an old one and has experience with mind manipulation and blocking."

"Really?" I wasn't sure I liked that idea. "You think that's a good idea?"

"Yes." Valen watched me. "Only a vampire would know how the art of mind manipulation works. He's a good friend of Arther's, and he's willing to help. He has time this morning, so I say we should take the offer."

Maybe having an ancient vampiress hunt my sister made me extra cautious about vampires in general.

"It'll be good for you too," said the giant. "Learning from another vampire, one that wants to help."

I looked at my sister. "What do you think, Shay?" If she said no, that's the direction I'd go. I wouldn't force her.

Shay fixed me with her green eyes. "I don't mind."

Valen gave me a *See?* look that said he was right and we should listen. Not that it bothered me. I had to admit mind manipulation was a foreign subject, and I didn't want to hurt Shay by making a mistake.

"Okay then," I answered finally.

"Can we eat first. I'm hungry," exclaimed Shay, shifting on the couch.

"You're always hungry." I looked around, not seeing any food out on the counter. Just a coffee machine. "Breakfast does sound kind of amazing right now. Coffee would be even better."

"Here." Valen handed me what looked like a full cup of coffee. "I just had a sip."

"Thanks." I gulped down some excellent coffee, rejoicing at the bitter taste.

"I didn't have time to get food," said Valen as he stood. "Arther told me most paranormals here eat in the common cottage. Families take turns cooking for the compound. I heard they have pancakes."

Shay's smile brightened at the idea of her favorite breakfast food.

"Okay. I'm in." So was my stomach.

"It's right here," said Shay as she pressed her finger on a spot on the map. "Let's go."

Before I had a chance to look where she'd pointed, my little sister leaped from the couch, grabbed her backpack that was plopped on the floor next to the front door, slipped on her Converse sneakers, and rushed out like she was being chased by demons, leaving the door open.

I looked at Valen. "Must be the fresh air."

Laughing, we left the cottage and followed Shay, who'd apparently memorized the compound's map to a T, because after walking for two minutes, we arrived at a long, rectangular-shaped building with a big wraparound porch. Picnic tables were spread around where paranormal families were already having breakfast—and of course, they were all staring.

We were met with curious expressions and murmurs as we passed them. It was awkward, yet I'd been in enough awkward situations to know that these paranormals weren't regarding us with contempt or disapproval that we were invading their compound. It was really just curiosity, wondering who we were. Maybe they were used to harboring strays.

But when their eyes fixed on Valen, I saw visible tension cross their faces, the same kind of stiffness in their postures I'd seen when people were around Valen.

Valen kept his expression blank, but it did nothing to hide his dominance and power. Strength oozed from him, so potent and intense, so incredibly ruling. Guess they knew he was a giant. Or they just felt those tremendous alpha vibes he was giving off like a cologne.

I wasn't bothered by the fear and control Valen instilled in others. In fact, I liked it… a lot.

Shay went through the door first, and we quickly followed after her. The room opened up to a large space with an arrangement of about twenty tables and chairs. The area was loud with chatter and the sound of happy people eating their first meal of the day. It was packed, but I saw a few empty tables. Across from us, at the end of the room, was a kitchen area with a long counter comprised of different stations, with stainless dishes set in a buffet style. It reminded me of an all-inclusive hotel's buffet layout.

"Sit," ordered Valen as we arrived at one of the empty tables. "I'll get you your food." I smiled at the giant, not used to having someone doing little things like that for me. Ever.

I pulled out my chair and sat as Shay let herself fall into hers.

"People are staring," she said, hanging her head low.

I did notice how the happy chatter had somewhat toned down as we entered. "It's normal. We're the *new* people."

Pink spots covered Shay's face, and I realized she was uncomfortable. "I don't want them to stare."

I felt bad for her. Guess she wasn't used to having this much attention on her. At her age, I'd be mortified too. Now, I couldn't care less. They could stare all they liked. I might even give out a few finger waves.

"They'll stop. You'll see. They'll get bored staring at us, and then they'll move on to something else. There's nothing exciting about us." Total lie. Our group consisted of a giant, rare as hell, and a Starlight witch, also rare. Add a Sun witch, rarest of all—and we were the special attraction at the paranormal zoo.

After a few moments, Valen returned to our table. "Here you go."

I glanced up to find the giant expertly balancing three large plates topped with steaming food. "Wow. Is there anything you can't do?"

The giant grinned. "Not that I'm aware of."

I smirked as dirty thoughts entered my mind of his expert hands over my body. He truly was exceptional in the bedroom.

Valen set Shay's plate of pancakes on the table and then mine, which was an omelet next to fruits. His, well, it was hard to tell what there was. It was packed so damn high. Still, I could make out cubed potatoes, sausages, bacon, a stack of six eggs, beans, steak, and five slices of buttered bread.

"You can eat all that?" I pointed with my fork at what I knew were some sausages.

Shay snorted at her plate. And I noticed she was paying less attention to those around us now that her pancakes had arrived.

Valen shrugged. "It's this place. Being in the wild is making me hungry."

I laughed and dug into my omelet just as a young teen male of about fourteen years came around and filled our cups with fresh coffee. He placed a glass of orange juice for Shay.

"Thanks, Tommy," said Valen, and I wasn't surprised he already knew the staff's names or, rather, family names.

The teen's face flashed red, and he hurried away. Yeah, Valen had that effect on people.

Shay laughed harder into her plate.

I don't know why, but it made me happy to see her eat and to see her smiling again like that cute little girl she was. I leaned back into my chair, feeling a sense of tension release around my shoulders and neck.

"I'm glad we came," I said, staring at the two of them devouring their breakfast like they hadn't seen food in weeks.

Shay dipped her fingers in the maple syrup around her plate and shoved them in her mouth. Then she pushed back her gleaming, empty plate and flashed me a smile. "I'm done."

"You eat like a starving street kid, you know that?"

Shay shrugged. "I was hungry."

"I can see that." With food in her, she'd be ready to train. "You'll need a few minutes to digest the mountain of food you shoved down your throat before your training. You don't want to be sick."

Valen's eyes met mine, and I could see the sudden alarm in them. Using magic to go into one's mind was a dangerous affair. Even training the mind to block the intrusion of others. Because if performed wrong, Shay might end up in a coma or even lobotomized. Worse, we didn't know this vampire either. And the more I thought about it, the more nervous I got and wanted to cancel this training session.

Still, it would be worse if Freida got her hands on Shay. No. She had to learn to protect herself, to protect her mind.

"I'm stuffed." I pushed my empty plate, not realizing that I'd finished it all. Looked like I was hungry too.

"Hi," said a young voice.

I turned my head and spotted the same girl with a round face who'd waved at Shay last night. Arther's niece, Eve.

I smiled at her. "Hi. You're Eve, right?" I asked her.

She beamed up at me, looking absolutely thrilled that I had taken the time to acknowledge her.

"Yes," answered the girl, blue eyes bright as she stared at me with the confidence of a young girl who was used to dealing with adults.

Eve was about the same height as Shay but with light brown hair, her eyes a blue like a sparkling lake. She wore a T-shirt with one of those Manga characters on the front, jeans, and plain sneakers. She looked like the typical girl next door from some posh suburban neighborhood. Not a young werewolf.

The distinct scent of wet dog rolled off her, confirming my inkling. "And you're Leana." Her eyes moved to the giant. "And you're Valen, the giant."

Valen grinned, not bothered by the fact this little girl knew who and what he was. Guess that meant everyone on the compound knew as well. "I am."

Eve's eyes settled on Shay. "And you're Shay."

Shay's face turned a shade darker, but she managed to utter a word. "Yup."

Eve beamed. "I saw you guys over here, and I wanted to come say hi."

"Well, we're glad you did," Valen said with a smile. "Are you here with your uncle?"

Eve nodded. "Yeah, he's just over there." She pointed to a man standing a short distance away and talking with a few other adults. "He's talking to my parents. He said it was okay if I showed Shay around the compound this morning."

Shay stilled. Her eyes flicked to me. Concern etched into her features. "Is that okay?" she asked softly, knowing how important her training was, but I could see the desire to go with this girl. It was obvious Shay would much rather hang out with kids her own age than train mind-blocking techniques with a stranger and her boring older sister.

I considered for a moment before nodding. "I don't see any harm in putting off the training until later today," I said, looking at Valen for confirmation. At his nod, I added, "Okay, sure."

Shay smiled at Eve, happy to have a new friend in this strange place. She had been nervous about coming to this compound, maybe even hated the idea, but meeting the kind and curious Eve made her feel more at ease.

"So it's cool about the training thing?" asked Shay, looking over at me.

I smiled at her. "A few hours won't make much of a difference."

"I'll let Arther know." Valen leaned back in his chair. "We can schedule the training later today."

Shay pushed her chair back and stood. "See you later." And with that, she and her new friend Eve strode across the room and disappeared through the front door.

"Well," I said, smiling at my giant. "Looks like Shay just made a new friend—"

My eyes spotted Catelyn standing next to Arther. She looked well and calm, and she was smiling?

I leaped up from my chair. "There's Catelyn," I told Valen. "I'm going to go over and talk to her."

Before Valen could stop me or change my mind, I hurried over. The giantess turned at the sound of my approach, her smile vanishing.

"Hi, Catelyn," I said. "Can we go somewhere and talk?"

Catelyn regarded me with deep loathing. "I have nothing to say to you." She looked like she wanted to spit in my face, or better yet, pound my head into the ground. Guess she still blamed me for her parents' deaths, though that had been the sorceress Auria.

"Please. Let me explain. I just want to talk to you."

Fury blazed in her eyes, and she took a step forward, her fists clenched at her sides. I winced and stepped back, instinctively afraid of her towering size and strength if she decided to change into her giant form and kick my ass.

"I don't want to hear it, Leana," she spat. "I don't want to hear anything from you."

"I'm sorry, so sorry about your parents," I said,

trying to keep my voice steady and refrain from recoiling from her hatred of me.

Anger colored her cheeks. "You're sorry? *Sorry?*" Her voice rose.

I took a deep breath, struggling to find the right words. "I know you still blame me for what happened to your parents, and maybe I am to blame partly. But I didn't kill them. It was Auria. The sorceress who'd cursed Jimmy and wanted revenge because I broke the curse."

"They died because of you," she hissed out, her voice laced with venom. "They'd still be alive if it wasn't for you. You did this to them. *You* killed them."

Her words cut deep, and I winced at the pain of them. She was right, in a way. None of this would have happened if I hadn't kicked Auria's ass and taken her grimoire. And Shay wouldn't be cursed.

"Catelyn, please. I'm so sorry. I wish none of this happened," I said, daring a step closer.

She flinched as if my presence were a physical blow. "Stay away from me, or I'll kill you!" she shouted, and I felt all eyes zero in on our conversation. Her face shifted, and for a second, I saw the mien of her giantess self. "I'll kill you! You hear me! I'll kill you!" She lunged forward, her hands going for my throat.

And I just stood there like an idiot, too shocked to move.

In a blur of clothes, Arther was there, his strong arms wrapped around Catelyn protectively. If I didn't know any better, it looked like he was protecting her *from* me, not the other way around.

Okay, weird.

"You should leave," said Arther, glaring at me like I'd done this on purpose, as though I wanted to make her angry.

It ticked me off to be spoken to that way by a stranger, no less, but what else could I do? He'd given us shelter.

Yes, I was humiliated, having the entire room look at me like I had murdered her parents, but I was more hurt at Catelyn's words and her reaction to me.

I spun around, my face hot and my eyes burning. Valen's voice echoed in my ears, but I wouldn't look at him. I needed space and time alone with my thoughts.

My only consolation was that Shay hadn't been there to witness this shameful scene. I had to accept the consequences of my actions. Catelyn's parents had died because of what I'd done to Auria. It was clear to me that she'd never forgive me. The pain was too deep. Some things could never be forgiven.

Because of my actions, I'd lost a friend forever.

And I'd have to live with that.

CHAPTER 6

I didn't know how long I walked, or rather, hiked on the trails. All I knew was that I'd been at it for about two hours. As soon as I'd stepped through the first set of trees, I saw a path. It was barely visible, even if you were searching for it, and you could easily pass by without noticing. Flat stones were scattered along its hard-packed dirt, and it took me beneath an archway of birch and ash trees with their branches reaching low enough to brush my hair in some places.

It was nice to get away, to be alone with my thoughts, and being with nature seemed to help calm me and lower my blood pressure. It was hard to stay mad and upset around the sound of the chirping of birds, the fluttering of leaves in the breeze, and the angry curses of territorial squirrels. It was peaceful, and soon my heart just accepted my fate. I had to move on. I had to think of Shay.

It was a good thing I'd snapped a few pictures of

the compound map with my phone. Otherwise, they'd need to send a search party for me. My sense of direction was hopeless. With the view of the compound map, I'd made it back to the cottage in one piece with only a few blisters. I needed better walking shoes.

"Valen? Shay?" I opened the door to find it empty. I kicked off my shoes and searched for the hiking boots Valen had brought me—in my size. As I grabbed the boots, I saw a note on the table. *Leana* was written on the top and in Valen's handwriting.

I opened the letter.

Go to Beaver Lake and you'll find me.

I flipped the note over, but that's all it said.

Beaver Lake? I checked my phone's copy of the map. Sure enough, Beaver Lake was there. But it was also about a forty-five-minute hike.

"Where are you when I need you," I muttered, knowing his healing magic could heal my blisters, though I wasn't supposed to let him use it on me. His magic was reserved for Shay.

Thinking of Shay, I pulled on the new boots, winced as they rubbed on my blisters, and headed out. I found Shay sitting on one of those picnic tables next door with Eve and two other paranormal boys.

"You okay?" I asked as I approached.

Shay looked up at me with a frown that said, *Please leave.* "Yeah."

"Hi, Leana," said a cheerful Eve.

"Hi, Eve." I smiled, and my eyes flicked to Shay. She looked fine, with no evidence of the curse or a fever. She looked good. Healthy. "Well. I'm going up to Beaver Lake to meet with Valen. Be back in about two hours. Should be back around lunchtime. You good here?"

"Yeah," she answered, giving me her round eyes and telling me to leave.

I laughed. "Okay then. See you later."

I winced and cursed most of the way to Beaver Lake, not understanding why Valen was there or why he couldn't wait for me, or instead, carry me. My heels and toes felt like I was slicing them open with razor blades whenever I took a step. This is the time I wished my starlight magic worked during the day. That way, I could use my newfound skill of flying and sail my butt over to Beaver Lake.

After an hour's hike, yes, I was slow, I followed the dirt-packed path down to a beautiful gleaming lake. A sign nailed to a nearby pine tree said BEAVER LAKE.

I hobbled forward to the lake's edge, where tiny waves hit a small gravel beach. Valen was nowhere in sight.

"Valen?" I called. "I'm here. If you made me come up here for nothing…" I waited but saw no sign of the giant. Where the hell was he, and why did he ask me to come here?

Tired, sweaty, and full of emotions, I didn't want to think of the hike back to the cottage when my feet were probably bleeding through my socks. Tall evergreens surrounding the lake reminded me of the *Dirty Dancing* movie "lift scene" when Johnny helps

Baby perfect the lift in the water. Loved that movie. Loved that scene.

The sound of water rippling pulled my attention up.

"Sweet mamma mia."

Valen stood up from the middle of the lake. And yup, the giant was naked.

He was glorious, the sun gleaming over his wet body. For some strange reason, seeing him rise from the lake like that made him hotter and more divine, like the god Poseidon.

"What are you doing?" I smiled, my eyes traveling over his fine muscled chest. Damn, that was some amazing male specimen, and he was all *mine*.

"You said you wanted to go skinny-dipping," said the giant, his voice rippling over to me from across the lake where he stood. Naked.

I raised a brow. "Skinny-dipping is usually done at night. You know… so no one can see your naked bits." Though I wasn't complaining. In the daylight, there was more to see… and it was quite the sight to behold.

Water droplets fell over the giant's face. "It took you long enough. Been here for over an hour."

I stared down at my boots. "I've got blisters from hiking for two hours straight. Didn't have the right shoes at first."

"Well, if you come here," he said, moving his hands around him in the water. Part of his manhood peeked from where the water hit just below his waist. "I'll take care of that."

"It's fine." I didn't want Valen to waste his healing magic on me when we had Shay to think about. "How did you even know I'd come? What if I'd gone to have lunch with Shay? You'd be here all by your naked lonesome with minnows nibbling your butt." And his *other* parts.

"Being naked and alone is a terrible thing," answered Valen. "I was in the cottage when I saw you coming down the path through the trees. I wrote you a note. And then split out the back door before you saw me."

I cocked my brow. "So your plan was to get me here and…"

"The water's great. Come," commanded the giant. "I've been waiting for you."

My pulse thrummed at the desire in his tone.

"Waiting for me for… what, exactly?"

"Thought you might need some cooling off after… after what happened with Catelyn."

I didn't need any reminding. "I did sort of run off."

"You did."

"I couldn't stay there. I couldn't…" I couldn't listen to any more of her words.

"I know," said the giant, able to read what I was feeling. "Give it time. Catelyn will come around. Eventually."

"No. I don't think she will." I shook my head, knowing in my gut she never would. "It's over with me and Catelyn," I said, feeling like I'd just gotten dumped. Any way you spun it, her parents' death directly resulted from my actions. "There's nothing I can do to change her mind. And it's fine. I've accepted it." It was a hard pill to swallow, but if I didn't, it would just keep haunting me. I had other priorities.

"Did you speak to Arther about putting off Shay's training with that old vampire?"

"Yes," answered the giant. "It's scheduled for two this afternoon. Should give Shay plenty of time to get to know her way around and hang out with her new friends."

"Okay. That's good." My stomach tightened at the thought of Shay training her mind with a stranger.

"Come," ordered the giant again. "Come join me. Let me rub off some of that tension."

"How can I resist such an offer?" I teased, though I was unsure if I should join him. My pulse thrashed as I looked around the lake and up the path I'd just come from. What if someone came here? What if kids wandered by? But then again, when would I ever get a chance like this again?

I hesitated for a moment, taking in the sight of him, the water droplets cascading down his broad shoulders and sculpted abs. I had always found Valen attractive, but this was something else entirely. Something primal stirred inside me, and I found myself not able to resist the urge to join him. I wanted to be in the water with him. I wanted to feel his hard body against mine.

So, without a second thought, I started to strip off my clothes. Valen's eyes followed my every move, and I could feel his gaze linger on my exposed skin. Was I self-conscious stripping in broad daylight for him to see my imperfections, cellulite, loose tummy, and glorious flabby arms? Nope. Not when such a man, naked in the middle of the lake, was regarding me like I was the most beautiful star there ever was.

Once I was buck naked, all my lady bits standing in the breeze, I stepped closer to the lake's edge, feeling adventurous, free, alive, and a little crazy. As soon as my toes hit the water, I felt a rush of excitement. It had been a long time since I had done something so spontaneous and daring. The last time was when I fake-cried to get out of a parking ticket a few years back with Martin's car.

Holding my breath, I walked into the water, hissing as it burned against my open blisters. The cool water wrapped around my skin, and goose bumps appeared on my arms.

"You said the water's great," I shrieked. "It's freaking cold!"

Valen laughed like I'd just told him a good joke. "It's really not that bad. You'll get used to it once you're in."

Easy for him to say. He was a warm-blooded giant, probably with an inner heating mechanism.

I stiffened, staring at the water around me and not seeing the bottom through its murkiness. "Are there leeches in this lake? If there're leeches in this lake, I might have to kill you."

The giant gave me a sly smile. "Are you scared of

a tiny leech? I thought nothing scared Starlight witches."

"Scared? No. Grossed out and wanting to scream at the top of my lungs? Yes. Hell, yes."

"No leeches. I promise."

I narrowed my eyes at him. Not sure I believed the smile on his face.

Valen swam over to me, and I couldn't help but admire how the water beads clung to his bulging muscles, his gaze intense and penetrating.

"You're so beautiful," he said, his voice low and husky. "I couldn't stop thinking about you all day."

"Really? Why's that? You wanted me to perform another round of humiliation in the dining hall?"

"No one cared about that."

"Sure they did. And I bet they're still talking about it."

"I was thinking more about that tight ass of yours," said the giant.

"Ah. Okay then." I felt my cheeks flush with heat, and my heart pounded in my chest. No one had ever made me feel this way before. And no one had even made me step into a possible leech-infested lake before either: naked *and* in broad daylight.

I continued walking into the lake until the water's edge hit my waist. *Here goes nothing.* Holding my breath, I ducked into the water, the cold flowing over my head. Then I jumped and broke through the water's surface.

"Well," I said, and I started to shiver. "That was a

stupid move," I added, lake water falling into my mouth.

The giant laughed as he swam closer. His hand reached out to take mine. His touch sent electric shocks through my body, and I shivered at the sensation. He pulled me back down into the cool water without a word, and I gasped as it enveloped me.

But once in, the water did feel amazing. He was right about that.

"I forget that you're not a shifter or a were," said the giant, his large hands finding purchase on my waist. "They have thicker skin and can take the cold better than witches."

"Like you, I presume?" I shivered as his skin touched mine, feeling his warmth and strength. His eyes bore into mine, and I knew there was no going back from this moment.

"Let me warm you up," said Valen.

"You better. Or am about to knock you over the head—"

Valen wasted no time in pressing his lips to mine. It was gentle at first, but soon it became more urgent, more passionate, his tongue intertwining with mine. I moaned, overwhelmed by the sensations coursing through my body. I had never felt so alive, so wanted. It was an awesome feeling.

I felt his hands on my back, pulling me closer to him, and I moaned as our bodies pressed together.

Valen lifted me, and I wrapped my legs around his waist, feeling the water lapping at our bodies as we continued to kiss. I hooked my arms around his broad neck, feeling the heat emanating from his skin.

Okay, so he was warmer, like a heating pad, and I did feel the warmth ooze into me. Or was that his healing magic?

Valen broke the kiss and looked at me with his piercing dark eyes. "Are you regretting coming here?"

I looked into his heady gaze. "Not anymore. I wish they would have mentioned this part of the activities in the brochure. This I like. Not so much the hiking."

The giant crushed his hard, muscled body against mine, pinning my breasts. "I have more activities planned for you."

"Like fornicating on moss-covered logs?"

"If that's what you like."

I laughed. A thought occurred to me. I don't know why it did in the middle of this hot, hot foreplay, but it did.

"Does Arther have a thing for Catelyn, you think?"

Valen cocked his head and stared at my lips. "You think Arther's into Catelyn?"

"Yeah." My gut told me so. "The way he went all overprotective of her. I think he *likes* her likes her."

"He's the alpha. Protecting his pack is what he does."

"You mean protecting her from me." The way he'd wrapped her up in his arms wasn't lost on me.

"I think he was just trying to avoid a fight between you two."

I shook my head, staring at his mouth, jaw, and eyes. "That's not how it looked to me. I think your pal has the hots for Catelyn." This might be the "right one" he'd been waiting for.

"Well," breathed the giant. "He's a grown man. He can take any mate he chooses."

"Even a human turned giantess? Won't the werewolf females have a field day with this?" I imagined a scene in my head like *The Bachelor*, where a group of devious single ladies fought for the affection of that one guy. Arther was a very good-looking man. I was pretty sure the claws were going to come out at some point.

The giant chuckled. The sound pinged my heart. "I don't know. It's his life. Why do you care?"

I shrugged. "I know I shouldn't. But I'm worried about Catelyn."

"You shouldn't be. She's well taken care of here."

"I've noticed." I let out a long breath. "Enough of that. Now. Where were we?"

Valen brushed his thumb across my bottom lip, and I parted my mouth in invitation. His kiss was fierce, and I felt the hunger and need in it.

The contact of our skin made me shiver, but it was a pleasurable sensation. I could feel the warmth of his body against mine and relished in it.

Valen pulled away, his hands still firmly on my waist. "I've been wanting to do that all day," he said, his voice deep and husky.

My lips pulled into a smile. "What took you so long?"

"Good question."

He loomed over me, his eyes dark with desire. I ran my hands up his chest, feeling the hard muscles beneath his skin. We kissed again, our bodies melding together as if they were one.

"You're so incredibly hot," he said, his voice husky with desire. "You make me crazy. I can't resist you."

I didn't want him to resist me. I wanted him to take me, make me his.

I'd never done it in the water before, not even a tub, so this would be new and interesting. I'd heard of a few incidents of having intercourse in water, specifically of "penis captivus" where the woman's vagina muscles clamped down on the man's pee pee like a Venus flytrap and got stuck.

Meh. I'd been in worse situations.

Valen continued to hold me, his hands roaming over my body. I could feel his firm muscles beneath his skin, and I knew he was strong enough to do anything he wanted to me.

I ran my hands through his hair, pulling him closer to me, and he groaned in response.

We continued to kiss, our bodies moving together in the water. I didn't know how long we stayed like that, lost in our own world. But eventually, we had to come up for air.

As we surfaced, Valen looked at me with a

mixture of desire and... affection? Not only did that have my lady regions throbbing, but also my heart.

I moaned as he pressed his lips to my neck, making me forget everything else.

No more Catelyn. No Freida. Nothing.

The world disappeared, leaving only the two of us in our little bubble of pleasure.

CHAPTER 7

We trekked through the forest, Valen leading as Shay and I took the rear. With my new hiking boots, I didn't feel any blisters anymore, and I had a feeling Valen had managed to heal those without my knowledge. Sneaky bastard.

"You nervous?" I asked my little sister.

"No," she answered, staring straight ahead as the path led us in a downward direction.

I raised a brow, not believing her for a second. "It's okay to be nervous. *I'm* nervous."

"I'm not."

I decided to drop it, hearing the nerves in her voice and realizing I was making it worse, making her *more* nervous by implying that she was.

Valen looked over his shoulder and gave me a knowing look that said *I* was making this worse for Shay. He didn't have to. I already knew that.

If I had to be honest, I was having a bit of a freak-out. I was nervous, and I wasn't ashamed to admit it.

This wasn't summoning your powers on the rooftop of a hotel. This was going into your mind and trying to block the voice that wanted to manipulate you.

This was hard-core magic that I wasn't familiar with. And it scared me to death. Not for me. But for Shay.

The deeper we went, the darker it got, and it felt more like it was late in the evening instead of barely 2:00 p.m.

I pushed some branches out of my face and kept on the bit of path I could see as Valen led us on. As we delved farther into the woods, the atmosphere became more intense and eerie. It was almost as if it could see us and didn't approve of our presence. With no signs of life other than us, the forest seemed to be holding its breath in preparation for something sinister to come. Maybe this was the forest's way of telling us this was a mistake and we should go back.

Light rose around us. The density of the forest thinned, and we stepped into a clearing of tall grasses.

In the middle of the clearing stood two males. My eyes settled on Arther first. His face showed no emotion at the sight of us, of me, and I wondered if my little conflict with Catelyn earlier had tarnished his view of me. Screw it. I wasn't here to make friends. I was here for Shay.

When my gaze finally settled on the other one, I gave a start.

Instead of the white-haired, wrinkled, and bent-with-age male vampire I was expecting, stood a young one.

Oh, he was a vampire, all right. Even from a distance, I could sense his strong magical energies and the scent of old blood rolling off him. He wasn't dressed like the usual posh vampires I'd see at the Twilight hotel in their designer clothes.

He looked like a lumberjack.

He wore cargo pants with a long-sleeve flannel red-and-black shirt, a jacket, and worn boots. His looks were the only thing from his appearance that gave him away as a vampire. His unnatural, flawless features seemed wrong and had all my red flags soaring in the wind.

The sun shone on his porcelain skin, highlighting his beauty in a captivating way. Though graceful and serene, I could sense the danger emanating from him. He appeared to be in his twenties, but vampires had the gift of longevity, and some were said to be over eight hundred years old. He could have been any age; his chiseled features and full lips were captivating. His jet-black hair was glossy and complemented his fair complexion. With a sweep of his hand, he pushed his locks back away from his face and gave us a smile that made my heart race.

I hurried next to Valen and whispered, "You told me he was old. He looks younger than me."

"He's old. Trust me." The giant's jaw twitched with tension. He was just as apprehensive as I was. Perhaps more.

I couldn't help but glance at Shay. She was

looking at everything except for the vampire. But him? His eyes were fixed on her, and my blood went cold at the creepy smile that stretched over his face.

Valen was the first to join Arther and his bloodsucking pal. "Arther," said the giant. I noticed how he didn't greet the vampire male.

Arther waited for Shay and me to arrive. He didn't offer a "hello" or a "how are ya," so neither did I. The werewolf alpha's expression was still carefully blank. There was no way to tell if he was irked by my being here or not. Or maybe this was just how he was when supporting a friend's family with his business-face on. I didn't know him, so who knew what he was thinking. I just didn't want it to affect Shay in some way.

Arther glanced at Shay and me. "This is my friend Nikolas. He's going to help Shay today."

We all looked at the old-young vampire, who gave a short bow of his head in answer. Weird. I wasn't sure what it was about him, but I didn't like him. Call it my witchy instincts, my female intuition —call it whatever the hell you wanted—but something was off with this bloodsucker. Or maybe I just didn't like vampires anymore after my encounter with Freida. Yeah. That was it.

Stifling my unease, I looked directly into the eyes of the vamp. "And you have experience in this kind of mind blocking? Or whatever it's called?" I asked, and I had to resist the urge to flinch when Nikolas's dark eyes flicked to mine. His nostrils flared as though he were taking in my scent. My skin tightened.

The vampire folded his hands before him and regarded me with a refined expression and manner that didn't fit the clothes he was wearing.

"Telethesia is the magic of closing one's mind against external penetration," he said. His voice articulate and holding the traces of a slight accent I couldn't pinpoint. "It prevents others from accessing one's thoughts and feelings or even influencing them."

"Wonderful."

"All vampires have the power of persuasion," continued Nikolas, as though I hadn't interrupted him. "But only the great are blessed with magical compulsion. The ability to transform *influence* into *action*. In our community, these individuals who hold such powerful mental dominance among our kind are referred to as Pushers."

"And I take it you're one of those?" I asked the pale bloodsucker. "You can do Jedi mind tricks too?" I crossed my arms over my chest, thinking of all those vampires with Freida. It meant every single one of them could try to persuade my little sister, with the vampiress probably being the most powerful.

A slow smile crossed the two-legged leech's face. "Indeed."

"And you believe you can teach Shay to block her mind from these Pushers?" asked Valen before I could.

The vampire's gaze held Shay's. "It will be difficult, especially for one this young and inexperienced. But it can be done. And from what Arther tells me, we must trust that she can learn what needs to be learned quickly."

I frowned and stared at Arther. He might be Valen's buddy, but to me, he was still a stranger, and I didn't appreciate him revealing information about Shay to someone I'd never met. I realized he had to give the vamp a story. I didn't know how much of it he told him, but it wasn't his place to tell.

"Shall we begin?" asked the vampire, forcing his tone to remain light.

Arther and Valen began to step back as Nikolas and Shay prepared to start. I held up a hand, stopping them. "Hold on," I said. "Let's review what you'll be doing so Shay is aware of the dangers associated with this type of training." I was also interested in knowing more about the risks. I glanced at my sister. "Right?"

Shay nodded, her eyes fixed on me. I could tell she was nervous, but at least she was willing to try. "Right," she said, with purpose. She knew learning how to protect her mind would be difficult, but she was determined to do it. Having experienced the consequences of Darius's destructive capabilities, I knew she didn't want to put herself in a vulnerable position again.

I took a deep breath, trying to calm my nerves. I looked at the vampire, waiting for him to answer.

His gaze slowly turned to my sister. "I'm going to teach you how to control your mind. How to block it from unwanted guests and any kind of compulsion. You will hear my voice inside your head." At that, Shay flinched, and when her eyes rounded, I was tempted to call this whole thing off. But then I realized that no matter how scary this was, she needed it.

"And you're going to try to *block* my voice from entering," continued the vampire. "It's going to be difficult, but it's necessary."

She nodded, but I could tell she was still scared. This was probably the most challenging thing she'd ever done, and my gut said Shay might not be able to do it on the first try or first day. But that was fine. She was a strong kid, and I knew she'd figure it out eventually.

I turned my back to the vampire and looked at Shay. "You ready to do this?"

Shay just nodded.

I squeezed her arm. "You've got this. And I'll be just over there if you need me or if you want to stop. Okay? If you want to stop, you just say so, and it'll be over like that," I said, snapping my fingers.

"'Kay," said Shay sounding a little more determined this time, but I could still hear a slight tremor.

With a last look at her tiny face, I walked back a few paces and followed Valen and Arther about twenty-five feet away from Shay and Nikolas. My heart was pounding as I turned around.

Nikolas walked back about fifteen feet from Shay and then turned to face her like two witches were about to duel—a duel of the minds.

Damn. I better not regret this.

"She'll be fine," came Valen's smooth voice, seemingly having noticed the tension oozing out of my pores. "She needs this."

I swallowed hard. "I know. It's just... I don't know this guy."

"Nikolas is a trusted member of this community," said Arther, speaking to me directly for the first time. "You can trust him."

Right. Coming from the mouth of a stranger. I didn't answer. I knew I'd only drive Arther further away from me if I did. I didn't want that. Not when he was Valen's best friend. Okay, so the Catelyn thing turned out worse than I thought. I'd have to make a reasonable effort to keep things from escalating further.

I crossed my arms over my chest, eyeing the scene before me. Shay and Nikolas weren't moving. They were just staring at each other from across the clearing. And for about a minute or so, nothing was happening.

And just when I was about to say something, Shay's face twisted and pulled like she was straining to keep from showing any emotion. Then her eyes narrowed, and her nose scrunched up like she had a nasty headache.

And then it just got worse from there.

Shay's face warped, and she shook her head. "No," she said and then clasped her head between her hands. "I don't want to. Stop."

Before my brain registered with my legs, I was

moving. But I got only one step before Valen's strong arm reached out and grabbed me.

He pulled me back. "You knew this would happen. It's part of the process. You have to let it happen."

I frowned, staring at my little sister's face. "She looks like she's in pain. It's hurting her."

Valen didn't release me. "You have to let her try. For her own sake. Remember. You don't want Freida to control her."

"I know that."

"Wait and watch." Valen let me go, but he stayed next to me, his hard body brushing up against mine like he was waiting for me to rush out again.

"Block my voice, Shay," commanded Nikolas, standing with his hands clasped before him again. "Stop my voice from entering your mind. Do it."

"I'm trying," Shay complained, irritated. She wiped the sweat from her forehead with the back of her hand. Her breath was coming in fast, as though she'd just jogged around the compound. I could see that determined frown on her face like she wanted to be able to block him. She was trying. I knew she was.

"Not hard enough," pointed out Nikolas, his voice rising. "Shay, you don't seem to understand the seriousness of this situation. If you don't stop me from entering your mind, you will not be able to stop Freida."

I stared at Arther, his gaze on Shay and Nikolas. Guess he told him more than he should have.

"You are a witch," continued the vampire, and I

had a feeling he was speaking out loud and not telepathically for our benefit. "Witches are capable of such magic, of this telethesia. If you don't want Freida or any other vampire to control you, you must step up and take command. You have to find a way to channel it yourself. If the Pusher gains control of your mind, you will lose. You will lose yourself, and she will win."

Shay nodded and wiped her forehead again. "Okay. I'm ready."

My heart just about shattered at how determined she sounded, but I could see that she was getting tired. If Shay wasn't cursed, she might have had more stamina. As it was, this telethesia was taking a toll on my little sister's body. And we'd just started.

Nikolas bent at the waist. His eyes narrowed on Shay.

She flinched as though he'd hit her. Her eyes filled with moisture, and she blinked. "Stop," she pleaded. "I can't do this."

"You must." Nikolas's eyes were hard chips of dark glass in an otherwise pale and handsome face. "Come on, Shay. Concentrate. Keep me from entering your mind!"

Again, Shay flinched like she was being assaulted with physical blows.

A growl escaped me. I sounded like a werewolf female wanting to tear out the jugular of that bloodsucking tick that was harming my pup.

"Leana," warned Valen, but I wasn't listening. My only focus was on my sister.

"Stop. Please. I don't want to do this anymore." She pressed her hands to her ears like she was trying to shut out his voice from her head.

Nikolas's face went hard with anger. "What you *need* is to get ahold of this power before it controls you and you kill someone."

"It hurts." A brief look of pain passed over Shay's features.

"This isn't right," I said, my thoughts swirling as I tried to control my emotions over the pounding in my head. "She's just a kid. This is wrong."

"She's fine," said Valen, though the tension in his voice betrayed him. "She has to learn this. To protect herself."

"It will hurt more if you let Freida in," said the vampire. "It requires just as much strength to control a compulsion like this. It's a job that no one can manage easily. It must become part of your nature. Like releasing an emotion but with more power. That is the only way to exercise control over such energies."

Tears leaked out of Shay's eyes. "I don't want to. I want to go home."

A tiny whimper escaped me. Okay, now I felt as though she'd ripped my heart out of my chest and stomped on it.

"Stop," I cried out. I felt my anger tighten around me until I thought I would scream. "This stops now. She doesn't want to do this anymore." I took a step forward, and this time Valen didn't stop me.

Nikolas was focused on Shay. "You *can* stop it."

He straightened, giving more emphasis to his words. "But first, you must master it. *You* are its master. You, Shay. All with your mind. Freida doesn't care about you. She only cares about what your body can do with this gift, and she wants to control it. Don't let her. Don't let yourself become her puppet. Again!"

Shay cried out like some invisible foe had hit her and fell to her knees. She bent forward, still covering her ears with her hands. When she turned to look at me, I felt the blood leave my face at what I saw on her expression—hurt, fear, panic. I'd told her she could stop at any time.

So when I saw blood trickling down her nose, well, I lost it.

And before Valen could stop me, I hurled myself at the vampire.

CHAPTER 8

You might be thinking that was a stupid move. And you'd be right. The old vampire was powerful. There was no mistaking that power radiated from him. But he was hurting my little sister. And he was going to pay for that.

It was like some animal took control of me. I saw red. I wanted to rip the vampire apart. I wanted to stop him from hurting my little sister ever again.

Savage fury made its way into my gut and stayed there. I was going to kill that two-legged leech. And I wouldn't feel bad about it later.

I reached out to the power in the stars as I moved, a desperate need for them to answer now, even though it was daylight. That vamp was going to regret ever hurting Shay. I felt a tug, a smidgen, and when I looked at my hands, droplets of starlight materialized.

And then they vanished.

Ah, hell.

Just when I was about five feet away from the vampire, Nikolas turned my way slowly.

Stop!

Commanded a voice in my head.

It was as though I was hit with an immobilizing spell. My legs and arms locked in place. I couldn't move.

Well, *this* isn't good.

"You sonofabitch!" I howled, glad my mouth was still working. "I'll kill you for this!" Not cool. Panicked, I struggled to keep it together. I couldn't fail now. I couldn't. Shay depended on me. I had to fight. I had to do this. And I had to kick this vamp's ass.

I battled with everything I had inside me, my starlight magic. I even begged the sun to let me borrow some power just this one time. But I got nothing from it. Yet… I felt a pang of energy.

You shouldn't have tried to harm me, said Nikolas in my mind.

And you shouldn't have hurt her. I told him using my voice in my head, unsure whether he could hear it. *I told you to stop. You didn't.*

Focusing on my will and all the magic I could muster to break away from the Pusher's mental attack, I felt a sudden release.

A tingling spread in my limbs, and I managed a step. "Aha! Not so powerful. My turn." Calling to my starlights, the smidgen of power I had, I raised my hand and—

No.

It was just one word, a tiny, two-letter word, but the power behind it was like being hit by a thousand curses at once.

I flew back and hit the ground with a roll. Holy shit. His mind control could actually *physically* move me like he also had the power of telekinesis. Not only could he use his mind to control the actions of others, but he could also use it like he was casting defensive magic. That, I didn't know.

But with the use of my limbs, I was up in no time. My head throbbed like I suffered from the worst migraine imaginable. I'd need a whole bottle of Tylenol after this.

But I wasn't finished yet.

As I tried to catch my breath, I looked up and saw Nikolas staring straight at me. The intensity in his black gaze sent shivers down my spine. I could feel the anger radiating off of him. He wasn't pleased with me. But then again, I wasn't pleased with him either. If I didn't know any better, it looked like poor Nikolas was about to vamp out.

I raised my finger at him. "If I see your claws come out, I'm going to put you down."

"*You* attacked first," snapped the vampire. "I merely defended myself." Was that a challenge I saw reflected across his stupid pale face?

"You hurt my sister and continued to hurt her when she begged you to stop."

At that, the vamp merely smiled.

Yeah. He was dead.

"Leana. Stop this," I heard Valen say. But I was

way beyond being rational at this point. And when I looked back at Shay, seeing her on the ground, looking broken, beaten, and bleeding, all the fury from before rose anew. She looked sick, like the curse was starting up again. Somehow the strain of the Pusher's attack seemed to have jump-started the curse. Bastard.

You dare challenge me? snarled a voice inside my head.

"You bet, you pale sonofabitch. Think of it as practice for when I meet Freida." Made sense to me, but I could still hear Valen's shouts.

Nikolas spread his hands in an invitation. *As you wish. Come at me. Let's see what you can do, Starlight witch. Let's see if you're as good a fighter as they say.*

"You can bet your ass." I couldn't use my starlight magic. That was an obvious blow. But I had arms and legs, and I would use them.

"Leana," warned Valen.

I turned to look at him and raised my hand to tell him to stay. "It's fine. Think of it as target practice." *And you're going to get your ass kicked for what you did to my sister.*

Part of me knew this was foolish. We'd asked the vampire to help Shay with the mind-blocking thing. But he'd gone too far. And part of me felt like he'd enjoyed it. She was already a sick little girl. And whatever mind tricks he'd done had made her worse.

"Look at her," I said to the giant. "Just look at what he did to her. It's like the curse is back in full effect. You think that's okay?" Before I finished my sentence, the giant rushed over to Shay.

I felt eyes on me. Arther. I didn't look at him. But if he tried to stop me, I would defend myself. His vamp friend had caused Shay's curse to rouse again.

You asked for my help, said the vampire, a cunning smile on his face.

"This is how I'm going to thank you." I shot forward, legs pumping with adrenaline.

Nikolas didn't move an inch. He stood there, his arms wide open, taunting, waiting for me. I could feel the power emanating from his body as I approached.

Stop, said the vampire's voice inside my head.

I knew it was coming. Hell, I wasn't that much of an idiot. So I'd mentally prepared for his strike. At least, that's what I told myself.

The voice rang in my head, my ears beckoning my body to obey the Pusher's command. I wasn't trained in this telethesia, so I just used my instincts to drive my actions and protect myself while fighting and purging the mind assault.

Again, my body locked like I was about to turn into stone.

You're a fool if you think you can overcome a Pusher's power.

"You're right. I am a fool."

Every witch has magic in her blood, in her DNA, if you will. Yes, my power lay with the stars, but I had my mother's blood inside me. And as a witch, she passed on to me my dark hair, eyes, and blood magic. Okay, so I couldn't call out to the power of the elements or make friends with demons, but I still had some magic in my veins. Innate magic. Magic that would help me now to fight against the pull of the vampire's compulsion. Or so I hoped.

I tapped into that power, that inner strength, that inherent part of me that was all my mother's.

And then I pushed.

I felt a sudden pressure in my head and a throb. Then just as it had appeared, I felt a release, like the removal of a really tight headband. A freeing of my mind. It worked.

I looked at the vampire, feeling the use of my legs again. "Looks like this fool's got skills." If Freida had the same amount of mind control as Nikolas, I could beat her too.

Yes, you are a fool, echoed Nikolas, *if you think that demonstration was a measure of my power.*

I cocked my head as I moved closer. "Looks like it."

Hurt.

I cried out in agony as excruciating pain flamed, and I convulsed, feeling like my body had been suddenly scorched with a flamethrower. Agony seared me, and I could barely breathe. I all but panicked as I felt my lungs squeezing out air. I fell to my knees, tears blurring my sight. I clenched my teeth, wailing when my entire body spasmed in pain.

Hurt.

The word came again, shaking me with terrifying strength. My spine felt like it was on fire, bones like rubber. Pain clouded my thoughts. More panic welled in me. I would not die. Not like this. Was the stupid vamp really trying to kill me? If he did, Valen would smash him into a puddle.

You think you're stronger than me, Witch? You're not. I can make you do whatever I want. You're nothing. You're weak. Pathetic.

"Screw you," I spat. I raised my head, seeing the vampire approaching, but I looked at Valen. The giant stood next to Shay like he was immobilized as well. But I knew this wasn't the vampire's mind power since I could see his fists clenching and the large vein throbbing on his forehead. The giant was barely able to control his temper, and I knew at any moment he would change into his much larger self and take on the vamp. Would he be subject to the vampire's power like me? That I didn't know. And I didn't want to find out. I'd had enough.

Determination boiled in me. Yes, I hurt everywhere like a sonofabitch, and I knew I couldn't get the giant's healing magic to put me back together afterward since Shay looked like she needed it more. But he was hurting me, not *immobilizing* me.

So I did the only thing I could do. When the vampire loomed over me, I swung up my arm and jabbed my finger in his eye.

Nikolas cried out as he sprang back, a hand going over the eye I'd stabbed. I don't have to tell you how gross that was. It was seriously disgusting. But a witch's gotta do what she's gotta do.

Having someone inside your head was a huge

violation. And I never wanted to feel so vulnerable and without control over my body ever again.

Seeing my opportunity to show off my one-on-one combat skills, which were nonexistent, I threw myself at the vampire.

As I got closer, a growl left his throat, and he lunged at me.

I sidestepped his attack, planted my foot firmly on the ground, and pivoted to face him. I swung my leg around, hoping to catch him off guard. But Nikolas was quick. The bastard ducked under my leg and tackled me to the ground.

Okay. Not the victorious move I'd imagined in my head. But at least he'd stopped with the Jedi mind tricks.

I gasped as the wind was knocked out of my lungs. Nikolas was on top of me, pinning me down with his powerful arms. As he growled in my ear, I could smell his breath, sweet and sour and sickly, like he'd feasted on cadavers just before coming here.

Julian was right about that. Vampires had horrible breath.

"You should set a better example for your sister. Your temper will get you killed," he said, his voice dripping with malice, and his eyes completely black. I felt something sharp graze the skin on my neck. Talons. He'd gone fully vamp on me.

I gritted my teeth and bucked, sending the vampire off of me. I rolled to my feet.

"And you should consider using mouthwash. That's a freebie."

Nikolas's eyes narrowed. "You're severely immature for your age."

I shrugged. "Immature is a word boring people use to describe fun people." I pointed to myself. "I'm fun. You're not." His face twitched, and I could see color spotting his cheeks. Ooooh. He was mad. Good. It seemed that when he lost his cool, he wasn't using his mind games on me. Excellent. That's what I wanted.

I attacked again. As I neared Nikolas, I feinted to the left before swinging my right leg toward his midsection. He moved to avoid it, but I was already spinning, my left leg coming around to connect with his jaw. The impact of my foot slamming into his face echoed through the clearing, and the vampire staggered backward for a moment.

But he was too quick to stay down for long. Before I could capitalize on my advantage, Nikolas had already regained his footing and launched himself toward me. I barely had time to dodge his first swipe, the sharp talons on his fingers narrowly missing my neck.

Nikolas wiggled his talons at me like a sophisticated version of Freddy Krueger. "You fight nearly as well as a man."

"Funny. I was just about to say the same thing about you."

A brow twitched on the vamp's face. "You won't win this."

"I'll take my chances."

I swung my fist in a right hook, but he deflected it

with ease, grabbing my arm and flipping me over his shoulder. I hit the ground hard, the wind knocked out of my lungs again.

Nikolas was on me in an instant, pressing down on my chest with one hand, his other hand raised in a fist. "I could end you now. My vampire strength is no match for yours. You're practically human without your magic."

"Let me guess. You eat humans for lunch?"

A grimace flashed on his face. "I don't *eat* humans."

"No, you just drink them up like a good wine."

Nikolas's eyes moved to my jugular, and I felt a chill roll over my skin. I was pinned, and I couldn't move. Well, I couldn't move my arms, but I could move one part of me.

I clenched my teeth and headbutted the bastard.

Please note: headbutting hurts a lot more than you might think.

We both cried out in pain, but at least the vampire rolled off me. I struggled to my feet, staggering as my head throbbed from both the mind control and now the aftermath of my headbutting.

I whirled, and just when I was about to kick the vamp while he was down—

Stop.

A tingling whispered in my mind, the only warning I got. I stiffened as the vampire's power rose through my mind, tapping into my head and tuning it to my body, my awareness.

I tapped into my magic again, desperate, enraged at having someone else controlling my body.

I wouldn't let it happen.

Letting myself fuel with anger, I fought back. I wouldn't let him control me. I heard Nikolas approach, my body trembling as I fought his mind control, and I could feel a release. I was going to break through.

Sleep, came the word inside my head.

Like a switch, everything went dark in my mind. My boots left solid ground. I was floating, suspended as though in water. I tried to cry out, but my mouth wasn't working. The words wouldn't come. Fear hit hard, and a ribbon of panic pulled through me. That's it. I'd done it. I'd pissed off Nikolas, and now he'd killed me.

My last thought was of Shay as darkness took me.

CHAPTER 9

I woke up with a colossal headache from hell and feeling embarrassed. Yes, I might have overreacted. I might have been a tad *emotional* as Clive liked to point out. But I had discovered something.

A Pusher's hold *could* be broken, which meant Shay had a good chance of conquering it and blocking Freida.

I blinked the sleepiness from my eyes and looked around. I was back at the cottage, and my throat was dry, like I hadn't had a drink of water in weeks. Parched, I noticed a tall glass of water on the side table. Once I pulled myself up to a sitting position, I grabbed the glass and downed the water in one go.

I had no idea water could taste this good. I set the glass down just as the murmurs of voices sounded through my closed door.

Shay.

I swung my legs off the bed, glad I was still wearing the same clothes. Although smeared with dirt, I didn't have to go looking for something to wear. I stood up, the world shifted, and a bout of nausea rose, threatening all the water I had just drunk to come out again.

I fell back on the bed. "Okay. Maybe I need a moment." I took a few breaths, waiting for the dizzy spell to leave, and tried again. Finally, I stood up slowly this time and stepped out while I controlled my breathing.

Valen stood in the living room with his arms crossed, staring at a small older man, with a headful of thick, orange hair past his ears and matching bushy eyebrows, sitting next to Shay on the couch. I didn't think I'd ever seen such a small man before. He looked... he looked like he might have gnome blood or something. He couldn't be taller than four feet.

They all looked at me as I approached.

If they expected me to feel badly for my outburst, or embarrassed, or even fearful, I wasn't. A swell of possessiveness had overtaken my better judgment, and I'd almost used my bare hands to strike down Nikolas. But I was okay with that.

The stranger narrowed his eyes at me. "You should be resting." His voice was as mousy as his appearance. "After what they tell me you went through, you shouldn't be on your feet just yet."

I didn't know him, but I sensed genuine concern in his tone, etched across his face. He cared.

"You're the healer?" I approached the couch. A

black leather medical bag sat on the floor, next to the man.

"Yes," he answered. He opened his mouth to say something else, but I cut him off.

"How are you feeling?" I asked Shay. Some of her color was back, but black circles still marred under her eyes, darker than they had been this morning.

Shay gave me a short smile. "I'm okay."

I didn't believe that for a moment. "I'm sorry. If I had known this telethesia would have made you sicker, I would have never agreed to try it. I thought it would help. I thought if you could keep that vampiress from inside your mind, you would be safe."

Shay looked at her fingers on her lap. "I know."

I wanted to say more, but I couldn't find the words. My heart ached at the defeat on her face. This was all my fault. I wanted to sit next to her on the couch, but there wasn't enough room, and I wasn't about to squeeze myself next to the tiny man. The energies he was giving off were different yet familiar. Like an old friend I hadn't seen since childhood but couldn't remember their name. It was like he was part witch and part something else. The other part was a mystery. He could have fae in him, just as he could have shifter. Possibly a gopher. That would explain the size.

Valen's dark gaze settled on me. "I was starting to worry about you. You took quite the... mental beating."

"Tell me about it." The memory of Nikolas using

his Pusher magic on me set my teeth on edge. "I might have lost my temper a wee bit."

"We noticed." Valen chuckled. "But we understood. Even Arther. It was your first experience with mind manipulation. You couldn't have known what to expect—how it works and how it affects the mind. You just... reacted. It was natural to want to defend Shay."

It explained why Arther or Valen hadn't interrupted us or stopped Nikolas from pushing further. Back when I was fighting the vamp, I really wanted to hurt him. I would have kicked his bloodsucking vampire ass if it had been nighttime.

"How are you feeling?" asked the giant.

"Like a metal rod decided to play piñata with my head," I answered. Though Nikolas had attacked my mind, it felt as though he'd also harmed my body, like *he* had beaten it with a metal rod. Weird. "I'm good. Don't worry about me." I still felt a little woozy, but maybe I'd feel loads better with some food in me.

"This is Olin," said the giant after a short pause. "He's the compound's healer."

"I figured as much." My gaze traveled over the stranger again.

His orange hair gave me pause. A pair of thick, black-rimmed glasses, maybe a little too big for his face, sat on a long nose. His green suit hung loosely on him like it was two sizes too big. Large feet with sandals peered from under the hem of his pants. His toes were immaculate and looked as though he'd gotten a recent pedicure.

Olin gave me a pointed look that reminded me of Elsa. "You should lie down. Your mind's suffered a traumatic experience. It needs rest. You're lucky he didn't send you into a coma."

I stiffened as I felt some anger returning. "Right. Nikolas. Could he do that?" I had no idea how strong these vampire abilities were. I needed to do some more research.

"Yes," answered the healer, his eyes serious. "The kind of coma you never wake from."

That sounded ominous. If he'd done that to Shay... I'd have killed him. "What happened after I... passed out."

"I took you and Shay back here," answered the giant. "I did what I could with my magic. But I wanted a healer to take a look at her. I asked Arther to get Olin."

Right. Arther. *Wonder what he thinks of me now.* Probably as much as a rock. "How long have I been out?" I glanced out the window and noticed how dark it was. The sun had set already, and shadows were quickly creeping in. I hated missing time, and judging by how dark it was already, I was guessing I'd missed a lot.

"About five hours."

"Five hours?" Damn. It only felt like moments between when the darkness had taken me and me opening my eyes now.

"You need rest," scolded Olin, staring at my head

like he expected it to erupt or that I'd start to bleed out of my ears. "If you don't, you risk sending *yourself* into a coma. A person's mind is a fragile thing. Just like a sprained ankle, it needs time to heal."

"I'm fine." I stared at Shay. "I'm worried about her. How is she?"

"Valen did his healing magic." Shay shifted on the couch. "I'm way better now."

When my eyes reached the giant, he didn't seem to agree with her statement. Though she did look better, she didn't look totally healed either. And Valen knew this. He knew this, and by the tightness of his expression, it worried him.

What if the session with Nikolas had worsened the curse? To the point that Valen's healing magic wouldn't work anymore? That was not something I wanted to think about.

My eyes rolled over the coffee table to an empty glass with some green particles resting on the bottom. A few containers also sat alongside some glass vials. Medicine, I gathered. Olin's medicine.

I glanced at Shay again, and from the softness of her features and her relaxed demeanor, I could tell she liked this healer. Or at least she wasn't afraid of him. Maybe it had something to do with the fact that he was smaller than her.

"What kind of witch are you?" I asked, and when I tried to tap into my starlight, a massive migraine throbbed against my forehead like it wanted to push out my eyeballs. Okay, bad idea.

Olin folded his hands on his lap and answered in

a way that implied I wasn't the first person to ask this of him. "I'm a mage, actually."

"A mage?" Huh. I'd never met one before. "But you're so... small?"

Shay snorted as her face turned bright red, and she was looking at everything but at Olin and me.

I tried not to smile at her reaction. She was just too freaking cute. "What? I'm just curious. No offense."

Olin smiled, not seemingly offended at all by my rudeness. "My mother was a goblin, my father a mage."

"No shit." I tried to visualize a goblin female and a mage together. I couldn't.

Valen's shoulders bounced as he laughed. I wasn't sure if he knew I was trying to imagine a goblin and a mage bumping uglies or if he thought I was hilarious.

Shay slowly slipped back into the sofa like she wanted to disappear, but I was intrigued.

I moved closer to the mage-goblin healer. "And you learned your magic through your father's teachings?"

Olin nodded proudly. "That's right. But I learned most of my healing abilities from my mother. See, Mum was a healer. One of the best. I could have gone to the Mages Guild, like my father. But the guild didn't want a half-breed like me to soil their great halls, and by then, I had already put effort into learning to heal rather than using my magic to hurt others. I gravitated naturally toward healing." I knew what he meant by that, just like I had a similar feeling, a pull from the stars.

I looked him over. Now that he mentioned it, his long, pointed nose and equally long fingers did give the impression of some goblin genes. But other than that, he looked like an ordinary yet tiny older man.

"You've given her some of that healing stuff"—I gestured to the empty glass—"and it's working? She's better?"

"Yes." Olin shifted on the couch. "I've given her feverfew and mugwort to speed up her recovery process and some sandalwood to give her a boost of energy. Her immune system was attacked, and it needs to be replenished." He looked over at Shay. "Don't skip any meals. You need to eat. Protein is best. Chicken or turkey, if you have it. You should carry some nuts with you for snacks." He waved his hands over the vial and looked at me. "She needs to drink one full glass of water with the added nutrients once a day for another five days. That should do it."

I smiled at my little sister. "So, she'll be fine."

The little man nodded. "Yes. But I must advise you not to try the telethesia again. *You* can, if you want, but only after a few days. But Shay must never be subjected to it ever again. For someone so young and in an already *fragile* state," said Olin, his eyes on Valen, and I could tell he knew we were hiding something. Guess the giant didn't tell him about the curse. Good. Olin was kind, but we didn't know him.

I let out a breath. "I had a feeling you'd say that."

"I understand you were only trying to protect her

from another vampire," said the healer. "But exposing Shay to another training session is a terrible idea. Because it will cause her to deteriorate further, too much stress on her mind and body."

"What are you saying, exactly?"

"That she cannot suffer another episode of a mental attack," answered the healer.

My mouth fell open. "So, even if another vampire were to, say, try to use their mind abilities on her... it would make her worse?"

Olin shook his head solemnly. "She wouldn't recover from it."

That was all the healer said, but the message was clear. If Freida tried to get into Shay's mind to do her bidding, to enslave her, it would kill Shay. Freida didn't know about Auria's curse. And if she tried to push into my sister's mind, Shay would die.

I rubbed my temples. "I need a drink." Even though we tried to help Shay, thinking that if she could block the vampires from manipulating her, that would save her, we ended up making it worse. But we also inadvertently discovered that because of Shay's fragile state, more mind compulsion would kill her. This was the grimmest possible outcome. Could things get worse? Of course, they could.

I hated to admit it, but coming here seemed like a bad idea.

"No alcohol for at least twenty-four hours," instructed Olin, eyeing me.

I opened my mouth to object, but instead, I said, "Yes, Doc." Seeing the tiny smile on his face and that twinkle in his eye, I felt myself relax around him. My witchy instincts said I could trust him. Could I trust him about Auria's curse? I wasn't sure yet. And I wasn't sure what good it would do to tell him anyway.

"And no other strenuous *physical* activities on the body for another twenty-four hours." Olin gestured with his fingers at Valen and me.

My face flamed. I knew exactly what he meant by that. Seeing Valen's smirk told me he knew too. Right. Okay, no sex for a while. Not like I was thinking about that right now, though some horizontal boogie with my giant would release some of that tension I felt fluttering inside me. Guess that would have to wait.

My eyes fell on my sister, and part of me wished we'd never come here. "I'm so sorry, Shay."

"It's okay," she said, looking at me. "You didn't know. At least we tried."

I sighed. "But we made you sicker." The thought of that vampire pushing Shay sent another volley of fury through my veins. But I couldn't stay mad at the bloodsucking leech. He was trying to help, though he did push Shay too hard. In his defense, he also was oblivious to the curse.

"Well, I should be going." Olin tried to rise from the couch but only managed to fall back. Then, with more effort, he rocked forward and pushed himself up, drawing several faint popping sounds from his joints. He grabbed his medical bag. "Should you need anything, anything at all, please come find me.

Doesn't matter what time it is. I'm just a few cottages down. The one with the red roof and green door. There's a sign. You can't miss it."

"Thank you so much," I said, feeling grateful and surprised at his willingness to help Shay since we were strangers here. Then again, he was a healer. It's what they did. But that big, genuine smile that spread over his face made me like him instantly. He cared. He cared about Shay.

I stuck out my hand—

The front door to the cottage burst open. Arther rushed in. His eyes first went to me, and then they darted to Valen as he declared, "Nikolas is dead."

Like I said, things could always get worse.

CHAPTER 10

The pine-and-hemlock forest pressed close on either side of the trail, which wasn't an actual trail but more of a break in the forest tree line. The woods were so dense and dark, I could barely see the twinkling white stars and the glowing moon through the gaps in the trees.

A chill rushed through me that wasn't from the cooler air.

Nikolas, the compound's old vampire, was *dead* dead. Not like I hadn't wished to do it myself a few hours ago, but I hadn't. Honest. And in my defense, I was in bed, passed out from the vampire's Pusher attacks.

Blood pooled around the head, oozing from the single gaping hole pierced on the side of his temple like he was hit with a sharp object. A dagger? Possibly. It looked like the blow had killed him. His eyes were wide and staring at the black sky, his face pale with blood loss. The vamp had been pale before.

Now his skin was nearly white. The air smelled of a mix of blood, pine needles, and wet earth.

I moved around the body, but I couldn't see any signs of a struggle. No defense wounds and no bruises on his skin. His hands were smooth and clean, not the rough and calloused hands of a warrior like Valen's, but like the hands of a banker or an accountant who handled paper and pushed the keys of a computer most of their lives. His nails were short, and his talons from before were retracted.

Blood spatter stained the shoulder area of his lumberjack shirt, which I still found odd on a vampire, in dark maroon blots. The spray pattern marked the source of the blood as coming only from the puncture wound on the side of his head. The killing strike. That's what it looked like to me.

But Nikolas was a mighty vampire with the skill to make any enemy bow down and kiss his feet. In fact, before this moment, I would have thought him invincible, given his exceptional talent. A non-kill vampire, or whatever it was called.

Looked like I was wrong.

Nikolas had been alive only a few hours ago, using his Jedi mind tricks to kick my ass. But now he was as lifeless as a doorknob.

"Who found him?" Valen knelt next to the body, his eyes rolling over the scene like he was looking for something. The murder weapon?

"A group of kids." Arther stepped forward. "They were pretty freaked out."

"No kidding," I said.

Arther turned his gaze on me, and it was hard trying to keep my face straight and refrain from showing any emotion. He kept giving me these intense looks since he arrived at the cottage, looks that made the hair on the back of my neck rise and the tension around my middle tighten.

My gaze shifted to the other side of the path. Standing, both with their arms crossed, were two werewolves. I knew they were weres, not because of how they were built—all burly muscled and looking like they spent too much time at the gym, since not all weres were built like Arnold Schwarzenegger—but because of the energies that radiated from them and their scent.

I didn't have to look very hard. Hell, just by the way they were standing in my line of sight, they *wanted* me to see them.

The werewolf male was a hulking figure. Huge pectorals bulged under his T-shirt, the seams straining to contain all that muscle. He had an intimidating stance, like that of a bear. Through his thick, black beard and shaggy hair, his expression was blank as he watched me.

But the female werewolf had my pulse quickening. Her long, black hair cascaded down her body like waves. She wore jeans and a jacket, ideal for a battle. Petite but fast, females were known to be more aggressive and vicious. Her posture was tense and her face stern, and there was no mistaking the potential violence in her gaze. I knew that look. It was the *I'm going to rip out your throat and eat it* kind of look.

Swell. I really had a knack for making friends.

The werewolves stood stock-still, their eyes on their vampire friend sprawled on the ground.

Soon the lingering dusk would be gone, and we would be left in total darkness. I was tempted to use my starlights to give us light, but something in my gut told me that was a bad idea, that the werewolves wouldn't welcome it.

The blood of the dead vampire was already seeping into the soil, and soon it would disappear. Though Shay had given me a hard time when I told her to stay in the cottage to wait for us, I was glad she didn't have to see this.

"I want to come," she'd protested as we prepared to leave.

"No," I'd answered, feeling another sense of déjà vu, knowing we'd had this conversation many times before. "Doctor's orders." I looked over to the healer, Olin, who was still standing in the cottage.

"Yes," he'd agreed. "You need to stay here and rest." He'd looked at me then, probably to tell me the same thing, but from his frown, he guessed I'd just ignore him. He'd imagined right.

"And don't try to follow us, Shay," I told her, knowing she excelled in stealth and had the uncanny ability to sneak out of tight situations. Until I knew more about what happened to Nikolas, I wanted her indoors and safe.

"I'll have Eve come over and keep her company while you're out," Arther had suggested.

"Thanks." That made me feel better, and judging

by the tiny smile on Shay's face, her too. And that would most likely keep her staying put.

And so, Valen and I followed Arther out, leaving Shay alone to wait for Eve.

My gaze flicked back to the dead vampire. There was no love loss here, and I felt absolutely nothing for him except for maybe the shock that he was dead. He'd hurt me. He'd hurt Shay. I could never like a person for that, even though my mind kept telling me that we'd *asked* him to, that he'd done us a favor. I couldn't shake it off. Still, someone had killed him. Maybe he'd pissed off a few too many folks here. Maybe he'd used his Jedi mind tricks too often, abused them, and someone finally had enough.

It's possible that whoever it was had surprised the vampire, snuck up behind him, and bludgeoned him to death. So where was the murder weapon? The fact that it was gone told me that it had been premeditated. They'd taken it with them.

Judging by the waxy, grayish-white color of his skin, the blue on the tips of his fingers, and the graying lips, the body was still in the "fresh stage" and hadn't begun the first stage of decomposition. I estimated he died about two hours ago.

"I'm guessing Nikolas had enemies," I said, looking at Arther. "Do you know who?"

A muscle feathered along the pack leader's jaw. "Nikolas was well-liked. He had many friends here. Not enemies. This was his home for four years." His gaze turned intense as he added, "*You* are his only enemy."

I choked on my spit. "Excuse me? I wasn't his enemy. I barely knew the guy, vampire. I met him this afternoon." I resisted the urge to roll my eyes. Something about the way Arther was watching me was unsettling. It kind of creeped me out.

Valen stood up slowly, his posture bordering on explosive. Yeah, he sensed the dangerous vibes his pal was projecting.

Arther gave me a contemptuous look, barely acknowledging Valen as he moved around the body. "You threatened his life."

"You're serious?" I repeated. I looked askance at him to see if he was joking. This had to be a joke. "He hurt Shay. You were there. You saw what happened. I was only trying to protect her from him." What kind of backward thinking was this? Like I said, I was really starting to regret our choice of coming to this compound. We should have stayed in New York.

"It looked like you wanted to kill him," said the alpha, his voice calm with an underlying deadly tone. "And if he hadn't beaten you, I think you would have."

I felt a sudden rush of anger and vehemence. "I wouldn't have, and I didn't." Not true. I just might have if I had the power of my starlights behind me. It was the only reason Nikolas had kicked my butt. And then the pieces started to fit. "You think *I* did this?" Yeah, I was a little bit slow tonight. I blamed it on the violation of my mind earlier. His silence was my answer. Damn. He thought I'd killed Nikolas. Yes, I'd imagined doing it, but I hadn't.

"Leana didn't do this." Valen came to my defense. "She's not a killer."

That wasn't entirely true. I had killed Auria, though it had been sort of an accident. And countless others. All baddies, so they didn't count.

Arther kept his gaze on me, unwavering. "That's not what I heard."

My brows rose my scalp. "You mean Catelyn? What's she saying about me?" Okay, she and I needed a chat. And it was going to be the kind with fists.

Arther looked at Valen. "She's the only one here who wanted him dead. And he is. Coincidence?"

"Yes," I said out loud.

"There're no such things," said the alpha with the same amount of animosity in his voice. I was starting not to find him so attractive anymore. Right now, he was butt-ugly.

I waved my hands around. "Listen. I didn't kill him. Yes, I might have wanted to, but I didn't. Despite whatever Catelyn's told you about me, I don't go around offing vampires that piss me off."

"You threatened his life," said Arther. "We all heard you."

Shit. There was that. "It was just me letting off some steam. You can't hang me for that."

The other two weres stiffened at my comment. They looked like they were waiting for their boss to give the signal so they could attack me. Okay. This wasn't going well.

"Arther." Valen moved closer to his friend.

"Leana was in bed for hours. Passed out. There's no way she could have done that. Trust me. Ask the healer. He'll vouch for her."

"Yes. This," I said, pointing at the giant, smiling. Damn. I shouldn't be smiling. It made me look like a crazy person. A guilty person.

Arther regarded me with an expression somewhere between annoyance and contempt as he let out a puff of breath. "I have a witness that says otherwise."

Horrified, I felt the blood leave my face. "Impossible. I never moved out of that bed until right now. You're bluffing."

Arther shook his head, and there was no way for me to know whether he was. "I'm not. She says she saw you about two hours ago. Here. In these woods."

"Bullshit." Okay, now I was pissed. "I wasn't here."

"She says you were. You had plenty of time to sneak out the bedroom window, kill Nikolas, and return before anyone noticed you were missing."

My tension rose, pulling my shoulders straight. "Wow. You've got this all figured out. Don't you? Who's your witness?" I had a feeling I already knew who she was, but I wanted Arther to confirm it.

"Why? So you can kill her too?" he said to me, venom in his voice.

"It's Catelyn. Isn't it?" Yeah, it was, and by the tightness in his jaw at the mention of her name, I knew it was her. Holy crap. She was trying to pin this on me. She must really hate my guts to lie about something as serious as murder.

"Listen," I said, looking at Arther and trying to reel in my emotions. "I didn't do this. The real killer is out there. Maybe you should stop to think for a second, realize that Catelyn's feeding you bullshit, and start looking for the real killer." Was I hurt that she was trying to do this to me? Maybe. But I was more surprised at how far she was willing to go because of what happened to her parents, even so far as pinning a murder on me.

"Right now, the evidence is pointing to you," said Arther, the expression on his face empty as he looked at me. "You wanted him dead. And here he is. Dead."

I raised a brow, a sliver of anger sliding under my skin. "If I wanted him dead," I repeated, my voice dangerously low, "this isn't exactly how I'd do it. I would have fried his ass with my starlights, not stabbed him in the head with some sharp object." I realized only afterward that I was shouting. I shouldn't be screaming, but this guy was starting to rub me the wrong way.

"Leana." Valen raised his brows at me, his eyes moving over my body like I was missing something important.

"What?" I looked down at myself. Crap. I was glowing like a freaking star. I'd tapped into my starlight magic, and I never even realized I was doing it. Not only did they blame me for something I didn't do, but I was also now threatening their alpha with my magic.

I let go of my starlights and took a calming breath. I didn't apologize. Why should I?

"What Leana is trying to articulate," interjected Valen, speaking quickly. "Is that she couldn't have done this. I know her." He looked intently at Arther. "And you know me. You know my word is good. And I'm telling you, Leana didn't do this. Trust me on that. Arther, you're wrong. Leana didn't do this. You've got this all wrong, man."

The alpha looked at his friend. "It's not for me to decide."

"Really?" I said. "I thought you were the big cheese around these parts."

A flash of annoyance crossed Arther's face, fleeting and almost not there. "When these types of events happen, we have a way of dealing with them at the compound."

"How?" asked Valen, unease rippling in his voice.

Arther didn't look at Valen. He looked at me and said, "With a trial. Leana will be put on trial, and the council will decide her fate."

Wonderful. I knew I loved it here.

CHAPTER 11

When Arther had mentioned a trial, I figured it would be in a few days, enough time for us to sneak out of this place and head back to New York. I never expected the trial to be held moments after discovering Nikolas's body. Like, right the hell now.

Valen looked just as pleased as I was to follow Arther and his bodyguards back down the path to a different part of the compound I'd never been to yet. The clearing was right behind a line of cottages. A few fire braziers lit the way, filling the air with the scent of burning wood, and gave us enough illumination to see what this place was. A small platform at the end of the clearing was raised several feet higher with three suspiciously throne-like chairs perched upon it. Only two were occupied at the moment. Was this the council? Looked like it.

The male who sat in one of those chairs might have been another were or shifter, and the other, an older female, reminded me of my grandmother.

Witch? Possibly, but I was too far away to sense any magical properties about her.

My gaze cast around at all the people milling about. Looked like the entire compound had come to see the show. And yup, they all turned their heads at our approach. Energy crackled against my skin: the powers from the other weres, shifters, and witches who stood facing the dais. Seemed like Arther was leading us there.

When Arther reached the dais, he pointed to a stone circle laid just a few feet away in the dirt. "You stand there." He didn't wait for me to follow his instructions as he climbed up on the dais and took the empty seat.

I looked at Valen standing next to me. "Any great ideas?"

"I'm thinking."

"Think faster. I'm not sure I'm liking what's happening right now." I felt like I was on trial for my life. How the hell did that happen while I was unconscious?

"It'll be all right."

"Ya think?" I looked up at the faces on the dais, their expressions all dour and severe. In their eyes, I was already guilty of a crime I hadn't committed.

The soft murmur of conversations among the gathered filled me with a sense of apprehension and dread. I shouldn't be here. I should be back at the cottage enjoying a glass of wine, preferably poured by a glorious giant. A *naked* glorious giant.

I had the sudden crazy idea that I could fly

away. Now that I knew I could with my new badass starlight flying ability. I wasn't worried about leaving Valen. He could take care of himself. They were blaming and attacking me, not him, but when I spotted Shay standing in the mob next to Eve, my dread replaced any remaining confidence at the fright that flashed in her eyes and across her face. I tried to tell her with my eyes that it would be okay, but I probably looked terrified, possibly constipated.

Damn it. My emotions were raw. And when I saw the confusion and the moisture in her eyes, I nearly lost it. But it would only end badly if I acted on my emotions right now. For me, yes, but especially for Shay. She was the only thing that kept me sane right now and not blowing up the dais with my starlights. *Accidentally*.

I searched the crowd for Catelyn, but I couldn't see her.

"Please step into the judging circle so we can begin your trial, Leana," ordered Arther again.

"Judging circle?" I hissed at Valen. "Did you hear that? I thought you said we'd be safe here?"

"We are." His jaw clenched, though his voice lacked conviction.

"Then why do I get the feeling my life's about to change? And I'm not talking about getting a new pair of shoes."

Valen looked from the dais to me. "Do as he says, Leana."

"No."

The giant took in a deep breath. "I'll protect you. Don't worry."

It was the one time I didn't believe him. I let out a shaky breath. "Don't think you can this time."

Reluctantly, I stepped into the stupid judging circle, resisting the urge to kick some stones on the way.

Arther stood up and addressed the crowd. "Friends. Family. We are gathered here tonight to resolve an urgent and troubling matter." His eyes traveled over the heads of the mob until they rested on me, and my heart gave a start. "Leana Fairchild, you are accused of assassinating Nikolas Bertram."

"Motherfrackers," I muttered. I knew it was coming. He'd said so before leaving the dead vampire's body just as another group joined us to pick it up. I shouldn't have been surprised. But now it felt... real. Because I was standing in some stupid judging stone circle, staring up at a council while the compound watched. I was going to puke. I knew I was.

Valen's expression was tight as he stood beside me, fury simmering in the back of his eyes. But it was nothing compared to the deep rage that boiled in my core.

Breathe, just breathe.

My body trembled as I tried to control my starlights from acting out. It was only natural and instinctual to defend myself under these circumstances. My starlights wanted to protect me. They wanted out. But I couldn't let them.

Yet I had the feeling I couldn't control them much longer.

I looked at Valen. It wasn't that I didn't trust him. I knew if they sentenced me to death or something, he would fight for me. Of that I had no doubt. I just didn't want it to happen. This was a gargantuan mess of things.

"How do you plead?" asked Arther, his face carefully blank, and I wanted to jump up and kick him in the throat. And I might even do it. Not sure how far I'd get, but still, A for effort.

"Not guilty," I said, my voice loud, still thinking this was seriously ridiculous. I'd never been on trial for anything in my life. Yes, Clive the douche had thrown me in a cell, awaiting a tribunal, but Darius had let me out. All part of his master plan to lead him to my sister, which, unfortunately, I did. But it ended up in our favor with Darius dying.

"Leana."

I spun around at the sound of my sister's voice. "It'll be okay. Don't worry," I told the terrified kid, the whites of her eyes showing in the semidarkness.

"Unfortunately, the council agrees that the evidence points to you," said Arther solemnly. I turned my attention back around toward the council and saw everyone nodding.

"She didn't do this," warned Valen, and my heart thrashed at the hardness in his voice. He moved to stand in front of me like an impenetrable wall of protection.

Arther looked down at Valen. "You'll be allowed

to speak on Leana's behalf after all the evidence has been viewed and witnesses have been heard."

"Evidence? What evidence? I wasn't even there." If I didn't know any better, I'd say this was arranged somehow.

"Catelyn, please step forward," announced Arther.

Voices erupted all around as I spotted the giantess cutting a path through the crowd and making her way forward. She stopped about twenty feet from me on my right.

"Why are you doing this?" I snapped at her, but she wouldn't look at me. Her eyes were on the council, on Arther. "Catelyn. Talk to me."

The alpha turned around and returned to his seat. "Catelyn, tell us what you saw."

"I saw her leaving Nikolas's dead body," she answered. The lie flew really smoothly off her tongue. As though she believed it herself and was rewarded by dramatic oohs and aahs from the crowd.

"You lying cow," I hissed. "I should have left you to rot in that aquarium." I regretted the words that flew out of my mouth when I saw her flinch. But I was beyond rational now, hearing her lie flat-out about me to a group of strangers, when she knew I had nothing to do with this. It all came back to her parents. She blamed me for their deaths, and it looked like she wanted me to be executed or something.

But I wouldn't go down without a fight. There

was no actual proof that I'd committed this crime. It was her word against mine, apparently.

I seethed, crossing my arms over my chest to hide my trembling hands. A cold shiver oozed down my spine. This was madness.

"And you're positive it was Leana?" Arther gestured to me with his head as though we didn't already know who I was. The one standing in the stupid judging stone circle.

"Without a doubt," answered the giantess. Was that a smirk on her lips?

I pressed my hands on my hips, glaring at the side of her face. "Really? Then why didn't you report it? Why was it a bunch of kids?" I took a breath, feeling dizzy from all the excess anger that welled in my veins. "Because you never saw me. You're lying."

The crowd stirred, most of the noise swallowed up by the space.

"Because I followed you," answered the giantess, still staring straight ahead as she spoke. "I wanted to make sure you didn't kill anyone else."

I gritted my teeth, my body tingling with suppressed starlight energy. "You're so full of crap. You know it. I know it. We all know it." My blood pressure rose like a tide as I faced the council, careful to keep my expression calm and blank. But I was failing.

"It was her," said Catelyn, her voice loud and clear for everyone to hear.

"She's lying," I said, my voice rising and as piercing as hers. "She blames me for her parents' deaths, and she'll say just about anything to make me pay for it." A thought popped into my head. "Did you kill the vamp to make it look like *I* did it?" I would have never thought of her doing something so evil and nuts, but then again, I'd never thought I'd be pleading for my life in a makeshift tribunal deep in the woods, with the flannel parade.

Catelyn's jaw tightened, and I could see the emotions spiraling through her as she, too, tried to control that inner beast that wanted out.

The female council member leaned over and whispered something to Arther. I watched as the three members entered into a conversation. Arther leaned back in his throne-like chair. The other council members put their heads together, and I waited, watching them.

"Leana, I'm sorry," said Valen.

"I know." I knew he meant he was sorry and regretted coming here because he'd said we'd be safe, protected. Not subject to this makeshift council and false charges.

The pressure in my head climbed, making me feel light-headed. My limbs began to tremble uncontrollably, and I was sure I was about to faint or possibly vomit.

After a moment, Arther spoke. "After much deliberation. The council has reached a decision."

"Steady, Leana," I heard Valen say. "Whatever happens, keep your cool. We'll figure something out."

"Easy for you to say." My gut knotted like my

intestines were playing a game of jump rope with the rest of my organs. I looked at him, unable to bring myself to say anything. What would be the point.

"It is the council's opinion," Arther went on, "that too much past exists between you and the witness to accept all of her testimony."

Ha. They knew she was lying. Maybe not Arther, but I was willing to bet that old lady and the dude were on my side. "Which means what?" I could tell Arther was holding something back. This wasn't finished. Not by a long shot.

"This brings us to a crossroads," Arther said as he placed his hands on his knees. "You can either stay in house arrest until we have more proof or more people come forward, or you can choose to end this tonight."

That didn't sound so bad. "And how would I end this tonight?"

He hesitated and said, "Trial by combat."

I burst out laughing. "Trial by combat? What is this? Are we in the medieval ages? Bring me my sword!" I laughed again. Arther wasn't laughing.

He paused before he spoke again. "The choice is yours."

"What kind of backward place you running here?" I'd never heard of trial by combat before. It sounded like something you'd see in the movies. It didn't sound real.

"If you win, you'll be acknowledged as innocent and exonerated from the murder allegations," Arther declared. "But if you don't succeed, the punishment for murder in this compound will apply to you. Depending on the gravity of the crime, a time in prison is likely."

"Lovely. And I'm not even one of you."

"Rules apply to all those who stay at the compound," answered the alpha.

"Spoiler alert. You need to rethink your rules."

But I was curious and hopeful. If it only took a fight, and the case was dropped, maybe a trial by combat wasn't such a bad idea. Primitive, yes, but I could work with that.

"Who am I fighting?" I had a feeling I already knew.

Catelyn turned to face me. "Me."

I grinned. "You're on."

CHAPTER 12

"Leana, no," warned Valen.

I looked at my favorite giant. "Don't worry. I've got this. She wants a fight? She's got it."

Catelyn was staring at me with as much open hatred and promise of violence as I was. One of the things I liked most about her was I could read her like an open book. She wasn't a hypocrite. She was a what-you-see-is-what-you-get type of person. She was real.

Arther rose to his feet and descended from the platform. "Let the trials by combat begin," he proclaimed, prompting a roar of approval from the audience. It seemed they had been eagerly anticipating this battle, looking like this was what they were hoping for.

I rolled my eyes. I hated this place.

Arther walked past us, ushering the crowd to make space for our fight. I met Shay's eyes and didn't see fear in her this time, but regret. She didn't want me to fight Catelyn. Or maybe she didn't wish Catelyn to fight me? She'd seen firsthand how strong the giantess was and how by dumb luck, I'd managed to knock her out. But here, no low ceilings or walls could hinder the giantess's movements. The space was open, and she could go wild on me.

Catelyn's eyes flashed with anger as we moved to follow Arther. "You won't be so confident once I'm finished with you."

I smirked. "We'll see about that." I wasn't about to let her pound my head in. "Don't forget. *You* did this. This is on you." Funny how we'd been friends one minute, and the next, we were enemies, wishing pain on one another. Life could be weird that way.

We trudged through the dirt to reach the makeshift arena, which had been compacted in a way that showed this place had hosted many fights before us. I couldn't help but feel a rush of adrenaline. This was it. The moment of truth. The crowd gathered around us, chanting and cheering. I was seriously going to hurl.

Valen stood at the sidelines next to Shay, his expression tense. I could tell he was worried about me, but I had to do this. I *had* to prove my innocence, even though this method was positively barbaric and made absolutely no sense. And it looked like proving it meant I was going to kick the giantess's ass. No biggie.

The only good thing was that Valen was with Shay. If something should happen, like if I died, he'd take care of Shay. I doubt he'd stay here. He'd probably head to that secret cabin of his where Shay would be safe.

I shook the morbid thoughts out of my head. I was not dying tonight. Catelyn wouldn't best me.

A loud wail erupted from Catelyn's mouth, and I snapped my attention back to her. Her body vibrated with magical energy before a bright flash of light enveloped her. She fell to her knees, still screaming in pain as her features swelled beyond human proportions. The ground shook as she managed to stand on two feet. Her face had taken on a bigger, more pronounced shape with larger eyebrows and a wider jaw, giving her that Neanderthal look, just like Valen. The fabric of her clothes didn't rip this time. Instead, they rippled and stretched, fitting her new enormous shape as though they'd been tailored to her. Magic. Her clothes were spelled to accommodate her new size. Very practical. Maybe Valen should get some like that.

Her fourteen-foot frame was impressive. So were her hands that could snap my neck like a twig. I couldn't help but feel a shiver run down my spine as I tried to take in the sight of Catelyn's transformation. This was going to be some kind of monstrous showdown. But there was no backing out now. I had to stand my ground and fight.

Catelyn growled, and it sounded like a feral animal. *"I told myself if I ever saw you again, I would kill you."* Her voice rasped and sounded like the grinding of rocks.

I flashed her a smile. "You look good. Have you been working out?"

The giantess snarled, showing me her flat teeth. "*Witch*."

"Big lady," I said with a shrug. "We can do this all night, you know."

"*Witch*," the giantess repeated with much more ferocity and malice, this time like it was the command word to pound in my head.

I shifted my weight and stepped back, readying myself for the oncoming attack. Catelyn let out a deafening roar, and I braced myself for impact. Damn. This was going to hurt. She lunged at me with deadly force, her massive arms swinging toward me like the sledgehammers of death. At the last moment, I dodged to the side, barely avoiding her blow.

As I turned around, I drew on my starlight and let out a loud clap of my hands. Countless miniature globes of light burst forth from my fingertips like fireworks exploding in the night sky. And hit Catelyn.

The giantess was enveloped in a swarm of sparkling stars that buzzed around her like a cloud of angry hornets. She thrashed and screamed, the scent of burnt flesh rising as the starlights burned her.

Was I sorry I was burning her? Nope.

But then, faster than I thought possible, Catelyn stopped thrashing as the brilliance of my magic vanished from her body like she'd summoned a protection shield, or her giantess form suppressed my starlights. But Catelyn couldn't do magic. And then it hit me. Her clothes. Her outfit was spelled with a built-in protection guard against my starlight. Looked like it. And it looked like she'd been planning all of this too.

Then she charged me.

I leaped out of the way as her fist smashed into the earth, sending a shower of dirt and dust raining down. The crowd cheered. Obviously, they were cheering *her* on, not me. Clearly, they wanted her to smash in my brains. Part of me wanted to stop and give them the finger, but I couldn't stop or get distracted. That's how you got killed.

"*You shouldn't have come here,*" said the giantess. "*You should have stayed away.*"

"Thought we could hang out. You know. Shoot the shit."

"*I will kill you.*"

I cocked my brows, holding on to my starlights. "You can try."

I stepped back, thinking of a way to take her down without killing her. I'd knocked her out once. I could do it again. I had to.

But Catelyn was relentless. She charged again, this time kicking out with her legs, hoping to step on me like you would a cockroach. I dodged her attack and countered with a swift kick to her stomach. It was like kicking a cement wall, and I cringed at the pain that reverberated all the way up my leg. She didn't even flinch.

Whoops.

I had to think fast. If my attacks weren't working,

I needed to try something different quickly before she pounded me into mush.

I pulled on my starlights. My hand glowed with a dazzling white light, and I aimed it at Catelyn's chest.

A beam of pure starlight shot out of my hand and hit Catelyn square in the chest. She staggered back, clutching at her heart. For a moment, she looked like she was going to fall, but then she regained her balance and charged at me again, this time even faster than before.

Shit. It was like her outfit was becoming increasingly resistant to my magic, or her giantess body was tougher than I expected.

I backed away, summoning my starlight magic, but Catelyn was already there. I felt the heat of her breath on my face as she closed in on me. I tried to dodge, but she was too fast. Her fist crashed into my side, and I went flying, hitting the ground hard. Pain coursed through my body, and I struggled to catch my breath.

Okay. That hurt. That hurt like a sonofabitch.

I could hear the crowd roaring with excitement. Wonderful.

I spat the earth from my mouth and staggered up.

Something hard hit me, and I went sprawling. I screamed as the giantess fell on me, pinning me on my back as I kicked out with my legs and struggled to wriggle out. Her weight crushed my lungs, and I couldn't breathe. Fear slid into me as I rocked my body. Her massive face loomed inches from mine as her hot breath assaulted my face. Her eyes shone with the desire to kill me. Yeah. This was *not* my friend. This was my enemy.

"All I have to do is stay like this and you will die," said the giantess.

I thought of something clever to say but came up short. This wasn't a joking matter. She was right. Another minute or so, and I was a goner.

"Catelyn! Stop!"

Was that Shay's voice that soared over the cheering crowd?

Catelyn seemed to think so because she turned her head in the direction of that voice. Her hard features seemed to soften for just a moment.

I used that moment of distraction to buck with all my strength, and I was surprised to feel a moment of release. I took it. Rolling, I managed to get away from the giantess and shot to my feet. And then I stabbed her with shots of my starlights.

Catelyn roared as my starlights enveloped her in a sheet of blazing lights, flaming her skin.

A cold panic ignited in my mind. The giantess was a mighty opponent. Without my starlights, I'd be dead right about now. She was strong, but her hatred for me fueled her with even more strength. It was scary.

My moment of triumph evaporated as she stopped moving, my starlights still very much burning her, and then rushed me.

"You're crazy," I muttered as I watched the now-glowing massive woman hurl another attack at me.

The earth shook, literally, as the giantess tore the ground with her bare feet and came thrashing at me with impossible speed for her size. "You *have* been working out."

She hit me in a blur of fists and my own starlights. She looked like a crazed polar bear with her body doused in starlight. One of her fists made contact with my chest. I felt a moment of the air leaving my lungs, and then my feet left the ground as I soared back. I smashed into the hard earth, feeling as though I'd broken a few ribs.

Damn.

I blinked the black spots from my eyes, trying to regain control of my body and focus. Something moved in my peripheral vision.

Catelyn stood over me, her glowing body looking like a burning demon with my starlights still attached to her. *"This is what happens to those who kill the innocent."*

Tension spiked through me. "I didn't kill Nikolas." I coughed as I struggled to catch my breath.

"You killed my parents." I was in too much pain to answer that. But we'd been over this many times. I didn't kill her parents—not physically, that is. But to her, it was as though I had used my own hands to end their lives.

"And now you're going to die."

I struggled to raise my hand and gather my starlight. I could do this. I had to do this. I needed to save my friends. I needed to save Shay. I had to protect myself.

Catelyn cocked her head just as my starlights vanished from her body. Her face was a blotchy red with burns.

I focused and tried to call out to my starlights.

And then she stepped on my arm. I could feel as if my bones were crushing under her weight as I cried out in pain and tears welled in my eyes. My focus collapsed, and I only had room for pain.

"*No more magic,*" said the giantess, a smile in her voice that made me sick.

Pain shot up my arm, and I fell back, struggling to keep consciousness and tasting blood in my mouth. I couldn't think beyond wanting the pain to stop. *Please make it stop.*

"*It's over. You're dead.*" Catelyn put more weight down on my arm, and I heard something snap.

I screamed as searing pain assaulted me, my cry drowned by the crowd's cheering, shouting, and stomping with glee as I struggled to move and get away from the giantess. But without the use of my arm, I couldn't do much.

All she had to do now was step on my head, and I was dead.

Agony shot through my arm as the giantess pressed her weight on it again. She was going to squish me into little witch bits.

I couldn't die like this for the second time tonight, especially not in front of Shay. Why did I agree to this? It was a stupid move. A stupid, impulsive move.

I was a fool to think I could best a giantess.

"And now because of you, Shay will have no more family," said the giantess. Her words hurt, possibly more than my broken arm. But when she laughed, actually laughed at the fact of what this would do to Shay, I lost it.

A savage roar escaped my mouth. I never thought I'd hear such a sound ripping out from my own throat, sounding primitive, feral.

Ignoring the pain in my arm, I reached out, pulled on my starlights, and with my free arm, slammed a blast of my magic into her chest with all of my remaining strength.

The giantess flew back like she'd suffered a kick in the gut. The earth vibrated beneath me as she fell, rolling to a stop.

I didn't wait for her to get up.

On my knees, I let out another scream as I yanked on my starlights again, and this time, I let out the rage and pain in my heart. It was like the starlights had exploded from my body and just kept exploding, faster and faster, until the whole forest was filled with the brilliant light of the stars.

And I kept hitting the giantess.

Again and again, like I was a semiautomatic weapon hitting my mark. I barely remembered standing up and walking over until I loomed over the writhing giantess.

And I kept hitting her with my magic.

The crowd went silent. Or maybe I couldn't hear them over the roaring in my ears.

I wanted it to end. I wanted her dead.

I kept slamming her into the ground again and again, pounding her with my magic. I knew Valen and Shay were watching. I couldn't see them, but I could feel them all.

"Kill her! Kill her!" someone shouted over the other incoherent wails of the crowds.

Kill her?

I moved my gaze around the crowd and noticed the two council members standing before the mob. The female caught my eye and gave me a nod.

No. That can't be right? She wants me to kill her.

Then, I looked at Arther. The horror on his face and his taut posture told me what I needed to know. This trial by combat was even more barbaric than I thought.

We had to *kill* each other. And the victor walked away free. I thought we just had to knock each other out or something.

Yes, I wanted her dead after what she did. And seeing as I kept hitting her with my magic while she was still down, it seemed I'd already made that decision.

"Leana. Stop. Please."

I spun my head around and saw Shay standing in the fighting ring just a few feet away from me, her face smeared with tears as she shook her head. She looked… she looked frightened *of* me.

I noticed that the crowd was silent. They'd stopped chanting for me to kill Catelyn.

When I looked at Shay again, seeing the pleading in her eyes, I let my starlights go.

The light trickled out of the forest, and I was left in darkness except for the flickers of light coming from the brazier fires.

My arm throbbed as I looked down at the giantess, her skin red, blistering, and scorched. She was alive. And I knew she'd heal fast. Was I sorry that I hurt her? Not one bit.

I only stopped for Shay. I didn't want her to see me kill someone she'd once considered her friend. Maybe she still thought Catelyn was a friend.

Wincing, I looked to the council, to Arther, who appeared relieved that I didn't kill his girlfriend or whatever she was to him. The other two council members' faces were unreadable.

Valen looked, well, he looked saddened and a bit angry. Not at me, but at the situation we found ourselves in.

"Now what?" I asked Arther. "I won't kill her, so what happens now?"

The alpha were glanced at me and said, "Now, you're on house arrest."

Of course I was.

CHAPTER 13

I'd forbidden Valen from using his giant healing magic on me. He was only to use it on Shay, and she needed it more than me. I wasn't the one living with a so-called incurable curse. She was.

So, this explained why Olin was back, making me drink questionable vials and rubbing dubious, stinking ointments on my right arm that smelled like a chicken coop.

"Reckless behavior," the healer mumbled, rubbing in a yellow ointment while he wore green garden gloves. His orange hair was standing up on his head, and he reminded me of those tiny luck troll dolls that were popular in the nineties with crazy hair.

Shay leaned on the table next to me, her green eyes filled with wonder as she watched Olin work on me.

I gave Valen, who was leaning against the kitchen wall, a pointed look. "She started it," I said in my defense. Totally true. I wouldn't have been caught up in this mess if it hadn't been for Catelyn and her grudge against me.

Olin looked at me, a flash of confusion on his face, and then it was gone, replaced by his serious frown that I had become accustomed to. "No. Not you. But yes, that was reckless too. I'm talking about those barbaric rules. Trial by combat. That sort of nonsense."

"I take it you don't approve?"

"Nor should you. We are not animals."

"Speak for yourself. Most of the compound are animals in a way. They're shifters. Weres. They have their beast side." Which could account for their more-than-primitive way of dealing with stuff.

Olin glared at me. With his bushy orange eyebrows and crazy hair, he really did look like those tiny trolls. "I prefer to live in a civilized society. Not one that thinks fists are the way to decide one's fate. It's absurd."

"So why don't you leave?" I hadn't meant it in a negative way. I was just curious.

The healer exhaled, and some of his anger left him. "Because I am old. I've made a life for myself here. I'm respected. It's too late for me to try again somewhere else. Besides, I like nature. And I can just walk out my door and find as many mushrooms as I like."

I narrowed my eyes. "You sure you're not a hobbit?" I teased.

Olin smirked. "Who says I'm not?"

I laughed and then regretted it immediately. "Ouch. I think she broke a few ribs." I glanced at my little sister. "I'm sorry you had to see that. I know Catelyn's your friend." She'd seen me at my worst. Hell, the entire compound had. But I couldn't care less what they thought about me. I cared only about Shay. Shay and Valen.

Shay shrugged. "It's okay. She's not my friend."

"She's not?" I looked at Valen, who shook his head.

"She wanted to kill you," answered Shay. "I saw it in her eyes. That's not my friend. And I know you didn't kill Nikolas. You were with us here."

I exhaled. "I know."

"Why didn't they consult me?" Olin grumbled. "I could have told them it was impossible. You were unconscious. You could not take on a formidable vampire such as Nikolas and defeat him! It's ridiculous. Outlandish."

"Glad you're on my side." Though it was too late. "She lied so she could fight me. So she could try to kill me." I shivered at the memory of that pure hatred in her eyes and the promise of death.

"But she didn't." Shay's eyes filled with sudden wetness. "I don't want you to die."

Ah, hell, my throat suddenly ached. I swallowed. "I'm not dead yet. So don't you go thinking like that. Okay?" I reached out with my good hand and squeezed her tiny fingers in mine.

Shay just nodded and pulled her hand away as

she blinked fast, doing her best not to shed a tear. Stubborn beast, that kid. Like her older sister.

"It was obvious to everyone there that the giantess set you up," commented Olin. "None of it made any sense. Only Arther—"

"Is oblivious because he's in love with her." There I said it. And it was the truth. I was certain of it. Men were stupid when they're in love. And if he was an alpha, that's a dangerous combination.

I grabbed the cup of steaming healing juice—didn't know what else to call it—and drank the last of it.

When I sipped the last of Olin's drink, I started to feel a tingling over my skin. Heat spread through me with the sensation of burning warmth, prickling through my skin and insides, beginning from my stomach and branching out to my limbs. I wasn't cured, my bone was still broken, but I felt considerably better.

"Will she be okay?" asked Shay, tiny concern lines on her face. "Her bones are going to heal, and she'll be like before?"

"Yes." Olin looked at me and said, "Your radius, your arm bone is set, should heal in a few hours."

My mouth parted. "Really? That fast? You must be a very good healer."

"I am." He said it matter-of-factly, not like some pompous doctor who thought he knew everything but more like he knew what he was capable of. He reached inside his black medical bag and pulled out what looked like a sling and carefully looped it around my broken arm.

As a witch, I could heal broken bones faster than humans, but I still needed time for the actual healing to work. And I still couldn't move that arm, at least not yet.

"Thank you," I told Olin. "Thanks for patching me up."

The healer beamed. "It's my job." He looked at me for a moment. "Try not to die in the next forty-eight hours."

"I'll do my best."

"I need to talk to Arther about this house arrest." Valen unfolded his arms, his brows low and matching the threat in his voice.

"What does house arrest mean?" asked Shay.

"Aren't you full of questions tonight." I looked at Valen, hoping he could answer for me.

"It means Leana can't leave the cottage," he replied in a menacing tone. "She's not allowed to step outside of this place. She's stuck here until they decide what to do with her."

Shay's eyes widened. "What happens if she does?"

That was a very good question. And Valen's silence was answer enough.

Shay's lips parted in shock as she, too, made the connection. "That's not fair. You didn't *do* anything."

"I didn't kill Nikolas," I said, my voice firm. "But they need a scapegoat, someone to blame, and apparently I'm it."

Valen cleared his throat. His gaze was still fixed on me. "Not for long. I'll talk to Arther. If I have to pound him a few times for him to see reason, I will." His voice was tight, his jaw clenched, and I knew he wasn't happy about the situation. None of us were.

I don't know why, but the idea of Arther's face being pummeled by Valen's fist made me smile.

"So we're stuck here?" Shay's face fell, and I could tell she was disappointed. We had planned on going for a hike in the woods tomorrow, but now that was out of the question.

"Not you or Valen. Just me," I said, trying to sound upbeat.

Valen gave me a small smile, but it didn't reach his eyes. I knew he was worried about me, and I didn't blame him. The last few days had been rough, and we were both on edge. But we were a team, him and me. We'd figure this out.

The giant nodded. "They think that by keeping her here long enough, she'll be more likely to confess to something she didn't do. That they'll get a confession out of her."

"That's stupid," Shay said, her eyes flashing with anger. "They can't do that to you. You're innocent."

I smiled at her. "I'm glad you think so. But unfortunately, it's not up to us."

"I hate it here. I want to go home," she said, her face determined.

I glanced at Valen, who shrugged. "I'm sure we'll figure something out." Home was also an issue for Shay, with Freida waiting for us.

"Well…" Olin sighed as he grabbed his bag. "If there isn't anything else, I'll take my leave."

"Thanks, Olin," I said. Shay and I waved at him as he stepped out the front door and disappeared into the night.

Valen shut the door and joined us. "How are you? Really?"

"Fine." I narrowed my eyes. "I know what you're doing. Don't go after Arther. He's probably pissed and worried about Catelyn. I did nearly kill her, you know."

"I have to talk to him. To clear things up. This isn't what I wanted for us."

My heart tugged at the sadness on his face, and then it crushed a little at Shay's own misery. Damn it. I would not cry. Not now.

"Is anyone looking for the real killer?" I asked Valen. "I mean. We all know it wasn't me. Look. I hate to say this, but it could have been Catelyn. She's angry enough at me to pull off something this disturbing. Or someone else out there who hated Nikolas enough to kill him."

Valen rubbed the back of his neck as he exhaled long and low. "I don't know. Maybe."

"This place is weird." Shay pushed off the table, walked over to the couch, grabbed her tablet, stepped into her bedroom, and shut the door.

"How long is this house arrest going to last?" I asked him. "I'm not going to confess to something I didn't do. And I'm pretty sure Arther knows that. I made it clear to them."

The giant shook his head. "I don't know that either."

"What do you know?" I teased.

Valen moved closer to me and positioned himself between my thighs, his big strong hands rubbing my legs. "I know how to make you feel better. How to make you forget about tonight."

"Oh, you do, do you?" Sex was really not on my mind at the moment. Well, it hadn't been until his bedroom eyes bore into mine.

Valen grinned. "You have a dirty mind."

I smiled. "There are worse things in life."

The giant laughed. "Come. You need to rest. And I promise I won't—"

"Touch me?" I finished for him. "You know I like touching."

Valen made a growl in his throat. Then he slipped his big hands under me and lifted me, careful not to touch my broken limb. "Taking you to bed."

"Yay."

Valen carried me to the bedroom, where he gently laid me down on the bed. He sat down next to me, his hand reaching out to brush the hair out of my face. "You've been through a lot," he said softly. "I just want to take care of you."

"I know," I said, my voice barely above a whisper. "And I appreciate it. And you can't use your healing magic." I caught his hand. "You can't." I kissed it, and seeing the smile on his face sent tingles all over me.

"You drive a hard bargain," said the giant. "But I won't. Promise. I'll keep it for the little squirt."

Valen leaned down and kissed me softly on the lips, his hand gently tracing my jawline. I felt my heart race as he deepened the kiss, his tongue exploring my mouth. I wrapped my arms around his neck and pulled him closer, needing him.

He pulled back, his eyes filled with desire. "Rest now. Tomorrow… tomorrow we make plans."

I watched as he leaned back, resting his arms behind his head.

"Okay."

We didn't have passionate sex or even make out again. We just held each other, and somehow that felt better. Even more intimate.

The warmth of Valen's body against mine, the steady rise and fall of his chest, was all I needed to feel safe and loved. I closed my eyes and let myself drift off to sleep, clinging to him like a lifeline.

As I drifted, I still had that gnawing feeling in my gut. There was still the fact that the real murderer was here at the compound.

And no one was looking for them.

CHAPTER 14

The next morning, I woke up to the sound of birds chirping outside. For a moment, I forgot about the previous night's events, the accusations, the house arrest, Catelyn's stupid face, and her lies. But then it all came rushing back to me, and I sat up with a heavy feeling in my chest, my heart pounding.

But as the scent of something sweet like pancakes filled my nostrils, the heaviness in my chest lifted.

"Nothing like the smell of freshly made pancakes to make a girl feel better about putting a few extra pounds on her butt."

Feeling the sling around my body, I checked my arm. When I felt no pain, I removed the prop and carefully moved the appendage. Okay, so it was a little stiff, but it was loads better than it was last night. And the throbbing, inner bone pain from having a broken arm was gone. The bone was healed. And it didn't hurt when I breathed, either, so I assumed my bruised ribs had also recovered. Was I

100 percent better? No. But I was closer to 90 percent. Good enough.

I leaped out of bed, using the washroom to brush my teeth and do my business. And after a quick shower, I dressed and went in search of that delicious smell.

Valen's wide back came into view, his muscles popping and shifting as he worked the stove. The sound of something sizzling reached me. Butter. Yum. Love me some butter.

And butter would definitely add to the weight on my butt as well.

Butt... but*er*...see where I'm going? *More* butt.

Shay was already at the kitchen table, her eyes fixed on the screen as she scrolled through her tablet. I walked over to them, feeling a little lighter and more optimistic than I had the night before.

"Good morning," I said, trying to sound energetic, even though technically I was still on house arrest for something I didn't do. Yeah. Gotta love the "off the grid" experience.

"Morning," Valen replied, looking over his shoulder at me, his hand still on the frying pan.

"Morning," Shay said, still glued to her tablet.

I made a beeline for the coffee machine. "Something smells scrumptious."

"Pancakes," said Shay, still not looking up from her tablet.

I smiled at Valen as he turned back around and busied himself with said pancakes. "Thought so." I grabbed a mug from the cabinet and poured myself a large cup of steaming coffee. After adding some milk, I took a sip while taking in my giant. My fingers suddenly ached to rake through his thick, tousled dark hair. My eyes roamed over his very nice backside, and I slumped against the counter, enjoying the view. I could get used to this.

As Valen worked the frying pan, flipping the pancakes, I couldn't help but notice how relaxed and comfortable he looked as he stood there in the tiny kitchen, wearing only a T-shirt and jeans that hugged him in all the right places. The combination of sexiness, brilliance, and strength was an irresistible force. I had a weakness for intelligent men, especially when their smarts were paired with such a handsome figure. I could watch him all day, all night...

Valen cut me a look over his shoulder as though somehow he'd heard my thoughts, or maybe he felt my eyes rolling over his body. He smiled mischievously as he met my gaze. A hungry expression flashed across his rugged features, making me think that maybe giants *could* read minds.

He turned back to his work, and I kept staring at him. What? It was hard not to, and he was right there.

Though enjoying the view and how natural it was for him to be the first one up and make us breakfast, I was still not used to it. However, I was accepting that's what it was like to live with him. He was always up before Shay and me, ensuring we had sustenance in our bellies before starting our mornings. He wanted to do it. Wanted to take care of us. I wasn't complaining. It was just such a change from what I was used to. Martin never prepared breakfast or cooked me anything. Ever. The only thing he enjoyed doing was throwing me insults and body-shaming me. He was an expert at that. He *loved* to do it.

I snorted in my coffee at the memory of his broken and horribly swollen penis.

"What's that?" asked Valen as he piled another fresh pancake on a plate.

"Hmmm?" I said innocently. "Nothing." More images of broken penises flashed in my mind's eye.

"You're laughing by yourself again." Shay was staring at me with that look she had that said I was crazy.

I frowned at her. "Again? You mean I do this a lot?" How horrifying. And I didn't even know I was doing it.

"All the time," answered Shay.

"*No.*" I shook my head. "I think I would know."

"Trust me. You do it," said my little sister.

"Huh."

"Here you go, squirt." Valen dropped a plate of three golden, fluffy pancakes on the table for her, next to her glass of orange juice and the bottle of maple syrup.

"Thanks," said Shay, already pouring an avalanche of maple syrup over her pancakes and cutting into them.

I stared at her openmouthed as she stuffed her

face, trying to fit as many bites as she could in that tiny mouth of hers.

"Careful you don't choke." I pulled the chair next to her, watching her eat.

Shay stopped mid-chew. "What?" she said, her mouth full.

"Fascinating how you can stuff all that food into that tiny mouth."

Shay shrugged and swallowed. "I've got skills."

"I believe you. I can't remember ever being this hungry as a kid. You devour your food like you've never tried it before. It's almost like each time it's your first time experiencing food."

"I'm a growing kid." Shay cut into her pancake. "I'm hungry. Stop staring at me."

I raised my hands in surrender. "Okay. Sorry." I wrapped my hands around my warm mug. "So," I said with a sigh. "How do I get rid of this house arrest?"

Valen dropped a fresh pancake onto a plate. "I'm going to see Arther after you've had your breakfast," he said as he turned around. "I think he'll be in a better mood now that he's had time to cool off."

"And you think you can have him remove the house arrest?"

The giant watched me. His lips pursed in thought. "I think so. He'll come around. Don't worry. I know him," he said, confident as he spun back around as though this house arrest thing would be all over soon. But I had a feeling it wouldn't be.

"This whole thing kept me awake most of the

night," I said, hearing Shay chew and doing my best not to stare. "We came here for protection. To get away. And instead…"

"I know." Valen's shoulders tensed. "I'll take care of it. I promise."

"Okay," I said, not feeling a glimmer of hope. I knew he'd try, but this Arther had it in for me because of Catelyn or whatever she'd been telling him.

"He needs to focus on finding out who really killed Nikolas," Valen said, his voice firm. "I'm going to help him with that. I don't think it was Catelyn."

"I'll help," I said before catching myself. "Oh. Right. Guess I can't." Not yet. "Any news on Catelyn?" Not sure why I cared. The woman tried to kill me and lied about my involvement with Nikolas's death.

"She's much better," answered the giant as he flipped the pancake over. "I met Olin this morning. He was leaving Arther's place. Says most of her burns have healed. She's up. Not on bed rest anymore. Her giantess healing took care of most of her injuries."

"Just not the one between her ears."

Shay laughed. "Good one."

"Thanks," I said proudly, glad we shared the same sense of humor.

"She's just confused." The giant placed a plate of pancakes before me. "She'll realize one day that she's lost a good friend."

I shifted closer in my chair. "Well. Too bad for her.

You're not eating?" I watched as the giant placed the now empty frying pan back on the stove and proceeded to wash his hands in the sink.

"I had my breakfast hours ago," he said.

I raised my brows. "Of course you did." I cut into my pancakes with my fork and took a bite. "Wow." I rolled my eyes. "This is amazing. You should consider opening a restaurant." I immediately regretted saying that, knowing that his restaurant was his passion, and I'd taken him away from it. He was still checking in on it and doing some office stuff remotely, but it wasn't the same as being there physically.

But then the smile he gave me shut down all those thoughts. "Maybe I will."

My heart warmed as I watched the giant scrubbing the pots in the sink, marveling at how pretty he was at doing the dishes. He was a *very* good scrubber. The best. It had to do with those big manly hands of his.

"See ya," said Shay, suddenly pulling me out of my thoughts as she leaped off her chair and rushed to the front door.

"Wait. Where're you going?" I called as she slipped on her sneakers.

"To meet Eve and the others at Rainbow Falls."

"The waterfalls?"

"See you later," she called and shut the door behind her.

I rose from my chair and spied on her through the kitchen window just as Valen's shoulder bumped against mine. Sure enough, Eve was waiting for Shay next to a tall birch tree. Eve jumped in excitement when she saw Shay and rushed over to whisper something in her ear that had both girls giggling.

I snorted in my coffee. "She seems... happy. Doesn't she? All bouncy." I wondered if I was bouncy, too, as a kid. Probably.

Valen smiled. "She does."

A young boy sauntered toward them. He was taller than them with a scruffy, bad-boy vibe about him. He gave the girls a sly smile that had them chuckle harder. He reminded me of Julian, only smaller. My chest tightened at the thought of the thirteenth-floor gang. I didn't realize how much I missed them until this moment.

"You know... we really shouldn't be spying," I said, watching as the boy's face took on a few shades redder as he gave covert looks in Shay's direction.

"We shouldn't."

"She'd hate us if she knew."

"She would."

I met Valen's eyes. "Let's get closer!"

The two of us, laughing like idiots, hurried over to the living room area with a bigger window, flattened ourselves against the wall, pushed the curtain over a fraction, and peered out.

As we leaned in, trying to eavesdrop on their conversation, I couldn't help but feel a sense of excitement for Shay. She didn't look too traumatized from last night. This was good.

"Should I intervene?" Valen whispered, a

dangerous undertone to his voice. His breath was hot against my ear, sending delicious tingles down my neck.

I laughed at first but then caught myself at the frown on his face and the seriousness in his eyes. "Wait. You're serious? Because of the kid? No, Valen. He's a boy."

The giant kept his gaze on the boy in question. "He looks like a few years older. I don't like it."

I cocked my brow. This was new. He was... annoyed. Irritated that a *boy* joined Shay's group. I watched him as he went all silent on me again, shutting me out of something he was feeling. What was that about?

"Valen..." I began, seeing a shift in him. "Is something bothering you?" I searched his expression, finding a tightness in his eyes that spoke of a past situation ill spent. My heart clenched at the tension around his face. I wanted to help him with whatever was causing him pain.

"I'm just concerned for her," he answered, his tone carefully blank of any emotion. But I knew he was lying. Guess he wasn't ready to tell me what that was. And I wouldn't press him until he was ready.

So I let it go. "Shay can have friends who are boys, not just girls. It's allowed, you know."

"I don't like the way he's looking at her. I think he's up to no good. Look. Why does he have his hands in his pockets? What's he got in there?"

I snorted again. "He's just nervous."

"Exactly. Why is he nervous? Because he's up to

something." A muscle popped along Valen's jaw. "I should go check it out."

A smile played on my lips. "If you go out there and act all... giant-like... you're going to scare the kid and embarrass Shay. You won't be her favorite anymore." Maybe that wasn't such a bad thing.

Valen gave a grunt in agreement, though he never took his eyes off the poor kid. If he knew he was being stalked by a giant, the kid would probably wet himself.

"Did you tell Shay about her father?"

The question surprised me. I hadn't given it much thought after. "Not yet. I haven't found the right moment to do it. I mean, poor kid. She's been through so much already. How do I tell her that the line of communication with her father has been disconnected?"

"Mmmm."

I knew I would have to, eventually. Something was just not right about the whole thing. Even though I barely knew him, he was my father too. And it felt like... like he was in some trouble. I loved trouble, which was why I was planning on trying to communicate with him in another way. I just hadn't figured it out yet.

"You know," I said, rubbing my hand over his large biceps. "You're really hot when you're overprotective like that. I like it."

"Yeah?" The giant leaned his hard body against me. "How much do you like it?"

"A lot."

"Like…" The giant brushed his lips over my neck and sent tiny kisses. "That?"

"Mhm. And more."

My heart raced in anticipation as his face slowly moved closer to mine, his gaze lingering on my lips. He kissed one of my cheeks, then the other, and finally the edges of my mouth.

His touch and his lips on me sent a wave of tingles through my skin. I stood there motionless, barely able to draw breath, feeling him, with the smell of him all around me as his kisses caused a surge of desire in me.

I pushed him back playfully. "You *are* trying to get me in bed," I teased.

The giant smiled devilishly. "Is it working?"

"It is."

He was still staring at me when I captured his mouth with my own, biting his lower lip.

His eyes, dark with hunger, and his hands, rough with greed, raced over me. It was an incredible feeling to be touched and kissed by a man who obviously wanted me so completely, so urgently.

He pulled back. "How's your arm? Your ribs?"

"Almost as good as new."

"Good enough for a little… I wouldn't want to hurt you. I'm not small, in case you haven't noticed."

"Oh, I've noticed. And the answer is yes. Yes, for sex. Yup. Totally." With Shay gone out with her friends, I didn't know when we'd get another opportunity to be alone together.

The giant growled as he smacked his lips on

mine, and his tongue swept in. He grabbed fistfuls of my T-shirt and pulled. I heard a rip and gasped as I looked down at my exposed bra and chest.

"Sorry," laughed Valen, letting go of the ruined T-shirt with a playful smile. "Didn't mean to do that."

"Sure you did. Don't lie." I cocked an eyebrow and bit my lower lip suggestively before crushing my mouth on his.

We pulled away, chuckling as we undressed in a tangle of kisses, eagerness, and limbs. We hurried as fast as we could to the bedroom without tripping over ourselves.

My need for him flooded through me. I pulled off my bra and panties and threw them across the room. Valen, now his gorgeous naked self, lifted me off my feet and lowered me onto the bed.

I reached out, wrapped my legs around his waist, and pulled him over me. He settled in between my thighs, pressing his body against mine. I could feel his heart beating against my chest, and his breaths were heavy with desire. His lips met mine, and all my worries melted away as we kissed passionately.

His hands explored my body as his tongue tangled with mine, and we moved in perfect synchronicity as if our bodies had been created for that moment only. I felt like I was floating away from reality, lost in the sensation of being loved so deeply by this amazing man. I wanted this moment of pure bliss and connection to last forever.

Which should have prepped me for what came next. But it didn't.

CHAPTER 15

I was going out of my damn mind.

House arrest was worse than I thought. The notion that I couldn't leave the cottage wasn't so bad in the beginning, not when only a few hours ago my body had been entangled with a giant and enjoying all of him. Yeah. That was pretty great. Fast-forward a couple of hours, and I started pulling my hair out.

The couldn't-leave part was getting on my nerves. I couldn't even step outside on the front lawn.

That's when I came up with my idea to sneak out. I had it all planned and even picked an outfit. I'd stuffed my hair into an old baseball cap I'd found in the entrance closet, added a flannel shirt that reminded me of Nikolas, and a pair of sunglasses, and I was all set.

I was going to sneak out incognito. Good plan.

When Valen told me he would speak to Arther to have him remove the stupid house arrest thing, I didn't realize it would take him this long. He'd been gone for two hours. That's two hours of me alone, not knowing what to do with myself. So, of course, I was going slightly mad with nothing to do. If I'd had my laptop with me, I could at least do some research on vampires with *Pusher* abilities. But in our haste, I'd forgotten to pack it. I was pretty sure I could find another computer on the compound, but I doubted they'd openly give me one, seeing as I was still under house arrest and they blamed me for Nikolas's death.

Even Shay hadn't returned, though she had answered my messages through the messenger app. She was still with Eve at the waterfall. Part of me had wanted her to return to the cottage to keep me company, but that was selfish of me. She was out there making friends and having fun, which was the main reason we'd come here. To get away and make plans for the future. We just hadn't factored in that I'd be blamed for a death.

Worse was that they weren't looking for the real killer. Once they removed the house arrest, it was time to get the hell out of here and let these fools deal with their problems on their own.

I had the daunting feeling that the reason Valen wasn't back yet was because he had bad news.

Arther wouldn't remove the house arrest.

Whether he was under Catelyn's spell, I didn't know. But the longer Valen was absent, the stronger my resolve. Yeah. Arther wasn't budging.

Cursing, I started to pace around the cottage. I couldn't help but feel trapped, like being in a metal cage with no way out. I silently wished I had my thirteenth-floor gang with me. Elsa would have probably given Arther a piece of her mind. The thought made me smile. Loved her. She might even have been able to get through to Catelyn too. She had a way with people, a way to talk to them that I didn't have.

My mind was racing with different scenarios, but they all led to the same conclusion. I needed to get out of here. I couldn't just sit around and wait for something to happen. That wasn't my style. I was a witch of action. A Merlin. I caught bad guys for a living. I didn't play housekeeper. Or rather, house arrestee.

I checked my phone to see if Valen had sent me any updates, but I had nothing. No texts. No missed calls. Nothing. I didn't know whether to be worried or angry. He knew how important this was to me. How important it was for us to be free of this place. To get the hell out.

A sudden chorus of shouts yanked my attention outside. I couldn't make out what they were saying. The words were faint, like thin whispers, as though they came from far away in the distance until I couldn't hear anything at all. Was that Valen's voice? I couldn't tell if the shouts were coming from the cottage next door or if they were coming from somewhere else on the compound.

I didn't want Valen and Arther to fight because of me. Judging by the increased intensity of the voices, it didn't sound good. If Valen hurt Arther in a fight, the whole medieval compound would want our heads.

Damn. Damn. Damn.

I pulled at my hair again. "I have to *do* something." I couldn't let Valen lose a friend because of me. Even though technically I was innocent, and it was all Catelyn's fault, it always came back to me. Like my life had a boomerang effect: one disaster after another that came back around to kick me in the ass on the way out.

Thumps and cries sounded from somewhere outside.

"Damn it. They were fighting."

As I continued to pace, my eyes landed on the door. I should just go. Screw it. Screw everybody. I would go next door and find out what the hell was going on.

With my heart pounding, I made a move to the door.

It burst open.

Valen came striding in. His eyes widened in surprise as I had to do an awkward jump back so the door wouldn't hit me in the face and take my nose with it.

"Leana?"

"Valen."

Color stained the giant's face. "What are you wearing?"

"Clothes."

He blinked. "But... you heard? How?"

"That you and Arther are throwing blows? Yeah. You're kinda of loud."

The giant just looked at me with a confused

expression. "What? No. Arther and I weren't fighting. The compound's under attack."

I stumbled back as though his words had hit me like one of his fists. "Shay…"

"I know." Valen closed the door and rushed to the bedroom, me following behind him like his shadow. "I'll get her. You stay here."

"Like hell I am," I growled as a mixture of fear and fury slipped into me.

Valen ripped open his duffel bag and pulled out what looked like a weapons belt, equipped with daggers and other metal things I didn't recognize, wrapping it around his waist. "Listen. If they see you, they might think you're involved in this."

I let out a frustrated breath. "What is the matter with these people? I didn't do anything. I didn't kill Nikolas."

"I know." Valen took a moment and looked at me. His eyes were gentle, but his expression was serious. "But right now, tempers and emotions are soaring. They're not themselves. They're scared. And Arther's frightened for his people. He cares about everyone here. They're supposed to be safe in this place."

"Right." I rubbed my face, trying to ignore the increased hammering of my heart. "Who's attacking the compound? Is it Freida? Did she find us?" I remembered Arther saying this place was basically impenetrable. Looked like he was wrong.

The giant shook his head. "No. Arther says it's another pack, one they've faced before."

"What? This is so nuts." I gritted my teeth. "Why

is there another pack—of what? Werewolves? Attacking this place?" I was really regretting coming here.

"It's a territory thing," said Valen. "The other alpha is claiming this land as his own. He insists that Arther has no right to the title of alpha here, and he will force them to leave or risk being killed."

"Wonderful." I let out a breath through my nose. "What's he going to do?"

"Fight," said the giant, like it was a totally normal thing to do. "He's recruited an army of troops and familiarized himself with strategies for this sort of takeover. He'll do whatever it takes to protect his territory. He's done this before and knows how to handle it. He'll fight for his stronghold until his dying breath. Everyone else who's not fighting has to stay inside."

"Super." I let out a frustrated breath. "So all this time, here I thought you were negotiating my release."

The giant looked at me. "I was. I did. I did for a long time."

I stared at his face. "And judging by the solemn look you got there, he didn't agree."

"He told me he'd think about it," said the giant, walking out of the bedroom. "But then... this. He needs me right now."

"I get it." Anger tightened my gut further. "Was Catelyn there?"

"She was."

I was sure she was to blame for Arther's hesitation. "Fine. But I'm still going after Shay."

"No." Valen glared at me. I could see plans formulating behind his eyes, trying to devise a way to make me stay.

I glared right back. "Don't you give me that look, *giant*. She's my sister. Mine. And I don't give a crap about their damn rules!" I realized I was shouting, but I didn't care.

Valen grabbed me by the shoulders. "If you go out there, you'll just make matters worse for yourself," said Valen. "Here, we have to follow their rules. Just until this is over. Okay? Stay here, and I'll get Shay. I'll be back before you know it." He leaned over and squeezed me into a hug. "I'll bring her back," he said, speaking on the top of my head. "I promise." He let me go and added, "I'll be back soon."

Before I could stop him, he moved to the door. "Stay here and lock the doors. Shay might find her way back before I find her."

I stood there, too angry to utter any words. Guess he figured out that part because he shut the door.

I saw his silhouette rush off as I made for the window in the living room. Paranormals were rushing into their homes, some dragging their kids by the arms, shutting doors as they barricaded themselves in, and getting ready in case the enemy pack found their way to the cottages.

I stood there with my arms crossed over my chest. Fear and anger, with the mix of adrenaline, were making me dizzy. I watched through the window, watching as the chaos continued outside. The sounds of growls and snarls mixed with screams and cries filled the air. It was a war zone out there, and it was only a matter of time before it spilled over to our cottage. I needed to do something.

I didn't know how long I stood there, watching. Maybe five minutes. Maybe a half hour. Maybe only one minute.

But my mind was made up.

I dashed to the bedroom and rummaged through Valen's bag. My fingers found something solid. I yanked it out. A dagger. I wasn't skilled with this type of combat, but since it was daylight out, my starlight magic would be almost nil. I needed something to fall back on.

Checking the picture of the compound's map, I'd taken with my phone, I found the spot where Shay and her friends were, Rainbow Falls. Memorized it. And then I went for the door.

Hopefully everyone was too panicked and focused on the attackers, they wouldn't even notice me. Well, that's what I was going for. I looked like a regular person, nothing unusual about me.

Valen would be furious if he knew I was leaving. But I knew he wouldn't stay mad. He was just worried about me, and I got that. But I wasn't thinking of him or me. I was thinking of my little sister.

I took a deep breath, focused on what I needed to do, and slipped out of the cottage.

CHAPTER 16

If I had the magic or the spell to glamour myself into invisibility, I would have. But as it turned out, without that kind of witchcraft, I was just another Starlight witch cursing the sun for being such a bastard.

Still, those who glanced my way barely paid attention to me as I rushed past the compound cottages, leaving them behind as I trekked deeper.

With the waterfall's location still fresh in my mind, I bolted for the nearest path, keeping my head down.

As I rushed along the trail, I saw a few paranormals bustling around, and again they hardly glanced in my direction. They were too busy running to their cottages or looking for somewhere safe to hide. A group of male and female paranormals dressed in black cargo pants rushed in the direction I was headed. Part of Arther's army? Probably. It was like I was invisible to everyone. Good. I felt a sense of relief wash over me. I was finally free. Well, not really.

As I ran along the path, I couldn't help but feel the adrenaline pumping through my veins. My heart was pounding so hard in my chest, I thought it would burst out of my rib cage. Every nerve in my body was on high alert. My senses heightened as I kept my eyes peeled for any sign of danger. I tapped into my starlight—what little I could—and got a whole lot of nothing. I glared at the sun. Yes, it made Shay uber-powerful, but it was a pain in the ass for me.

Frustration aside, I needed to find Shay and get her back to the cottage and away from this angry mob of weres. I didn't want us to get in the middle of this war. It wasn't our fight. Then I'd text Valen. Look at me. I was the queen of plans today.

As I galloped through the woodlands, thankful that Olin had healed me enough to do this, I found the woods eerily quiet for so early in the afternoon. The only sounds were the crunch of leaves under my feet and the rustling of branches in the wind. It was a strange feeling, like I had entered a different world, where anything was possible.

My pulse raced as I sprinted toward Shay's location. I was determined to find her and bring her back to the safety of the cottage, no matter what it took.

As I ran, I could hear the sounds of fighting in the distance, the clash of weapons, and the snarls of shifted werewolves. The hairs on the back of my neck stood on end as I realized I was getting closer to the action. I could see flashes of movement between giant hemlock trees, the glint of metal as weapons were drawn and swung.

I knew I had to be careful to stay hidden and avoid being seen by either pack, compound members, or whatever they were calling themselves these days. I took a deep breath and stepped off the path, moving through the underbrush as silently as I could.

I took a moment and checked the map on my phone again. "Should be here." I looked around, trying to pinpoint the markings of the waterfall, and saw a carved sign nailed to a tree with the words RAINBOW FALLS with an arrow pointing upward to the route ahead.

I stuffed my phone in my pocket and galloped in that direction. As I got closer to my destination, I could hear the faint sounds of voices in the distance. I slowed down, trying to blend in with the surrounding trees as I made my way closer.

A twig snapped behind me.

I whirled around.

A young girl with blonde pigtails smacked into my chest.

"Ow," I exhaled, holding on to my boobs. "There goes my dream of fitting into a 32 C Victoria Secret bra." I stared at the wide-eyed girl. "Eve?" I looked at her and the young boy I'd recognized from spying on them earlier. It was just the two of them. "Where's Shay? I thought she was with you?"

Eve stepped back and rubbed her nose. "She went back to the cottage when we heard the screaming."

"Shit." I should have met her on the way. "Which way did she go?" A heavy lump of dread formed in my chest.

Eve pointed in the direction from where I came. "She said she was going back to check on you."

Damn. She shouldn't have been going anywhere alone. My heart thudded against my ribs. Shay was heading straight into danger. Yes, she had the sun's power behind her and could obliterate a were or shifter if they tried to harm her, but Shay was just a kid. She was only just learning how to use her powers. If she got spooked, she might freeze. And then she'd be dead.

I let out a breath. "She must have taken a different route. Possibly because she wanted to stay off the path." Smart. But now I had no idea where she was. She could be anywhere in these woods. "How many acres is this compound?"

"Three hundred and ten," answered Eve proudly.

"That's a lot of trees and squirrel poop," I looked around, knowing in my gut that my sister would find her way back to the cottage. I glanced at the many possible routes Shay might have used. I shook my head, my thoughts a jumbled mess. This was not good. If Shay went back to the cottage looking for me and found out I had left, she'd head out again.

"You guys can't stay here," I said, turning my gaze on them. Up close, they looked even younger than I'd first thought. "You need to get to safety. The other group is coming this way. And if they find you, I don't know what they'll do." Would they attack and kill kids? I had no idea what would happen to them. Crap. I couldn't just leave a couple of kids on their own. They were barely older than Shay and didn't have her magic.

The young boy stepped forward. "We can defend ourselves," he said, sensing my hesitation to leave them alone.

"I'm sure you can, but you're both coming with me," I said firmly, having made up my mind. "Your uncle would have my ass if he knew I'd left you out here alone while another group of werewolves was trying to take over."

Eve cocked her head. "Yeah, he totally would."

"I'm Leana, by the way," I told the young man, boy.

"Jason," he answered.

"Okay then. Eve. Jason. Follow me." I turned to go but froze mid-step.

Voices.

I grabbed the two kids by the scruffs of their necks and pushed them down into the earth with me behind a large dogwood shrub. A bit too forcefully in my haste, but I'd apologize later. I let them go and pressed a finger to my mouth, their eyes wide and filled with terror.

After a few seconds, shapes came into view. Five paranormals. They were too far away to get a reading on them or what kind of shifters they were, but the throbbing of cold energies told me they were powerful. The brash breathing and tread sounded incredibly loud in the otherwise oppressive silence of the forest. Of course, if I had my starlight on full power, five shifters wouldn't have been a problem. But with it on low-battery mode, plus having two young ones with me, hiding was our best option.

I felt Eve's body shaking against mine. Even Jason had a nervous tic happening with his jaw. They were terrified. It was a good thing I didn't leave them alone.

The kids and I stayed like that for another few minutes after the shapes disappeared through the forest, and another good three minutes passed before we finally stood from our hiding place.

"That was close," I whispered as loudly as I dared, knowing weres and shifters had super hearing. "Don't talk unless it's absolutely necessary."

Both kids bobbed their heads in agreement. I felt a pang in my heart at the fear that marred their faces. Their parents must be going out of their minds with worry.

I nodded and pointed in the direction of where they were to follow. Then using Shay's logic, I stepped off the path, far enough so we would see if anyone was coming and close enough not to get lost. Though I had the feeling these kids knew these woods like the backs of their hands. Maybe they should be leading.

But I hoped this attacking group wasn't as well-acquainted with these woods. Did they know where the cottages were? I surely hoped not.

Together, we trekked back through the forest as fast as we could while being as quiet as possible. Shouts rang close, and we had to duck and hide a few times.

My heart was racing as we made our way through the dense woods. I felt the sting of branches against my skin as I darted through the trees, the pain only fueling my adrenaline. The fear of being caught by the paranormals was palpable. I didn't want to think about what would happen if we were captured—not the kids. My insides twisted in a feral rage, like a lioness protecting her cubs. They might not be *my* kids, but they were innocent kids nonetheless.

My mind kept racing, trying to come up with a plan to get us all out of here alive, and I was coming up short. We needed to find cover, a place to hunker down that was one of the cottages.

Suddenly, a loud growl echoed through the trees, making us freeze in our tracks. I could feel the fear radiating off Eve and Jason, which only heightened my own anxiety and fear. We had to get the hell out of these woods.

The sounds of hissing reached me, followed by a bloodcurdling chorus of battle cries. I heard the unmistakable roar of pain and then a howl. The growling grew louder, and for a horrible second, I thought we'd been discovered. I yanked out the dagger I'd taken from Valen's bag, trying to steady my nerves as we waited. I was not skilled in using the dagger, but I knew I had to defend the kids. I'd wing it. I always did.

Go for the eyes, I told myself. *And if male, go for the eyes* and *for the cojones.*

I took a deep breath and positioned myself in front of the kids, ready to face whatever was coming for us.

But as luck would have it, the growls and sounds of battle moved *away* from us, and we were left once again on our own in the woods.

Looked like the goddess was on our side.

"Let's go," I whispered as I shot forward, Eve and Jason running behind me.

After a moment, I realized in my haste to get away from the battle, I'd lost sight of the trail, and I had no idea where I was going.

I halted, keeping low as I looked around. Crap. I'd gotten us lost. *Way to go, Leana.*

Eve grabbed my arm and pointed through a gap in the trees. "This way," she said, her voice low and barely audible. "A back way to my uncle's cottage." She nodded and took the lead. This time I let her.

I followed Eve as she rushed through the forest like a wild child raised by wolves. Guess that was sort of true. Jason ran behind us, looking just as wild and probably anxious to get to their people.

But after what felt like forever, we finally saw the back of Arther's cottage up ahead. Relief flooded through me, but it was short-lived as I saw two figures hovering over the front porch as we rounded the side.

"Uncle!" shouted Eve as she ran faster and right into the arms of her uncle.

The big alpha lifted his niece into his arms and hugged her fiercely. "We were so worried." His eyes fell on me for a second, then they settled on Jason. "Go. Your parents are waiting."

Jason nodded and vaulted toward a cottage with a yellow door. Before he reached the front porch, the door swung open, and a teary-eyed woman came out, wailing, as she grabbed him.

I blinked fast as Arther lowered his niece. "Get inside, quick. Your parents are there." He motioned to his own cottage.

I didn't stay for the reunion or his wrath at seeing me not in house arrest and abiding by his orders. Instead, I bolted to our cottage. I pushed the door open and cried, "Shay!" as I stumbled inside.

Valen turned around, his eyes narrowed and looking all dark and furious. Oops.

"Where the hell were you? I told you to stay inside." He stabbed his finger in the direction of the living room like I didn't understand that part.

I raised a finger. "First, I don't do well when people give me orders, and second, especially not with that kind of attitude." I knew his anger was geared toward his terror at not finding me or Shay in the cottage. So I gave him a few moments to gather himself, all the while giving him my angry eyes.

Visible tension left the giant, and his posture relaxed. "I just... I didn't want to have to worry about you too. And when you weren't here... It's crazy out there."

"I know." I let out a long breath, trying to reel in my emotions. "You didn't find her either." Obviously, since I was sure if he did, he wouldn't let her out of his sight.

The giant shook his head. "I searched the waterfalls and then the sand volleyball area, where Arther told me most of the kids hang out. When she wasn't there, I thought she'd be back here with you. Where did you go?"

"To the same waterfall. I found Eve and Jason, the boy you wanted to pummel, but no Shay. They told me she'd doubled back when she heard the screaming and came here." But it didn't look like she made it back. I didn't have to say the words as Valen and I just stared at each other, both thinking the worst.

Valen cursed and paced around the cottage. The giant's dark hair cast shadows over his eyes. He opened his mouth to say something but then shut it like he couldn't bring himself to say whatever was on his mind.

"I'm going back out. And you can't stop me," I challenged. No way was he going to stop me from trying to find Shay.

"I'm coming with you."

I bolted from the cottage, Valen a step behind me. We raced down the road that cut between our homes, where Arther was greeting a group of twenty paranormals wearing similar dark cargo pants.

The alpha male whirled around as we approached, his features set in a dark cast and his expression grim. "Stay inside your cottage," he ordered, making eye contact with me. "It's the safest place for you."

Right. Again, with the orders. "Shay's missing. We're going to look for her." I did my best to keep the rising panic from my voice, but it was useless.

"You can't go out there," grunted the alpha male. "The other pack have broken through our defenses and are killing everyone they encounter. If you go out there, they'll kill you. They'll reach the cottages soon. Valen, talk some sense into your female."

Oh my God. He did not just say that. My blood boiled at his words. "Valen doesn't control me, you overgrown dog," I shouted at him, feeling myself shaking with rage. "She's only eleven years old. She's out there, probably hiding in some burrow, terrified out of her mind. And I'm going after her. I'll fight you if you try to stop me." I'd had enough of his shit.

His soldiers were obviously surprised at my outburst. They'd probably never seen a female stand up to him like that before and not back down from being bullied. Tough. He didn't know me.

Their leader held his tongue, looking toward Valen for help instead of shouting back at me. But the giant just stood there with his arms crossed firmly over his chest, silently backing me up and looking at Arther like the asshat he was at the moment.

Arther sighed. "You saved my niece. And I'll be

ever grateful for that. But if you go out there, I can't protect you."

I frowned. "Doesn't look like you *can* protect me anyway." Or anyone.

Anger rushed into Arther's eyes, and I braced myself for a vitriolic explosion. For a second, I thought he was about to rip into me, but he surprised me when he said, "Go then. I hope you find her before they do."

"They're here," said Valen, his gaze focused on something ahead of us.

From the shadows of the tall trees, twenty figures stepped forward. Their perfect features, their hypnotic gazes, bizarre elegance, and extravagant attire made my heart race. The smell of old blood, their black eyes, and talons, a dead giveaway.

"These are not weres and shifters," I said, my voice filled with a sudden terror. "They're vampires. Freida's found us."

CHAPTER 17

"What did you say?" Arther stared at me in confusion.

"It's not your other pack," I said, feeling a surge of alarm rushing through my blood. I met Valen's hard expression, and the tingling of magic told me he was about to beast out into his giant form.

I looked around the compound, searching for the vampiress, but I couldn't see her. But that didn't mean she wasn't here.

Out of the corner of my eye, I saw Valen move. With a swift tug, his garments dropped to the floor. His six-foot-four figure had been replaced with a massive eighteen-foot version of himself. He had bulging arms and hands strong enough to crush metal and easy for him to snap a person's neck.

Taking his lead, Arther and his soldiers rushed forward. Some hit the ground on all fours, transforming into their beasts as some ran off in their human forms. I saw huge gray and black wolves, coyotes, and black bears.

With a pull of his muscled arms, Arther ripped off his clothes. By the time they fell to the floor, instead of his human frame stood the largest white wolf I'd ever seen. I would have taken the time to admire it, seeing as it was nearly the size of one of those bears, but I had the vampires to deal with.

I yanked out my dagger and focused on the threat. First, I needed to find Shay.

"Find Shay," came Valen's deep giant voice. *"Watch your back."*

I nodded, feeling slightly light-headed from the amounts of adrenaline and fear that were pumping through my veins.

With a great leap of his legs, the giant bounded forward and rushed to join Arther's pack.

The vampires shifted like shadows through the darkness. Their movements were so rapid that if you blinked, you'd miss them.

Arther launched himself at the nearest vampire in a blur of fur, limbs, and fangs as he crashed into his enemy with ferocious strength. With an earth-shaking collision, the massive white wolf and the vampires met in battle, unleashing their hatred and sharp claws.

I froze for a second, flabbergasted as Arther flew sideways, evading the talons of a mighty vampire with a shaved head and muscles like Vin Diesel. He crawled up the side of a cottage wall, his nails tearing up the wood paneling. He snarled. His canines shone in the light. He flipped from the roof and came down hard on the bald vampire, knocking him down.

And then I was moving, dagger in front of me. Not sure what I was going to do with it, but it was all I had.

I started forward and spun around a vamp in time to see one of the wolves backing away as two other vampires, a male and a female, were spinning around it like tops, tearing up the wolf's flesh as they went. The wolf growled as it batted its big paws at them like it was swatting away flies.

The vampires were pushing hard, not giving the pack a single moment to get on top.

I started forward again but stopped as another vampire flipped into a cartwheel and pitched forward, feet first into the giant's chest. Valen, the giant, stumbled back but straightened in time to grab the vampire by the leg, swing him forward, and with a flick of his hands, snap the vamp's neck.

The vamp fell, blood gushing out of his neck like a garden hose. I gritted my teeth. Yeah, that was gross.

The air was filled with agonizing howls and hisses, a chaotic chorus of screams and rage. Each screech of pain seemed to echo through my bones, the desperate cries shaking my body with a mixture of fear and anger.

Pulling my eyes away from the battle, I rushed behind one of the cottages. I crouched for a second, trying to figure out where Shay might be. Hell, she might be anywhere.

I pushed my trepidation away. Shay was a smart kid. She'd lived on the streets for weeks following her mother's death. She'd be hiding somewhere, scared out of her mind, waiting for me or Valen to find her.

I just hoped I found her before the vampires did.

And then I was moving again.

I sucked in a breath as a vampire leaped in my line of sight, thrashing at me and blocking my way.

"Well, shit. Where'd you come from?" Driving on instincts, I pulled on my starlight, calling to the stars —and nothing.

Damn you, sun!

So I did the next best thing.

I swung my knife, but the vampire struck out faster, catching me by my arm and slicing my skin open.

"You're the Starlight witch." The bastard had the nerve to laugh. "I thought you'd be taller," he said. "Pretty. But not enough to tempt me."

"Good," I seethed, my blood trickling down to my hand and making my grip on my knife slip. "I don't need looks to bust open up a can of whoop-ass on you," I said and threw the dagger, hoping for a lucky shot. But I missed, and it landed with a thump on the ground. "Yeah. Thought so."

In a blur, the male vampire threw himself at me. I jerked back, but the vampire was faster and wrapped his hands around my arms, yanking me to him. I screamed as his head dove for my neck.

Have you ever been bitten by a vampire? Yeah, me neither.

Panicked, just as his hot breath assaulted the skin on my neck, I rammed my knee up, colliding with his balls. He cried out, and I felt his hold on my neck loosen and let go.

"I'm getting pretty good at this," I said. Not giving the vamp a moment to recover, I lurched forward and gave him a solid kick in the gut. Grunting in agony, he stumbled back, but it didn't last long. The bastards were resilient to pain, just like most paranormals.

"You're dead." He lunged forward, a black streak of motion as if a cat had set its eyes on a mouse. I just managed to block his talons with my arm, but he followed up with a powerful punch to my gut. Before I could counterstrike, the vamp catapulted himself backward in an acrobatic flip, kicking me square in the face.

Stars exploded in my vision, and I staggered back, my eyes watering as blood filled my mouth. I'd bitten my tongue. I spat on the ground, my eyes meeting the grinning vampire as he waited for me in some martial arts stance I'd never seen before.

"Not bad," I said, complimenting his style as I rubbed my jaw, foreseeing a giant bruise. "You're a tricky sonofabitch. Aren't you? What is that? Kung fu?"

He let out a hoarse laugh. "Something like that," he said arrogantly, grinning wider this time and sending a chill down my spine. "Our mistress predicted this fight. She predicted you would lose, and we would win."

I whistled slowly. "Did she now? You sound pretty confident there, vamp boy."

He smirked, and something about the way he did it had the hairs on the back of my neck rising. "And we will take what we came for."

Shay.

I tried to look inconspicuous. The fact that he said they "will take" meant they hadn't found her yet, which gave me hope and the strength for this next move.

Raging, my leg came up, and the vamp's eyes bulged as my boot slammed into his chest. The kick sent him flying, and his body crunched as it hit the ground.

Panting, I searched the ground for my dagger. Silver winked up at me from a few feet away. I gripped the knife, posed myself, and let it fly, watching it sail through the air in slow motion. The dagger landed in the vampire's left eye, sinking all the way to the hilt. I'd aimed for its chest, but whatever. He fell forward, landing dead on the ground with a wet thump sound.

I blinked and stared at him for a second, making sure he was dead and also contemplating whether I should remove the dagger since it was my only weapon.

Resolute, I moved forward. Wincing, I wrapped my hands around the hilt and pulled.

The dagger came out more easily than I thought

accompanied by a disgusting suction noise. I didn't stay to see if he was truly *dead* dead. I needed to find Shay. And the vampire had basically told me they hadn't found her yet, so I needed to get to her fast.

I took off again, following the same route behind the row of cottages. Roars, hisses, and growls were loud over the beating of my heart. The sound of battle shook the air, now that I could actually listen. The weres' shouts were eerie and animalistic, but they didn't make me squirm away in fear. And then the vampires let out a rasping, snarling cheer that made my skin prickle.

I caught sight of a massive woman bashing the head of a vampire with her fist. Catelyn. I'd wondered when she'd show her lying ass and do something productive with that strength. My eyes found Valen trying to shake off a vampire who'd attached itself to his back like an overgrown tick.

I would have blasted that vamp easily with my starlights. But without them, I couldn't give much help. Besides, Valen could handle his own.

A sudden blast of light illuminated the forest, pulling my attention to the left of the cottages somewhere deep in the woods.

"Shay!"

Terror struck, and I ran forward like a madwoman into the woodlands, only thinking of my little sister.

Something hard caught me on the side, and I went sailing forward.

I rolled over on the ground and stood, my hip

throbbing in pain as I caught sight of my would-be assailant.

"What do we have here?" said a female vampire with short blue hair and some tribal tattoos that marked half her face. "A scared little pig running away from a fight?"

I really hated these vampires. "Out of my way, leech. I've got things to do." I glanced at the dagger still in my hand, thinking it was a damn miracle I hadn't impaled myself when I fell. I took that as a good sign and smiled.

The vampire flashed me her canines. "Yes. Like running away. I wonder what your pack might think of you if they saw what a coward you are."

"Not my pack. Not a coward."

She tsked. "But don't worry. I'll be nice. I'll make sure you live through this little battle so you can tell your alpha you were trying to sneak away before I caught you."

She charged, feinted left, and her foot flew into my side, knocking me off-balance. I staggered as she roundhoused my face.

Stars exploded in my head, and I flew back. My entire body screamed in protest from the abuse, but I ignored the pain and got up, looking around frantically.

My head snapped to the vampire. "Get out of my way."

The blue-haired vamp laughed. She licked her lips and said, "You said Shay, just before. You know where she is? I'm looking for her. Tell me where she is, and I might give you a quick death, Little Pig."

"Go to hell," I snarled. I knew I had to fight her to get to Shay. Might have to kill her. So be it.

The vampire sneered. "I think I might like to play with you, Little Piggie. After a few bites of my fangs, you'll be begging for a quick death."

Murderously silent, the vampire shot forward in a series of spins and butterfly kicks. She moved with inhuman speed, too fast for my eyes to register. I whirled toward her and brought up my dagger, hoping to slice me a few vamp-chops, but her legs and arms were a blur, moving everywhere at once.

A startled cry escaped me when a sharp pain shot through my leg. Blood seeped from the wound, and I crumpled to the ground in an ungainly heap of arms and legs. Immediately, I pushed myself off the ground, spinning around to deliver a powerful kick to her kneecap.

She howled and stumbled back, landing on her feet with a snarl. The little bitch wasn't knocked back. I let out a roar and charged her.

I rammed the dagger forward. When she moved to dodge it, I grabbed the front of her shirt and threw her to the ground. Before she could recover, I kicked her again, this time sending her into the trees. She hit a trunk and fell, yowling in pain.

But she was fast. One second, she was lying on the ground. The next, she was standing straight up in front of me with her talons at the ready. Her eyes shone with a black, wild light—a true predator's eyes. Yikes.

I saw a flash of her claws a second before they sliced my hip.

Pain exploded in my chest, and I staggered back, the sting of the wound running up my hip. I looked down. Blood was seeping out of the cut and stained my T-shirt. Not much but enough to tell me that I'd need to see Olin.

My self-assurance quickly boiled to anger at my first hint of pain and blood. The blue-haired leech had managed to cut me. She was grinning in the *I'm going to kick your ass kind of way*. That was *my* way.

The vampire stood before me, her black eyes wider than before, her fangs gleaming. "You're mine now, Little Pig."

I braced myself, ready to rush her, but before I could move, the vampire moved with all the swiftness of a cheetah, her talons up toward my heart.

I sidestepped and spun, kicking out with my legs, and felt something hard. She tripped but righted herself in a flash, and the next thing I knew, she knocked the blade out of my hand. Then she had me by the throat, her sharp nails digging into my soft flesh. Damn that vampire speed.

"Told ya, Little Pig." Her face was inches from mine, her skin flawless and wrinkle-free like she had a daily supply of Botox and used it. She squeezed my neck harder. I kicked out with my feet, trying to get her off me. My hands grasped her forearms, trying to pull her off me, my vision blurring.

A cruel, bloodstained chuckle erupted from her lips. "You're pitiful," she hissed. "By the time I'm done with you, you'll be begging to die. I will feast on your lifeblood and watch as your powerless shell crumples into nothing more than a meat sack, like the pig you are."

"I like pigs. Pigs are cute."

She snarled at me. Her eyes swelled, her fangs lengthening. Yup, she was going to eat me.

And I could do nothing about it.

Even as my body filled with fear, I watched hopelessly as she pulled her free hand back, her clawed hand ready to strike through my heart. "Say goodbye, Little Pig. I'm—"

She froze. She relaxed her grip on my neck, and I slid to the ground in a heap of limbs. I took gulps of air into my lungs as I blinked and looked around.

The blue-haired vampire was on the ground with a massive foot planted at the back of her head.

Valen.

He crouched over the vampire, his hands on her shoulders, his muscles taut like a spring ready to go off. He was grunting, and he was pissed. Of course, he was. She was about to kill me.

The vamp buckled and slipped from under his foot. She was a slippery little bitch.

"You shouldn't have touched her, vampire," said Valen.

"Fuck you, freak," she said, pushing herself up. The vampire hissed at him, her eyes scorching with hate. And then she threw herself at him, all crazed, spazzed, and teeth.

But the giant caught her in midair like he would a baseball, and with a sickening crunch, he snapped her neck and tossed her to the ground.

Once my ears stopped ringing, I realized everything was quiet. Unnaturally quiet.

I looked over to where the fight had been. I spotted bodies scattered across the grounds, the surviving weres and shifters standing. Catelyn was there next to the big white wolf, his fur covered in blood, though I wasn't sure if it was his or his enemies'. And the vampires? Well, they were leaving.

"Did we win?" I couldn't believe it. Guess Arther's soldiers were better than I thought.

Valen shook his head. *"No. We were losing."*

"What?" I got to my feet. "Then why are they running away?" Okay, not running, but definitely going in the opposite direction and back into the forest. Something wasn't right here.

And then I understood why.

One stepped forward out of the cluster of vampires still facing the compound. Her long black hair hung loosely over her shoulders, framing her porcelain complexion that was stretched tightly over her sharp features. She wore a white pantsuit made of some kind of shimmering material that moved with her every step. Her jet-black eyes were filled with malice and directed straight at me. I felt fear beginning to course through my veins as I took in her intimidating presence, but I forced myself not to show it. No way would I give this vampire woman the satisfaction of watching me cower in fear.

Starlight witch, said a voice inside my head. *We meet again.*

Freida smiled at me from across the path, that cold, satisfied smirk of someone who'd won. But won what?

And then I knew as my eyes dragged over to the person next to her.

There standing next to Freida was Shay.

Even from a distance, I could tell something was off about her. Her eyes were glazed like she was in some trance. The vampiress's hold.

"No!"

I was moving before I even knew my legs were advancing.

Die.

It was just one word, just one word…

I staggered to a halt. My arms and legs started to shake uncontrollably as though my own body were fighting me. A cold darkness spilled through me: alien, strong, blending with my soul and my will to live.

It was like I was struck with some virus, and my body was trying to fight it but couldn't. It was shutting down before my eyes. I could feel it. Inside. First, my lungs gave way. Then my heart stopped.

My body went limp. I felt myself fall. In a dream? Nope. I was dying.

And then it was lights out.

CHAPTER 18

I should have been dead. Freida, the Pusher, had commanded it. But when the darkness lifted from my eyes, and I blinked, I realized by some miracle, I was not.

But I did hurt like a sonofabitch.

Voices reached me. They were muffled. Was I in a bed? Blinking, I looked around. Outlines took shape as the haze lifted from my vision. Valen's face. Olin. Arther.

Shay…

Terror slammed into me, and I sat up. Then nausea hit, and I hurled whatever contents were in my stomach into the small trash bin beside the bed.

"Easy, now," said Olin, reaching out and giving me a washcloth. "You've been through quite an ordeal. No sudden movements. If you don't want to suffer more… *accidents*."

I took the washcloth and wiped it against my mouth. "Thanks," I said, shocked at how rough my voice sounded and how much my throat hurt, as though I'd put some bleach in my coffee this morning. But then again, everything hurt, like every single cell in my body ached.

Valen came and sat on the edge of the bed. He took my hand and rubbed his thumb along the inside of my wrist.

"Why am I not dead? Not that I'm complaining, but you know..." I stared at the room's walls, recognizing it as the cottage we were staying in. So I was back here. And surprisingly *alive*. "Freida used her Pusher magic on me. She said *Die*."

"You almost did," answered the giant.

My heart sank as I looked at him. His face showed clear signs of fatigue and illness with dark circles under his eyes and a pallid complexion. Dampness gathered at his hairline, making him look like he was sick with a fever.

"Valen," I breathed, knowing exactly what he did. He'd used his healing magic, perhaps too much of it, to heal me from death. But now he looked like he belonged in a hospital.

The giant just nodded. "Olin was also able to use some of his medicinal concoctions to keep you alive."

"It was touch and go for a while," said the healer, looking grave. "But you came back. Your witch blood is strong in you. It kept you alive long enough for us to reverse the effects. Well, somewhat."

I shook my head. "I told you not to waste your magic on me." He wouldn't, not unless... I swallowed, feeling bile trickling down my throat. "And… Shay?"

Valen looked away from me, though he was still holding my hand. "I couldn't get to her. You collapsed. And then they were gone."

Tears welled in my eyes, and I let them fall. "And the compound? What happened to the vampires?"

"They left after you collapsed," said Arther, leaning on the doorframe of the bedroom door. "All of them. They just disappeared."

Because they had what they'd come for. My little sister.

"We know now that this vampiress is responsible for Nikolas's death," I heard Arther say, though it was hard to concentrate on anything other than the loss of my little sister. "He was probably killed because he was perhaps the only one who could stop Freida since they share that power."

"They took him out so nothing stood in their way," agreed Valen.

"I'm sorry we doubted you," said Arther, and I wondered at his use of "we." Was he trying to include Catelyn? I didn't want to think about her right now, and I couldn't care less about his apology. It meant nothing. I felt nothing.

"If I hadn't been stuck here in this prison of a cottage, I might have been able to save her," I voiced, my anger giving my voice strength.

Olin stared at his medical bag uncomfortably.

Arther looked away from me, scratching the back of his neck. "I'm sorry. This is my fault."

I wanted to say, *yeah, it is,* but I bit my tongue. It wouldn't do any good now to rip the guy's head off, even though I really, really wanted to.

"I failed her," I whispered, feeling the weight of guilt crushing my chest. Shay was under the vampiress's compulsion, a captive to her will, and I couldn't do anything to help her.

Valen squeezed my hand. "If she's with Freida, we'll find her. And we'll bring her home. But first, you need to rest and regain your strength. You're not completely healed yet."

"I'm fine," I lied, feeling drained and exhausted. My whole body felt heavy, as if someone had filled me with lead. But maybe Valen needed rest. If he looked as good as I felt, it seemed we both needed a breather.

But how could I when my little sister was stuck with strangers who would force her to do their bidding? She was trapped in a mental prison. What would happen to her in the long run? Olin had said that Shay couldn't take more mind manipulation. More of these Jedi mind tricks would kill her.

Images of Freida's twisted face, her black eyes drilling into mine, filled my mind. Her voice, cold and emotionless, saying "Die." And then the pain, so much pain.

Hot tears spilled down my face. My father had left her in my care because he trusted me. Trusted that I would keep her safe.

But I'd failed.

She was out there somewhere, alone and vulnerable, and I wasn't there to protect her. She'd tried to fight back. I'd seen it. The light, her sun power. And the thought just rattled me more as more tears gushed down my cheeks. The guilt that filled me was overwhelming. I had to find her, no matter what it took.

Shay...

"I have to go," I said, trying to sit up, but Valen pushed me back down gently.

"Easy, now. You're not in any condition to go anywhere," he said, his voice firm.

"He's right." Olin moved over to the side of the bed. "This is much worse than when Nikolas attacked you. There you'd fainted. But this vampiress used a kill word. It's not the same."

"I'm going. And you can't stop me." I felt like I was about to jump out of my skin. "Shay's cursed, remember? Olin, you said she might not survive another mind attack. And it looks like she already has. She won't last long. She's going to die." The last word came out in a sob.

"What curse?" Olin waited, watching us as his foot tapped the floor, clearly expecting an answer. "Might as well tell me now. I know everything else."

"The Mark of Death curse," I blurted. "But it's been manipulated. By a master curse sorceress. We tried to find a counter-curse, but I killed the sorceress before I could make her tell me." Okay, that didn't come out right, but I was too tired to try and fix it.

"Hmmm." Olin's face screwed up, and he

thought about it. "Well. I always say things happen for a reason." He smiled and said, "You're in luck."

I blinked. "I am?" I looked at Valen, who seemed just as clueless as me.

"You see…" began Olin, excitement in his tone. "Vampire blood is very special."

"You say it like you like it."

"It is unique. Horrible and revolting, yes, but it has its purpose. One of which is its capability to fight against viruses and infections. Even curses."

I felt my mouth hang open, and I thought I was drooling. "What are you saying?"

"I'm saying that this vampiress Freida is old, very old, much older than our late pal Nikolas. I know who and what she is. This is not the first time I've had an unfortunate encounter with that vampiress, but I hope it will be my last." The healer tilted his head, his eyes vague, as though searching through old memories. "You see, Freida's kin are what we call the First vampires. They've been around a very, very long time. And the older the blood, the *stronger* the blood. So if you can get a sample of that vampiress's blood, I believe you can rid your sister of the curse."

"Are you shitting me?" My heart pounded against my chest.

Olin's eyebrows shot up at my vulgarity, but I was too excited to care. "Ummm. No. Definitely not."

My heart was about to explode out of my chest. "I said you looked like a good-luck troll, and I was right."

Olin blinked at me, clearly confused. "I'm sorry?"

I reached out, grabbed the little healer's face in my hands, and kissed the top of his head. "I think I love you right now." I let him go, laughing at how red Olin's face was.

The healer watched me for a moment. "You are a *strange* witch."

"Tell me something I don't know." I glanced over at Valen, feeling a sense of hope filling my gut. "I need to do this."

"I know." The giant stood. "And you're sure you're okay?"

"I am." More like 50 percent, but with the long drive back, I figured I'd be as good as new once we reached New York.

Valen let out a breath. "We still need to figure out where she is."

I met the giant's gaze. "I know where she is. She's in New York."

Valen frowned, thinking it through. "You sure? Seems a bit too easy."

I nodded. "She's there. I know she is. At that bitch's lair. And I'm going to get my sister out of there."

"Not without me, you're not." The giant smiled. "I'm your ride, remember?"

"Right." It's not like I would go without him. He loved Shay fiercely, and I knew he wanted to smash a few vampire heads again. I wasn't about to deny him something he enjoyed doing.

A sound like the door to the cottage opened. A few seconds later, I caught sight of Catelyn hunkering in the living room near the bedrooms. Arther pushed off the doorframe and joined her, their heads bowed as they spoke.

I found Catelyn staring at me. I saw regret flash on her face as I glared at her. Yeah. This was her fault. Shay would still be with me if she hadn't orchestrated this clusterfuck. I looked away. I didn't want to deal with that one right now.

But one thing I knew for sure. I would *never* forgive her.

I turned my back on her. "Let's go."

My gut told me that the vampiress would bring Shay back to her lair somewhere in Upstate New York, where she felt most comfortable and protected.

Not for long. Because I was coming for her.

And when I was finished with her, she would wish she'd stayed in her coffin.

CHAPTER 19

Freida's lair was just as I imagined it: a gaudy, ostentatious McMansion from hell. And it was red. Blood red. Of course, it was.

The light from the moon illuminated the scene rather dramatically, giving us a lot of details. A redbrick nightmare with three levels, as far as I could tell. It had a castle feel with turrets, but it was mismatched like the architect got bored and gave the project to his five-year-old to complete. The windows were tinted black. In fact, all the windows were black tinted, so there was no telling if any lights were on from the inside. Gothic arches were the main theme in this design along with what looked like gargoyles perched on the roofs, glaring at intruders. Or they could be really short and ugly vampires.

The front door was a heavy, dark wood, an intimidating barrier to enter with iron bars beyond. A patio edged the front of the property, complete with a redbrick wall and a black iron gate.

A long gravel driveway led to the front entrance, and the only landscaping I could see were the rosebushes that lined the property at the front and the sides. And you guessed it. The flowers were blood red.

By far, it was the ugliest building I'd ever seen. And I felt sorry for the neighbors.

I'd gotten the address from Jade's Facebook pal. Well, her husband, that is. After the four-hour ride back to New York, I'd been on the phone with the thirteenth-floor gang, mainly Elsa, as we went over the events leading to Shay's capture and what I'd learned about the curse from the healer Olin. When Jade had passed along to Margorie that Freida had kidnapped a minor—my sister—her address had miraculously come about a few minutes later. Seemed like most of the Gray Council members were furious with the vampiress. Unfortunately, now with her new weapon, my sister, they feared her even more.

So it was up to me, to us, to get her back. And we would.

As soon as we'd reached the Twilight Hotel, we—the thirteenth-floor gang—packed up some gear and went north in Valen's Range Rover.

By the time we got to Kingston, New York, it was two in the morning. And by then, I felt replenished, my starlights ready to go. Okay, I wasn't *completely* healed. Freida had almost killed me, but I still managed to find a reserve of energy and was in good enough shape to fight back and battle that vampiress to retrieve my sister.

"Here. We all need to wear these," said Elsa, her face cast in shadow as she crouched beside me behind an unruly rosebush and handed me a light-blue headband.

I took it. It was made of hard, shiny plastic. "And why do I need to wear a headband?" As I held it, I felt a sudden pulse of energy. Magic.

"They've been spelled for protection." Elsa handed out the rest to Jade, Valen, and Julian.

Julian laughed as he balanced the pink headband in his hand. "I'm not wearing this. I'll look like a ten-year-old girl."

The redheaded witch gave him an annoyed look. "You will if you don't want that vampiress in your head. These are to protect you from her mind compulsion."

"I'll trade you for the pink one," said Jade, handing over the red headband.

Julian grumbled something, but in the end, he switched his pink headband for the red one.

I inspected mine closer, impressed. "Wow. And they'll work?" I had no idea Elsa knew this kind of magic. It was higher magic. Being able to cast a spell on objects, especially one that could act as a shield for our minds from invasion and manipulation, was advanced magic. It was the kind of magic I longed to harness. But that would never be the case for me.

Elsa regarded me as though I'd just told her garden clogs had been out of style since the '90s. "Of course, they'll work. I'm not just a pretty face. I *can* do magic. It's something I've been working on since I heard of that vampiress and her mind tricks. Barb's been helping me too. We've packed a lot of magic in them. They're hot. So don't lose them."

Julian inched back. "Why are you staring at *me*?"

Elsa pulled her attention to Valen. "I couldn't find a bigger one. You might have to wear it as a bracelet when you… you know… *change*."

"It's fine," said the giant, holding his lime-green headband in his hand. "It's awesome."

"I don't know how effective it will be on a giant," continued Elsa. "I don't know what your limits are when it comes to conniving old vampires and their mind tricks. It might not even work on you."

"I'm sure it'll work," answered Valen with a smile. "Thank you."

Even in the gloom, I spotted Elsa's cheeks darkening as she held her head high. "You're welcome."

I took a breath. My nerves heightened every feeling, every emotion. I stabbed my head with my new awesome headband. My scalp tingled as I felt its magic seep inside, like cold fingers wrapped around my head. If it truly worked, it would allow me to fight back Freida's mind compulsion. I pulled out the syringe and stared at it, wondering how I would stab the bitch with it and live to see another day.

"Do you have a plan on how you're going to get her to stay still while you jab her with that and take some of her blood?" asked Julian, the light of the moon twinkling on his red headband.

"The plan is to knock her out or hold her down somehow while I draw enough blood," I said, stuffing the syringe back in my pocket. "And she has to be alive while I draw out the blood." At least, that's what Polly had said back at the hotel after I'd told her what Olin had said about the vampiress's blood and how it would remove the curse. "But first, we need to find Shay. Then I'll deal with Freida." It sounded all very plausible in my head. But we all knew things never turned out the way we wanted them to. They always took a turn for the worse. Well, in my case, they did.

A beep sounded behind me, and I saw Valen pull out his phone and text someone. He slipped his phone back into his pocket. He caught me looking and said, "Gave Arther the address."

That was a surprise. "He's coming here?" I was about to tell him to tell his friend not to come, but we needed all the backup we could get. I had to focus on Shay, not my dislike for the alpha.

"Yeah. Should be here soon. Left sometime after we did. He's bringing a team with him."

"A team is good." A team would really help.

"I think he's feeling guilty about what happened to Shay and blaming you for Nikolas."

"He should be," interrupted Elsa, having eavesdropped on our conversation. "He should be on his knees, begging for forgiveness."

I smiled. That was a funny image. I doubted Arther ever begged for anything, especially not forgiveness. But I'd take his help if it meant we could get my sister back.

"Catelyn." Elsa was shaking her head, a look of defeat on her face. When I'd first told her about the "trial by combat," and how Catelyn had lied about me murdering Nikolas in the hope that she could fight and kill me, Elsa didn't believe me. Or she did, and she was in denial. It was still something that bothered her, but she would have to let it go. Catelyn wasn't part of our gang anymore, not after what she'd done.

"Bedrooms are on the first floor. That's what your friend said. Right?" I looked at Jade for confirmation.

Jade nodded. "That's right. So either Shay is in one of those bedrooms, or she's kept in the tomb."

"There's a tomb?"

"Apparently," answered Jade. "More like a creepy basement. That's what Margorie said. The only person they know who's been in that house claimed to have seen one. It's where they keep all the blood."

My mouth fell open. "All the blood?"

Jade nodded. "Yeah. And she says they think they saw bodies too."

"Wonderful." I let out a long breath and rolled my shoulders. "It's time," I said and directed my gaze at the giant.

Valen nodded and began to strip, folding his clothes in a neat pile. A pulse of magic thrummed over us, and with a flash of light, Valen the giant towered over us. He leaned over and pulled up a pair of those giant shorts I'd asked him to have made so he could cover up his colossal manhood while in his giant form. Not that I minded, but it might knock over a few things.

Next, he grabbed his lime-green headband and fastened it to his wrist. "*It goes nicely with my coloring*," said the giant, catching me staring.

"It does."

"It won't be easy." Julian crouched low. "A lot of vampires will be in there. Old, powerful vamps like Freida."

"I like a good fight." I flashed him my teeth. "Besides, we have the element of surprise with us."

Julian raised his brows in question. "Really? You don't think she's expecting us?"

"No," I told him. "She thinks I'm dead. Remember? I shouldn't have survived that attack. But I did." My gaze turned to the garish mansion. "She has no idea we're coming."

"I like it," said Elsa, stabbing her rebellious red hair with her own orange headband.

"We ready?"

"Ready," chorused my band of witch misfits and giant.

With our magical headbands on, we rushed forward as a team toward the front of the mansion.

As we approached the looming mansion, I could feel my heart pounding in my chest. This was it, the moment that could make or break us. I still believed we had the element of surprise on our side. But there was a chance that Freida expected some retaliation from the paranormal community. She must have heard by now that the Gray Council knew of her abduction. She wasn't stupid. She probably had put up some sort of security. Fine. I expected that. But she didn't know *I* was coming. And I wasn't leaving without Shay. No matter what.

My eyes scanned the building for any signs of movement, but all I could see was the grand entrance with the double doors that led inside.

The closer we got, the more I could feel the power of the headband surging through me. It was like a shield of energy that kept me focused and ready for whatever Freida had in store for us. I could hear the sound of pounding footsteps as Valen's giant form drew closer to the front door.

We approached the doors cautiously, and I pulled on my starlights, feeling the rush of their power and filling me with the courage I needed. I was ready for anything.

Jade tapped her pink headband, seemingly for good luck. Seeing her do so, Julian and Elsa followed her example and did the same.

Then I did the same. I needed all the luck I could get, though I didn't have a good-luck troll to rub his hair and bring me said luck.

With my heart pummeling the inside of my chest, I grabbed the handle, twisted it, and pressed against the door with my shoulder. The doors creaked open, and I stepped inside.

CHAPTER 20

I yanked on my starlights, hands out, and twin balls of white lights bloomed in my palms like I was about to fire them at some vamps.

But no one assaulted us at the entrance. At least, not yet.

Lowering my hands and starlights, I looked around. We stood in a grand foyer, the inside even more garish than the outside. The walls were adorned with gold-and-red wallpaper, interspersed with the occasional painting, tapestries, or other eclectic art pieces. A red crystal chandelier hung from the ceiling, casting a warm red glow. Red-cushioned chairs were scattered around the room, and a small table was tucked away in one corner, holding a bowl of what looked like vials of blood.

"I just love what she did to the place," I muttered, feeling sick to my stomach.

A grand staircase curved from the entrance hall and led to the upper floors. The atmosphere was cold and damp with a faint hint of blood lingering in the air, and I had to fight to keep myself from gagging. It was like stepping inside a freezer packed with the blood of a hundred donors.

The sound of a gag came from behind me, and I saw Jade cover her mouth with her hand, looking a few shades greener than before.

Valen ducked and squeezed through the doorway without so much as a crack in the frame.

I raised a brow. "Not bad, big guy," I whispered, impressed at how flexible he was.

The giant gave me a thumbs-up. No doubt if he started talking, his deep giant voice would probably wake up the house and the neighbors. He turned around and shut the door behind him with a soft tap.

A hand grabbed my arm. "Which way?" asked Julian. "Up or down?"

I'd thought about it. I didn't believe Freida would stash her new toy in some dingy basement. No. My feeling was that Shay was in one of those bedrooms upstairs. Maybe she was still under the vampiress's spell and was lying on a bed like a vegetable, in pain and feeling sick. After seeing what had happened to her when Nikolas tried to train her mind to shut out unwanted guests, she was probably in worse shape. Possibly dying.

If not, knowing Shay, she would have escaped by now.

"Upstairs," I whispered and pointed to the staircase. I looked over at Valen. Would his big frame even make it up, or would his big feet break through the stairs? Guess we were about to find out.

With me in the lead, we sneaked over to the staircase and started climbing. The stairs smelled of old dark oak and polished varnish. I looked over my shoulder as the giant took the first step.

The stairs creaked under Valen's weight, and I halted, my heart in my throat.

I waited, frozen on the spot, to see if any vampires had heard that. Elsa, Jade, and Julian's eyes were round like moons.

Valen leaned forward and chanced another step. Again, the staircase groaned under his weight, and the tension rose between us. But after a few moments, no one came.

So we kept going.

The scent of blood and something fouler intensified as we climbed, and from the corner of my eye, I saw Jade wrinkle her nose in disgust. She wasn't wrong. It smelled like a slaughterhouse, as though the automatic air fresheners were scented with blood. Gross. So, so gross.

As we hit the first floor, a faint whisper of music and voices reached me.

"Sounds like the bloodsuckers are having some private party," muttered Julian next to me, a devilish grin on his face, which would have worked if not for the girlie headband over his head. "Should we crash it?"

On another given day, I would have said yes. But

we needed to focus on the plan to get Shay safely home. Nothing else mattered.

"Keep climbing," I instructed.

As we ascended, I couldn't help but feel nervous. I had no idea what to expect and in what condition I'd find Shay. I gritted my teeth, attempting to calm my nerves as best as I could. I tried not to let my imagination run wild, which was hard at the moment.

We kept trekking farther and didn't stop until we reached the third and final floor. A large hallway branched out in two directions, left and right. Wall sconces with red bulbs illuminated the hallways, their eerie light accentuating the already over-the-top décor.

"Which way?" asked Elsa, her head snapping in both directions.

Now came the fun part.

I closed my eyes and opened myself up to the well of magic, feeling the core of power emanating from the cosmos above me. The air vibrated with raw energy. My skin bristled as I sensed the energetic hum of power from the stars, waiting to be unleashed.

My eyes opened to the sight of a white sphere hovering in the air over my palm.

I took a deep breath and blew on the globe. With a sudden pop, the sphere split into thousands of tiny stars of light. The starlights flew forward, leaving behind a glowing trail of magical dust.

"I just love it when she does that," whispered

Jade, an envious look on her face as she marveled at my starlights.

"They'll find her," I muttered, knowing that even though our powers were different, my sister and I still shared a connection in blood and magic. If Shay was somewhere on the third floor, my starlights would find her. I had no doubt.

The starlights split into two groups. One group zoomed to the right while the others went left, down the hallway and out of sight, like hundreds of white pixies. I waited, my pulse throbbing. And then the starlights that had gone right came rocketing back and fired off to the left, where the other group had gone.

Restless, I called out to my starlights, my little buddies, my sensors. Tiny ripples of cold energy prickled my skin as my starlight answered back.

"They found her," I said, my voice low, and relief poured inside me. "This way," I hurried left, not waiting for my friends or Valen's response as I moved down the corridor that led deeper into the mansion. "Stay frosty," I whispered, glancing back.

The ceiling height was high, probably around fourteen feet, but Valen still had to stoop low or risk his head smashing through and the entire ceiling collapsing. His eighteen-foot frame was too big and thick for these halls. But he was still coming. The height of the ceilings wasn't slowing him down. His dark eyes flicked back and forth as he moved, searching the hallway. No doubt he wanted to punch a few vampires. I knew he'd come for Shay, but I suspected the added bonus was the prospect of crushing a few vampire heads for fun.

Suddenly, a door opened to our right, and a male vampire stepped out. He wore a black robe over his body and nothing else, judging by his junk enjoying a bit of a breeze.

He stared at us, a look of surprise on his face. He opened his mouth, fangs out, and lowered himself in a crouch before leaping at Jade.

Valen stuck out his hand, caught the vampire in midair, snapped his neck like a toothpick, tossed him back into the room, and shut the door.

"That'll work." I smiled at my giant, who grinned back, seemingly a tad happier than he'd been when we first arrived. Yeah. He was enjoying this.

We moved on, silently and quickly, as we followed my starlights, our eyes scanning every inch of the corridor for any sign of trouble.

I was channeling a lot of magic as I held on to my starlights. If not for my near-death experience, I would have been fine and peachy. As it was, I was tired, exhausted, sweaty, and shaking. I was beginning to feel the effects of pulling on my abilities and, by doing so, draining my magic and energy. Channeling my starlight magic like this was taking its toll. Soon I'd have nothing left to pull from.

But I wouldn't let the others or Valen know. Especially Valen, who wasn't keen on allowing me to come tonight. But I couldn't let Shay stay with that two-legged leech for another minute. I understood his worry. I wasn't completely healed, and he'd also taken a hit reviving me a few hours ago. He looked fine now and probably had already healed himself. But I wasn't a giant.

We tiptoed down the hallway, me in the lead, following my starlights.

I halted. "Wait." A bout of energy hit my senses, and my skin erupted in goose bumps.

Jade bumped into me. "You got something?"

I nodded. "Yes. Definitely." The thing with my starlights was I felt what they felt, and right now, they felt something. And they were happy about it. The energy they were giving off was warm, inviting, and familiar, like an old friend.

I hurried forward, past maybe six doors or more, wasn't really counting, and then I saw them.

My starlights clung to a door, creating a canvas of light. Something—perhaps an eleven-year-old girl—was beyond that door.

I tugged on my starlights, releasing their hold on the door, and the luminosity on the surface faded away.

"She's in there," I said and met Valen's eyes. I could see the light in them, the hope, the elation that we'd found her. Our Shay.

"Wow, that was seriously impressive." Julian crossed his arms over his chest. "You know, we need to sit down and discuss the endless possibilities I could do with some of that starlight power. Maybe I could bottle it up."

Jade shoved him on the shoulder. "Only you could think of making a profit at a time like this."

Suddenly, I heard a faint noise coming from behind the door. It was a muffled whimper.

"Shay."

She could sense the starlights. Of course she could. She knew we were here.

"We're coming, Shay."

I reached for the handle. And it twisted easily. Feeling the breath of Julian and Jade on my neck, I pushed the door open, and we stumbled through.

But it wasn't Shay standing beside the tall, tinted window with a surprised expression on her porcelain face.

It was Freida.

CHAPTER 21

My eyes scanned the room. A king-size, four-postered bed stood in the middle of the space over a large Asian rug. A red comforter embroidered with gold thread lay above it. It could fit three people lying sideways. Grotesque, screaming vampire faces were carved into the wood. Nice touch.

The dresser and all other furnishings were made of that same wood species with similar creepy faces etched into them. Guess you had to be a bloodsucking leech to appreciate them.

A single door was to the left, could be a closet or a bathroom.

Shay wasn't in this room. Yet my starlights led me here. To this room. I couldn't see her, but they had felt her. She was here. And I was guessing behind that closed door.

The vampiress wore a long, red satin nightgown with long lace sleeves, a deep V-neck, and a belt. Her long, dark locks cascaded down her back, setting off the porcelain hue of her complexion. The shock on Freida's face at seeing me, very much alive, was my only consolation. Yeah, she thought I was dead. It was a small victory. And I took it.

I gave her a finger wave. "Surprise."

A slight frown formed on the vampiress's perfect visage. "How is it that you stand here now? You should be dead." I could tell that was pissing her off, the not knowing, and I liked it.

I shrugged. "I'm harder to kill than you thought. Where's Shay? Where's my sister, you overgrown leech?"

Freida had the poise and confidence of someone in control. She didn't look at all bothered or frightened by our presence. Not good.

The floor behind me squeaked as the giant moved closer to me, his presence adding another layer of confidence. Now was the time to test Elsa's magical headbands and pray they would work because my master plan relied on them.

The vampiress turned her body slowly toward me. Her head dipped to the side. "My dear, you're mistaken if you think you can just barge in here and demand things from me." Her tone dripped with superiority. "You're a nuisance. A thorn in my side."

"Blah, blah, blah. I didn't come here to play games, *Freida*. Where. Is. Shay." I demanded, my patience wearing thin. I pulled on my starlights, and my body thrummed with magic. Oh, I was ready to take on that fanged bitch.

Freida smirked, not at all impressed with my show of magical ability. "She's safe for now. She is where I want her to be. Where she needs to be."

I wanted to use my new flying ability, soar over there, and kick her in the fangs. "Safe?" I repeated, my fury rising. "She's not safe with you. You took her by force, you Draculina wannabe. Tell me where she is. I won't ask again." *No. 'Cause next time, I'm going fry your vamp ass.*

"Are you *threatening* me? Witch?" mocked Freida, her eyes glinting with malice. "I remember you thrashing on the ground like a fish the last time I saw you."

Had I thrashed? Couldn't remember. Too busy dying.

I felt a wave of anger wash over me. "If you've harmed her in any way, I swear to whatever deity you pray to that I'll make you regret it. You'll be gasping for breath in a pool of your own blood when I'm through with you."

Freida laughed. "You have no idea who you're dealing with, little witch."

"I'm not the one you should be worried about," I said, my gaze flickering to Valen, who was flexing his massive muscles and cracking his knuckles. Yeah. He wanted a piece of her too. But I wasn't in the mood to share right now. She was all mine.

I stepped forward. My eyes moved to that closed door to her left. "She's in there. Isn't she?"

"You'll have to be more specific, witch," Freida

drawled. "I have many *toys* in my collection. Which one are you referring to?"

My stomach churned at the thought. She could be lying, but I had a feeling she did have some poor bastards chained in here somewhere, slowly emptying them of their blood, most probably in the basement. "You know exactly who I'm talking about," I spat and took another step.

Freida's eyes flickered with amusement. "You think you can come here, in my home, and steal what is mine?"

"Shay's not an object. She's a person. You don't own her. And I'm here to get her back, you trampire."

"Trampire?" came Julian's laugh behind me. "I like it."

"I do *own* her." The vampiress's smile was chilling. "And I don't share my toys. Not with anyone. Just as I don't share power."

"No shit. Now, why did I know you were going to say that?" My starlights pumped me with magic. And I dared another step.

Freida's eyes locked on to mine.

Die.

Uh-oh. That same word popped into my head with that same cold voice.

I felt a ringing inside my head, just as the last time she'd pushed her ability on me, and my body went rigid. For a horrible moment, I thought I was going to fall to the floor in searing pain as my body shut down. As I began to die.

But I also felt a tingling, cold sensation, like brain freeze, after you shovel ice cream down your throat too quickly. Then the feeling turned warm and soothing, like hot water poured over my head.

The headband thrummed its magic, its counter-magic, and I felt the compulsion—on my body, my limbs, my mind—break free.

The vampiress scowled at me with a look of puzzlement, the wrinkles marring her otherwise pristine face, making her appear almost grotesque. Oooooh. She didn't like that. Tough.

Die!

Her voice filled the inside of my head again, and again, the headband pushed it back.

Take that, True Blood, I scoffed in my head, hoping she could hear me.

I gave her a wide grin. "Double surprise!" I added an extra flourish by raising both of my middle fingers to emphasize my point.

I leaned over to Elsa and said, "It worked."

"Of course, it *worked*," answered the older witch, though she did look a little green.

"Your Jedi mind tricks won't work on us," I told the vampiress, calling to my starlights. "It's my turn to do some tricks."

Freida ran her eyes over me with a hint of amusement. "Such confidence for a little witch."

I looked down at myself. "And here I thought I'd gained weight. Thanks."

I steadied myself, pulled on my starlights, and aimed right at the vampire's head.

In a blur of that damn vampire speed, Freida ran to the closed door and disappeared inside.

The window behind her, though, blasted into thousands of shards of that tinted glass. The air that swooped in was fresh and a nice welcome from the constant blood aroma. It was a hole, like a missing tooth, sheared off. A slice of the night visible.

I ran after the vampire as fast as I could, my friends and Valen right behind me. I charged into the room and skidded into a bathroom nearly the size of the bedroom.

Freida stood next to a tall window, clutching Shay against her like a prize.

"Shay?"

My sister's gaze fell on mine, with lids drooping followed by a series of slow blinks, like she was waking from sleep or was still dozing off. Her eyes weren't focused, and I knew she was still under Freida's mind control.

The vampiress giggled, threw Shay over her shoulder, and jumped out the window.

"No!" I rushed over and caught a glimpse of the vampiress disappearing into the window of the lower level like some ninja.

Damn it. I'd lost Shay. Again.

CHAPTER 22

"Hurry. They went through a window on the second floor." I doubled back and dashed out of the bathroom.

And halted.

The room was teeming with vampires.

"Well, shit."

A mix of males and females, their faces held that eerie beauty all vampires held: just too perfect, too beautiful, unnatural. The air was thick with the pungent odor of old blood mingled with the thick musk of their bodies.

They all had something in common—fake smiles. And their eyes were locked on us in a way that said *we* were the entertainment.

I counted about twenty. Twenty very powerful, killer vamps.

Okay, so the odds were against us. I'd been faced with worse odds, though.

"Where'd they come from?" asked Jade, brushing up against me. "I didn't even hear them."

I wanted to tell Jade that vampires were blessed with stealth and could sneak up on their victims without making a sound, but we didn't have time. "They were here the whole time," I said. "This is their home. And we've just broken in."

"Well, I'm up for a fight," snickered Julian, his hands in his jacket, which I assumed were packed with vials of poisons and potions.

With greedy gazes, the vampires glided forward on silent footsteps. They bared their fangs and hissed, eager to sink their teeth in hot flesh. My flesh.

They'd formed a wall, I realized. And to get to Shay, I needed to break the wall.

No problem.

Valen growled, a crazy smile on his face. "*Showtime.*"

In a display of strength, the giant smashed his fists on the expensive parquet wood floors, sending up shards and splinters of wood and dust. No point in keeping quiet anymore.

My tiredness from before was barely noticeable, replaced by buckets of adrenaline pounding through my body.

One of the vampires, a black male, pointed a taloned finger at me. "I was in the mood for a little witch flesh. And here you are. Ripe for the plucking."

I rolled my eyes. "Promises, promises."

He looked over to my left. "Or maybe I'll take the

old one first. I like me some older female flesh. My teeth sink right through."

"Ew." He sounded like he wanted to eat Elsa. Maybe he did.

"You're not getting near my flesh," hissed Elsa. The air thrummed with her magic as muffled words escaped her lips, and her fingertips began to emit a subtle yellow light. She stepped forward, reciting clear and composed syllables while her figure lit up with power.

Jade spoke in gruff, clear words on my other side and was suddenly engulfed in energy.

I inhaled deeply, pulling on my own starlight magic, and met the vampire's gaze. "Your mistake was stealing my sister."

The vampire cackled. "Her blood is so tantalizing, so many enchanting flavors. It's exceptional—like no other."

My anger hardened. Had they been feasting on my sister's blood? The idea sickened me. Maybe he was lying just to get me riled up. And maybe not.

Furious, I sent a volley of my starlights directly at the vampire as he bolted like a shadow, and the other vampires moved in on us. The bloodsuckers drove in rapid flurries of talons and fangs.

My starlight shots went wide, hitting the walls and furniture and lighting up the room in white light.

"Whoops. I really thought I'd get one."

Movement to my left caught my attention as Valen threw himself at the nearest vampire, his giant hands coming down with frightening speed like hammers from hell. I heard the bone-snapping sounds of impact. Then with a downward motion, both fists sank into the vampire's abdomen. When he pulled back, little was left of the vamp. His chest was as flat as the floor. His entrails spilled from the two huge holes in his abdomen to land in a slopping mess around his body.

I gave him an approving smirk. "I knew bringing you was a good idea."

"I'm just getting started, witch." Valen beamed, and then he swung out his arm as another vamp came lurching at him. The giant was still crouched as he fought, limiting his movements. But that didn't stop him from kicking out and landing a killing blow to the vampire's head.

I would have loved to watch him fight, but I needed to get to Shay.

Electricity thrummed in the air as Jade and Elsa, locked in deep concentration, chanted ancient words in Latin. Their spells were cast with precision, sending fireballs of orange, bolts of purple lightning, and shock waves that shook the room and the floors beneath our feet.

I caught sight of Julian firing vials from inside his jacket that exploded on impact on one of the vampires. A sonic boom was followed by a cloud of yellow smoke. Then a bat fluttered away from where the vampire had once stood.

"God, I love clichés," laughed the tall witch.

"I had no idea you could do that," I told him, seriously impressed.

"Darling, there's no limit to my potions." The witch beamed.

I spun around and staggered. Though the air was hot, a cold sweat broke along my forehead as tiredness crept into the edges of my mind. But I wouldn't let it. Not yet.

The faction of vampires attacked with purpose—to kill, to annihilate, focused on my friends. And by doing so, they gave me a clear path to the doorway.

So, I took it.

I shot toward the door, my legs pumping with desperation. "Valen!" I shouted. I wanted him to know where I was heading. A girl could always use the help of a giant.

A vampire came out of nowhere, and I crashed right into it.

Well, my face made contact with his chest. Yeah. This one was half-naked, with only a teeny-weeny red G-string to hold his junk.

Awesome. Never mind how gross it had been to touch his cold, sticky flesh with my own face.

I waved a finger at him. "Think you can put some clothes on? That's seriously distracting."

"How about I rip yours off? Then we can call it even," answered the vampire.

Crap. I wanted to keep my remaining energy and magic to use against Freida. But to get to her, I needed to get past him.

The noise of a battle drifted up, the blasts of magic with the hacking of flesh and bone. Probably Valen's doing.

The vampire's black eyes burned with lust and excitement as he licked his lips. "You're pretty."

"Are you coming on to me? That's just so... wrong on so many levels." I looked over his shoulder. I had to get through. Shay was somewhere on the second floor, and I needed to go before I lost her. What if Freida jumped into a car and took off? I might never find my sister again.

His eyes glinted with wicked amusement as he rolled his eyes over me. "Have you ever been with a vampire? I can assure you there is no better lover."

I really didn't want to look, but I did. And when I saw the tent on his puny undies, I really did lose it.

With a flick of my wrist, I sent a burst of starlight magic hurtling toward the vamp.

The blast hit him head-on, sending him flying backward. He hit the ground hard, moaning in pain. I stalked toward him, a sense of disgust coursing through me.

I leaned over and said, "You need to brush up on your pickup lines."

The floor shook, the bloodcurdling chorus of battle cries resonating around the room at the vampires' continued attack.

I straightened, and my eyes found the giant.

"What do you need?" shouted Valen as he tossed a vampire through the window I'd blasted like he was doing his spring cleaning.

"Keep them from coming after me. I'm going after Shay," I yelled back, over the crashing sounds of combat and the constant hum of magic and the blasts of Julian's potions.

A female vampire snapped her attention my way. And with a burst of speed, she rushed me.

Valen reached out and grabbed her by the neck, lifting her up. His eyes were dark and dangerous. *"Go. We'll take care of these."*

Tapping my headband for good luck once again, I ran out of the bedroom. Terror-fueled adrenaline rushed through me and kicked me into high gear as I galloped down the hallway. I reached the stairs and thought about using my uber-cool flying skills to hover on over to the second floor, but that would require too much energy. I was already stretching my starlight power to its limits, so I couldn't risk it.

Instead I took the stairs. As I jumped down, two stairs at a time, I silently prayed that I wasn't too late. That Shay was still in the mansion and Freida hadn't slipped away in one of her luxury SUVs.

I was almost down the staircase. Two more stairs to go.

A vampire appeared at the bottom of the second floor. He looked up and spread his mouth open, showing off his fangs.

The thing is, I *would* have stopped to fight him if I could have actually *stopped*. But my forward momentum was already in full gear. No way *could* I stop.

So I did the only thing I could.

I crashed right into that sonofabitch—headfirst.

The vampire stumbled back, caught off guard by my sudden headbutting tactic.

"You hit me in the neck," said the vampire, with a shocked expression, a hand holding his neck. "Who does that?"

"Apparently, I do. I was aiming for your head." I took advantage of his confusion, delivering a swift kick to his gut. He doubled over in pain, grunting.

He glared up at me, his fangs glinting in the dim light of the hallway. "You'll pay for that."

"Story of my life."

The vampire recovered quickly, snarling as he lunged at me. I dodged to the side, slipping past his outstretched black talons. But I tripped on the polished floors, and the pain that followed in my ankle had me cursing.

I scrambled to my feet, cursing the same stupid ankle I'd sprained running after Shay from school while readying my magic. I gritted my teeth as I faced off against the vampire. Starlight magic crackled around me. The air sizzled with energy as I gathered my power.

He came at me again.

Limping, I blasted a stream of my starlights at him. But the bastard leaped to the side, and my shot went wide, hitting the staircase's railing and lighting it up like Christmas garlands.

"You're too late," said the vamp. A red welt on the side of his neck where I'd hit him was clearly visible. "She's gone."

The fear that rose in me was choking. "I don't

believe you." Terror was heavy on me, like a boulder in the pit of my stomach.

The vampire laughed, seeing what must have been panic on my face. "You'll never find them. You'll never see your sister again. Give it up."

"You're lying," I said, feeling the prick of tears. Was he telling the truth? It had been at least five minutes since I'd seen them crash through the window. Maybe they were gone.

The vampire cackled again. "It's over. Shay belongs to us now. She's our... secret weapon." He laughed like some dark plan was happening that I didn't know about.

I clenched my jaw. "She doesn't belong to anyone, especially not a group of lowlife bloodsuckers."

The vampire snarled, baring his fangs as he sprang again.

This time, I was ready.

I darted back, my ankle screaming. I could feel my starlight magic coursing through me, strengthening my muscles and sharpening my senses. I flung a volley of starlight, which hit the vampire in the left thigh, throwing him back with a wail.

But he was faster than I'd expected, catching me off guard with a swift punch to the gut. I doubled over, gasping for breath, and he took advantage of my vulnerability, grabbing me by the shoulders and slamming me against the wall.

"You think you can stop us?" he sneered, his breath hot on my face. Damn, that vampire breath was nasty. "You're just a pathetic human with a few tricks up your sleeve. Now that we have our secret weapon, the vampire race will rise again. And we'll be in control."

I pursed my lips in thought. "I've got one word for you."

The vampire leaned forward. "What's that?"

"Listerine."

A grimace rippled over the vampire's unnaturally beautiful face. "You think you can defeat me?" the vampire sneered again, his black eyes glowing with bloodlust. "I've been alive for centuries, little witch. You're just a witchling, a newborn. You're practically a fetus."

I smirked, my confidence growing. "Age doesn't necessarily mean strength." With a flick of my wrist, I sent a blast of starlight magic at his chest. The vampire released me and dodged to the side, but the blow caught him in the shoulder, leaving a smoking hole in his shirt.

"Looks like this fetus can kick your ass."

He snarled in pain and lunged at me once more.

I didn't have time for this crap. I had to find Shay.

Clenching my jaw, I summoned all the starlight magic I could muster. Sparks of light danced around my fingertips, and I channeled them at the vampire. He screamed, writhing in pain as sheets of starlight enveloped him like white fire.

Without looking back, I limped past him, trying not to let his words consume me. Shay was here. She had to be. Because if she wasn't…

I shook my head as I shambled forward. Damn,

this place had too many doors. Too many corridors. It was a freaking maze.

Again, I pulled on my starlights and blinked as I let them go in search of my sister.

I held my breath as they went, but they didn't go far. My starlights attached themselves to another door a few shambling steps away. Shay.

And then I was running. Okay, more of a hop-curse run, but I got there.

I pushed the door open and stepped into what appeared to be a plush living area. I blinked, adjusting my sight from the dark hallway to the light in the room. The room was richly decorated with sofas and chairs upholstered in soft red velvet. I was surrounded by opulence, a room full of gold and silver, ornate and gaudy. A giant wood fireplace stood across the room, its mantel carved by the same artist, by the looks of the screaming, pained vampire faces etched into the wood.

My eyes darted at the vampiress still clutching my sister, a hand around her neck.

Freida smiled that cold, conniving smile I was getting familiar with.

And then she turned to my sister and said, "Kill her."

CHAPTER 23

Well, *that's* not good.

I stared into my sister's distant and clouded gaze. "Shay? It's me. Leana."

"Kill her now," repeated the vampiress. I wasn't sure if she was saying the words out loud and in her head at the same time, using her Pusher abilities on Shay.

Shay's green eyes sparkled, and then, with a burst of energy, she shone like a brilliant star, just like that day when she'd fried Darius. Her sun magic rippled around her, glowing. Rays of light emanated from her like heat waves, brushing my face.

Guess the question of whether Shay could use her power at night was solved. She could.

And then a beam of light shot out of Shay's middle—straight for me.

"Oh shit."

I threw myself behind a couch and felt a brush of heat zoom over my head as I landed hard on the floor. The scent of burnt hair told me that, one, I was alive, and two, I was most probably bald. I reached up and touched my scalp. I felt something smooth. Damn. I *was* bald, at least partially.

Crap. I'd been lucky. But the next time Shay hurled her gargantuan powers my way, I might not get another break.

My little sister was trying to kill me. Well, not exactly. But it fueled me with deep hatred that the vampiress would use an eleven-year-old kid like that.

"You're killing her," I screamed. "Can you see that? Look at her!"

"She's perfectly fine," I heard Freida say.

"She's not," I howled back. "The sorceress Auria cursed her with the Mark of Death. And each time you use your mind tricks on her, it drains away her life force. She's not going to make it. You keep pushing, and she'll die. Ask any healer, and they'll tell you."

"You're lying," said the vampiress, a laugh in her voice. "What's next? You'll ask politely for your sister back?"

"If it'll work, I'm up for anything, really." I army-crawled to the edge of the flaming couch that, a second ago, could have been me. I leaned over and spied them from my hiding place.

My eyes locked on Freida, her repulsive features standing out with unnerving sharpness, her expression lacking emotion.

Shay hadn't moved from her spot, her sun magic

briefly radiating before fading away. I could easily make out her expression, the glassy look in her eyes, and the trancelike state she seemed to be in.

"I'm not lying. She's sick. And you're making her sicker. You're killing her."

Shay's eyes flickered, and for a moment, I saw a glimmer of recognition. "Leana..." she whispered, her voice barely audible.

"Shay, listen to me," I said, daring a crawl closer to her. "You have to fight her hold on you. Like Nikolas was helping you do. Remember? Fight her. You're stronger than her. Fight."

Shay looked at me with a mix of confusion and fear. "I can't... I can't..."

"Yes, you can. You can do this. Fight her!"

The vampiress hissed, stepping forward and snatching my sister by the neck again to draw her back like a puppet. "I'm growing tired of your interfering with my plans," she snarled. Her face changed, it went still, and I knew that look. She was using her mind tricks on Shay.

The next thing I knew, Shay's body glowed in bright light again. And then another beam came straight for me.

Damn it.

Using my starlights, I thrust my power out of my hands, like a Mandalorian jet-pack thruster, and shot sideways in a blur. I barely escaped my sister's deadly sunbeam.

It missed me by millimeters, hitting the wall behind me with a loud bang.

I hovered in the air, using my starlights as thrusters. I caught a glimpse of Freida, eyeing me curiously. She probably never heard of a Starlight witch who could fly. This one could.

I wanted to smile and show off my new skill, but I had three major problems I needed to solve. First, I had to save my ass from my sister's sunbeams. Second, I had to free Shay from the vampiress's hold. And lastly, I had to figure out a way to draw blood from the vampiress. Yeah. No problem.

My heart broke when I looked at my sister's face again. Tears were coursing down her cheeks, and despite the magical aura around her, her face was drained of all color, with dark circles visible under her eyes. She looked frail. Sick. She looked like she was dying.

Rage hit me hard and deep. Yet Shay wasn't attacking me. Not yet. It was as though she was struggling, fighting Freida's hold on her. Good. Shay was still in there. She could fight this.

Maybe if I could reach her in time and give her my headband, she would be safe. But then I'd be at Freida's mercy, so that wasn't any better. I couldn't save my sister if the vampiress was in control of me.

I shifted to the side, still hovering in the air. It was good that I took the weight off my ankle, but I was also draining all my starlight. "Let her go." I knew this was a long shot, but it was the only thing that popped into my head at that moment.

Freida smiled without humor. "Or what?"

I shrugged. "I'll throw you a party? You know how it goes."

She laughed harshly. "And what can a Starlight witch do to an ancient vampiress?"

"Plenty," I answered. "But you don't seem so powerful without your mind tricks. Are you? I mean, that's why you're using my sister. Because you're not as powerful as you make others think you are. Am I right?"

The vampiress narrowed her eyes at me. Yup, I'd hit a nerve with that one.

"You're just another power-hungry leech. Nothing more." I smiled, losing my focus, and dropped a few inches as I lost some control on my starlight jet pack. Oops.

She noticed.

"Trouble with your magic?" She laughed, moving toward my sister.

I shrugged. "Gas. Beans for lunch."

Freida wrinkled her face in disgust as she moved about the space. She stood in the middle of the living room. "Glad your sister has more class. And more power than you."

"You're using her as a weapon, and that's not right. She's just a kid."

The vampire bared her fangs. "That's not your concern."

"It is my concern," I said, floating forward. "Shay is my sister. I won't let you hurt her. Not anymore."

"Your sister is a powerful weapon," the vampire

said, her voice low. "She has abilities that no one else has. And we will use her to gain power."

"No," I said firmly. "Shay's not a weapon. She's a person. She's my sister. And I won't let you use her like that."

The vampire snarled, her eyes blazing with anger. "I can. I will. And you can't stop me." She stood next to Shay and said, "Burn her alive."

I knew she'd spoken out loud for my own benefit, so I'd know what command she'd used on Shay.

Like a robot, Shay rotated on the spot until her eyes and body faced me. Tears flowed down her cheeks as her tiny hands trembled and her lips shook.

"Leana…" she said in a barely audible voice.

My eyes burned at her suffering. I wanted to kill that Freida with every fiber of my being for doing this to a little girl. People like her didn't deserve to live. But I was stuck. I couldn't move.

"I know. It's okay." I slipped farther toward the ground, my eyes never leaving Shay.

She raised her hand. Though her body shook, her hand was steady, aimed straight at me. "I can't stop her. I don't…"

Slowly, I held my hands up in surrender. "Shay, it's okay," I said calmly. "You don't have to do what she says. You're stronger than that. You can fight this." Goddess, I hoped so.

"Get away." Shay's voice shook, her eyes pleading and filled with tears. "Go. Please."

"No. I'm not leaving you." My throat was raw at what I saw, my sister's suffering.

And then Shay's body burst into rays of light. I knew what came next.

I heard Freida's laugh as I reached deep within myself, calling forth every ounce of my power.

A beam of sunlight fired from Shay's chest.

My body hummed with energy as I channeled my starlights into a single, focused ray of energy. And let it rip.

My streak of starlight hit my sister's sunbeam.

The magics collided, and a blast radiated around us like a clap of thunder. I wasn't aiming to defeat my sister's magic, just to keep her from frying my ass.

The two beams coiled and pushed, sending sparks of energy in the air like faulty electric wires. They pressed and heaved against each other as if two bulls were competing for control and dominance.

At first, I thought this might work, that the two powers would counteract each other and diminish. We were both Starlight witches in a way. Maybe it *would* work.

But it was clear my starlight power wasn't as strong as Shay's sun magic. And I'd already used up most of my energy fighting the vampires and using it as my magical jet pack to keep me afloat. I was drained. And it showed.

Shay's sunbeam was stronger than mine.

It pushed mine back.

I could feel my control slipping as Freida's evil laughter filled my ears.

"I told you, Starlight witch. You're not as powerful as you think. And you can't beat me."

I could feel my starlight running out. I was slipping, the distance to the ground shortening.

I refused to give up. My sister still had a slim chance of overcoming Freida and reclaiming her mind. I could sense it; she was struggling inside her own body, trying to come out on top. Trying to push out Freida's compulsion.

Our eyes met, and I could see her in there still. My sister. She was fighting this.

But then my starlights faltered, and Shay's sunbeam pushed through.

My world shifted, and all I saw was white.

CHAPTER 24

They say you see your life flash before your eyes as you're about to die.

All I saw was a beam of white light. And then some more white light, just as my starlight magic ran out.

I fell.

Shay's sunbeam whooshed over my head, and the wall behind me exploded, dust and bits of wall and masonry striking my back. The force knocked me to the ground. Scorching heat seared my scalp, and I cried out as though I'd placed my head directly on a stovetop element. The smell of singed hair told me that whatever follicles were left were now fried.

I was bald.

My first reaction was, *What will Valen think?* But then reality hit, and I rolled onto my knees, searching for Shay, more like getting ready to leap out of the way at another sunbeam. Yet that beam should have killed me. I was too close for her to miss, yet she did.

And when I spotted her, I saw why.

She lay on the floor, her eyes closed. She'd either fainted from exhaustion, or she was...

I crawled toward her, my ankle throbbing, calling her name. "Shay? Shay!" My voice was raw and hoarse from exhaustion. I could feel the burn on my scalp throbbing, but I ignored it and touched my sister's face. Her skin was pasty and hot.

"Oh, no. Shay." I pulled her up on my lap, not caring that the vampiress could just as easily slash my neck with her sharp talons. I cradled my little sister. "What have you done?" I turned my hate on the vampiress who was staring at Shay with disappointment, like she'd paid a lot for a new car and instead got a lemon. "Look what you did. I told you. I told you this would kill her!" I shouted, the vampiress still regarding Shay with displeasure.

"How disappointing," she said, a mixture of irritation and contempt coating her voice. "I believed her youth would have sustained her, made her more powerful."

"She's just a kid, you evil bitch."

The corners of her mouth twisted at my defiance. "Now she is."

I rocked Shay slowly, holding her. She needed Valen. I could hear the sound of boots treading through the ceiling. Valen and the others were still at it. How could I reach him?

"Shay?" I wiped the wet strands of hair that stuck to her face. "Shay?"

"She is dying," said the vampiress. "I can feel her

life force slowly ebbing away even as we speak. She'll be dead in a few minutes." Freida gave an irritated glance at Shay before returning her eyes to me. "Such a waste."

"She was fine before you did this," I seethed, tasting salt in my mouth as my tears kept falling.

The vampiress sneered, her features pulled back making her look feline. "I have no more use for her."

I wrapped my arms tighter over my sister. "Come near her, and I'll finish you."

Freida threw back her head in a laugh. She sounded like a hyena. It was creepy as hell. "What? You?" She paced around us, circling like a predator stalking its prey. "You have no more power. Your magic is spent. Oh, yes. I can *feel* it. You're finished, Starlight witch. Both of you."

The vampiress pressed her ruby-red lips into a thin line, her face shining with a sudden terrible beauty. Freida drew herself up, her eyes dark with murder. The energy in the room iced.

Shit. My heart pounded hard, and my breath came fast.

"Shay? Wake up," I repeated, running my fingers through Shay's hair. I shifted her in my lap and held her tightly. "I'm so sorry," I whispered, my whole body shaking as I listened to her labored breathing. I had no idea what to do. I was exhausted, but I couldn't let Shay die. I couldn't lose her. I needed Valen, but I couldn't leave Shay. And I knew the moment I stood up, I'd be an easy target for Freida.

I had nowhere to go, nowhere to hide. I was screwed.

"Such a shame," said Freida, though I could hear the edge to her words. "I had hoped to make her my weapon. She could have brought great glory to my people. To our cause."

"Screw you," I growled, not caring anymore. I held Shay securely in my arms. I could feel her heart beating weakly against my chest.

"And now you die." Freida's face twisted in a wicked smile. She flung herself at me, at us, and I covered Shay with my body, using it as a shield to protect her.

I'm so sorry, Shay.

The floor reverberated, and I braced myself for Freida's attack, knowing the pain would soon follow.

But after a moment. Nothing happened.

I lifted my head, daring a peek.

Catelyn, in her giant form, stood in the room with Freida dangling in her hand in a death grip.

"Don't kill her!" I shouted. "If she dies, Shay *dies*."

Catelyn turned her head and looked at me. *"What?"* Her eyes narrowed. *"What happened to your hair?"*

I'd forgotten about that. "Yeah," I reached up and cringed at the baldness that spanned my scalp. "Too much Head and Shoulders."

Catelyn threw back her head and laughed. I missed that laugh. And that smile. But I was supposed to be angry with her. Wasn't I?

An orange headband dangled from the giantess's wrist, belonging to the hand that gripped Freida. It was Elsa's.

"You've seen Elsa?"

Catelyn nodded. "*Just now. She gave me that. Says it's to protect me from this one,*" she added and gave a tug on the vampiress. "*Valen asked me to go find you.*"

Loved Elsa. Catelyn wouldn't be handling Freida like a puppet if it hadn't been for that headband. It would be the other way around.

If Catelyn was here, it meant so was Arther.

Shouts resonated over the growls, tearing of flesh, and other various sounds of battle. They sounded like voices. Like commands.

I blinked through my tears as I felt Shay stir. I looked down and saw two green eyes staring up at me.

"Shay?"

My sister just blinked. Her lips moved, but no words came.

"Don't try to talk. I'm going to lay you here, okay? I need to get some of Freida's blood. It'll cure you."

Shay closed her eyes and didn't respond.

"I think she passed out again." I laid her on the floor as gently as I could. I stared at her for a beat longer, yanked out my syringe, and limped over to the giantess. I noticed she was not naked but had on those clothes that had magically stretched when she'd changed into her giant form during our trial by combat.

"I need a sample of her blood."

Catelyn lowered her arm but not her hold on the vampiress. Freida's face was turning a blue color. Blue looked good on her.

I grabbed Freida's arm, lifted her sleeve, and looked for a vein. I found a big juicy one and stabbed the syringe into it, none too gently.

The vampiress groaned.

"Ironic, isn't it, Freida?" I said, though I knew she couldn't answer. "A witch taking your vampire blood." When I filled the syringe with blood, I pulled it out of her arm and stepped back. "That should do it."

"Can I kill her now?" asked the giantess.

I was tempted to say yes, but I figured the Gray Council would prefer she stand trial and suffer the consequences. The thought of a swift death seemed too merciful. She deserved to rot in some prison for the last of her days.

"No," I answered instead. "But you can knock her out."

Catelyn's other hand appeared out of nowhere, and I heard a crunch as it hit Freida's temple. She tossed the vampiress to the ground like a discarded garment.

If she wasn't dead after that, she wasn't in very good shape.

My gaze fell on the giantess. She'd come to help. I wasn't sure how I felt at the moment. I was still not over what she'd done. But I'd think about that later.

"She needs Valen," I told the giantess.

SHADES OF WITCHES

"*I'll get him.*" Catelyn bounded out of view.

I knelt back on the floor and slipped Shay over me again. I held on to my little sister, sobbing as I rocked her. She would have been mortified that I was rocking her like a baby if she were conscious. But she was still a baby to me. She was just a little kid. Too young to have gone through this.

And if she died…

"*Leana.*"

Valen's voice turned me around as the giant lowered himself next to me. "*Put her on the floor.*"

I did as he instructed, and when I was finished, Valen had transformed back into his smaller human form. I watched as he placed one of his hands on Shay's shoulders and the other on her forehead.

Magic chimed my senses as light sparked from Valen's touch, his healing magic.

The golden light of Valen's healing magic engulfed Shay's body. I held my breath as I watched, too afraid to speak. Fearful that even Valen's magic couldn't save her. Not this time.

But then her pallid skin shifted and turned pink, and the dark circles under her eyes brightened. I grabbed her wrist. Her heartbeat was strong.

"Will she…" I swallowed, clearing my throat. "Is she okay?"

"Not okay," said Valen grimly. "But she will recover." He looked over at the syringe I still clutched in my hand. "Is that the vampiress's blood?"

"It is." I stuffed it in my pocket to keep it safe. "We need to get Shay to Polly right away."

Valen nodded just as the ground trembled. I looked up to see Catelyn march back into the room, still in her giantess form, and sit next to Freida, guarding her.

"What about the other vampires?" I asked.

A storm of emotions shifted over Valen's face. "We've beaten them. With Arther's help." He looked over at Catelyn and smiled. She smiled back. She looked at me, but I looked away. I wasn't ready to forgive her. Even though she had technically saved our butts.

Valen reached out and took my hand. "You okay?" His eyes rolled over my head. "You look—"

"Bald?" I should have been mortified at him seeing me like this. God only knew what I looked like, but there were worse things in life than being bald.

"And your eyebrows are gone."

Okay, maybe… not.

"Hell. My eyebrows too?" I reached up. Sure enough, I felt a smooth piece of skin where I should be feeling some hair. "I must look like Gollum."

"Gollum's wife," said a smiling Valen. "You look pretty good bald."

I pushed him playfully. If Shay could see me now, she'd be laughing. I looked down at her. She was still sleeping.

"What will happen to the vampiress?" I asked,

my eyes moving to the bundle on the floor beside Catelyn.

Valen followed my gaze, then looked back at Shay. He looked grim. "Gray Council officers are on their way. They'll lock her up for a very long time. I can assure you."

"But what about her mind compulsion?" I tapped my headband, relieved and surprised that it hadn't burned along with my hair. That was powerful magic. "If they don't have protection, she can pretty much *persuade* her way out of jail." Now that I thought about it, she'd probably compel her way into a seat on the Gray Council too. Freida might be down now, but she was extremely dangerous.

"They have tools to keep her from using it," said Valen, his eyes on my headband. "Maybe not something as stylish as these headbands. But she's not the first vampire with this ability." He flicked his gaze to Shay. "They won't let Freida return to what she was."

I frowned. "What does that mean?"

"They'll remove her *special* talent."

"Remove?" I shifted my weight. "Like physically pull it out of her head? Like a lobotomy?"

"In a way, yes." Valen rolled his shoulders. "She'll never be able to use it on anyone ever again."

"That's intense." I wasn't sure how I felt about that, but she was a psychotic trampire, and the notion that she could never harm anyone ever again did make me feel a tad better.

Shay stirred, and I looked down at a pair of fluttering green eyes.

My heart lurched in my chest. "Welcome back."

"Hey, squirt," said Valen.

"Hey," she whispered, her voice gruff. "What happened?"

I gave a relieved smile. I was about to say, *You almost died,* but instead, I said, "You passed out."

Shay's eyes flew wide open, and her face paled. "She made me do it. I didn't want to—"

I pulled her into a hug. Even though she might not want this, she needed it. I needed it. "It wasn't your fault. And I don't want to hear you apologize for this. Ever. You got that?"

Shay nodded over my shoulder. "'Kay."

I released her, and she shifted to sit on her own.

A tiny frown appeared on her face. "You're bald. And you don't have eyebrows."

Valen snorted, and I ignored him. "Just unforeseen circumstances with the job. It happens sometimes."

"You look weird," she said as a tiny smile quirked her lips.

I beamed because her telling me I looked weird meant she was on the mend. "I know. If you want, I could shave your head too."

"No." She wrapped her hands around her middle, and I laughed.

Then an army of about fifteen or more paranormals swarmed into the room. Some were dressed in black clothes. Some were in their animal forms as I spotted wolves and bears. Another group just outside the hallway was shoving cuffed vampires down the staircase. The vampires hissed. Some fought back, trying to escape from the onslaught of Arther's army. But they were just punched and kicked back into line.

"Leana! Shay!"

Elsa waded her way through the soldiers. "Out of my way," she commanded and rushed up to us. Behind her came Julian and then Jade. My throat wobbled with a sudden surge of relief. Thank the cauldron. They were all alive.

"We were so worried about you when we saw you leave," said Elsa. "Both of you." Her eyes rolled over Shay and then widened when they settled on me again. "Cauldron help us. What happened to your hair? You look like a crystal ball."

Here we go. "It's a new style. You like it?"

"No. But I believe Polly can remedy that," said Elsa, trying to smile but instead pulling her expression into a grimace. From the constant shifting in her face, like she couldn't settle on one emotion, I had a feeling I looked pretty bad.

"At least she looks good. I could never pull off the bald look," said Jade, throwing a smile my way. "I have about twenty wigs you could borrow. And in all colors. You can be a redhead, a blonde, or if you're feeling a little crazy, blue or green." She had a busted lip, and her right eye was swollen.

"Thanks. Are you okay? You look pretty banged up," I asked.

Jade straightened her shoulders. "You should see the other guy."

I laughed and smiled up at my friends. "What did I miss? Looks like I missed a lot."

"Well, it was touch and go for a while," said Julian, with a confident smile, his hair disheveled and wild like he'd just come from a trek in the woods. "We'd beat one down, and two more would show up. The vamps kept on coming. Hundreds of them must have been living here."

"But then Arther showed up with his pack," said Jade. "Kicked their asses."

"Good." I exhaled. "That's good." The alpha was still not my favorite person, but I'd thank him later for helping and perhaps saving my friends.

"That Freida?" Julian gestured over to the fallen vampiress.

"Yes. Catelyn did that."

At the mention of the giantess, she looked over at us. She was back in her human form. I hadn't noticed her change, but I did perceive that none of my friends acknowledged her.

Elsa knelt and inspected Shay's face. "How are you feeling, dear?"

Shay shrugged. "Okay."

"Hmm." Elsa pressed the back of her hand on Shay's forehead. "What she needs is some of my chicken soup. And then rest."

The idea of soup sounded amazing, but I knew that wouldn't happen. I felt the vial of blood in my pocket. "Not yet. We need to get back to the hotel. And I need Polly."

"You got the blood?" Jade's eyes moved to the bundle that was the unconscious vampiress.

"Yes. We need to leave." We still had about an hour's drive back to the city. "I'll call Polly on the way."

"What blood?" Shay was staring at me, confused, and I could see a little fear flickering behind those green eyes.

I searched her face. "Blood that'll make you better. Blood that'll take that curse away for good, and you'll be just as you were before. I promise." I hoped Olin wouldn't make a liar out of me. If Freida's blood didn't work, I was back to square one.

Elsa stood up. Her eyes met mine. "And you, my dear, need to get some rest too. You look like you're about to fall over."

"I'm fine," I protested, but the moment I tried to stand up, the world spun around me. Straining, I pushed to my feet, my ankle crying out in protest, and I put my weight on my other limb.

"Fine, huh?" Julian said with a snort. "You're about as fine as a newborn deer trying to walk for the first time."

I shot him a glare, but I knew he was right. I was exhausted, my muscles ached, and my head was pounding. All I wanted was to curl up in my bed and sleep for a week.

Valen scooped Shay into his big arms, and my little sister giggled as he swung her around his shoulders.

"Come on," Elsa said, wrapping her arm around my waist. "Let's get you home."

As we made our way out of the tacky room, I couldn't help but feel grateful for my friends. We had been through so much together. I felt a sense of relief wash over me. We had made it out alive, but just barely. It had been a close call.

I turned to take one last look at the chaos that had unfolded behind us. The room was in shambles, broken furniture scattered everywhere and scorch marks staining the walls that weren't destroyed. It was a mess, but at least we were safe and together.

Catelyn looked up, and our eyes met. None of the gang went to talk to her, not even Elsa, her devoted friend, although she had given the giantess her own magical headband. I was pretty sure the rejection stung. And from the sadness on her face, it was clear that it did. With her shoulders slumped, I watched the play of emotions on her face: regret, anguish, shame.

We all mess up. It's part of being human—and paranormal. It's also in our nature to forgive. Unfortunately, not every mistake warrants a second chance. But sometimes they do.

And maybe, just maybe, this time, it did.

CHAPTER 25

The drive back to the hotel was a blur of exhaustion and anxiety. I kept reassuring Shay that everything was going to be okay, but my own doubts and fears were beginning to creep in. What if the blood didn't work? What if we were too late? What if the curse had been inside Shay's body for far too long for anything like a counter-curse or antidote to work? What if Polly wasn't the healer to work it? Should we risk driving back to the compound to find Olin?

Now that Shay was with us, and because Valen's SUV could only fit five people, Julian surprised us when he said he'd catch a ride back to the hotel with Arther's gang. No one objected.

When I'd caught a glimpse of myself in the reflection of the Range Rover's windows, I nearly had a heart attack.

"Holy hell," I muttered, reaching up to touch my very bald head. It hadn't hit me as much since I hadn't *seen* it, only felt it. But now that I had, I was mortified.

"I think I will take one of your wigs, Jade," I said, pulling closed the SUV's door and doing my best not to take another peek at myself as I heard Shay laugh.

"I'll lend you my *best* one," said Jade, a smile in her voice.

Why didn't that make me feel any better? Because I had a feeling her *best* wig was a curled monstrosity styled with an eighties' perm.

When we finally arrived at the hotel, I stumbled out of the car and practically collapsed, cursing my damn ankle. Once Valen had Shay in his arms again, we all made for the doors.

Polly was waiting for us at the entrance. She didn't look like I'd woken her out of bed. Instead, her eyes were alert, focused. Her white chef coat was spotted with orange and green stains. She eyed my bald head. "I can fix that."

I let out a little whimper of relief, making Shay laugh. "Okay. But Shay first."

"Blood," instructed Polly as she stuck out her hand.

I dug out the vial from my pocket. "How long do you need to make the counter-curse? Or is it an antidote?"

Polly took the vial of blood. "It's a bit of both. We'll need a counter-curse to play with the magic part of the curse. And an antidote to counter the blood aspect. Shay'll need the vampiress's blood in hers for it to work. I've been working on it since you called. But I'll need a few minutes to prepare. Best if you get her upstairs. I'll be up in a minute."

Following Polly's instructions, we—me, Valen, Shay, Jade, and Elsa—piled into the elevator. Not a soul was in the lobby, and the only sound was the emptiness of the space, like a roomful of furniture with nobody inside. Seeing as it was about four in the morning, it made sense that the hotel was deserted except for the night concierge. His bloodshot eyes tracked us warily from behind the front desk. But he did not utter a single word before the elevator doors shut.

Once back in my old apartment, Valen settled Shay on the couch. She did look better now than when she was under Freida's control. But the ashen color to her skin had returned, and so had a darkness around her sunken eyes. It was as though the giant's magic was failing, as though it wasn't working anymore.

And from the concerned frown on the giant's face, and the way he'd withdrawn again, I knew he'd come to the same conclusion. His healing magic was becoming ineffective. If the vampiress's blood didn't work, we'd be in serious trouble.

I watched Valen. His jaw kept clenching, and he was wearing a permanent frown now. If I didn't know any better, I'd say he was about to lose control. That Shay's illness, or curse, was affecting him in a way that would only affect a parent. Like he had felt this before, and it was killing him that he was going through it again. Was this about his wife? I didn't know.

Part of me wanted to go to him and wrap my arms over that big chest to try and calm him down. But I didn't want to take my attention away from Shay.

She was looking pale, and her breathing was shallow. I wanted to reach out and touch her, but I knew it wouldn't help. All I could do was wait.

I kept my face blank, from showing the emotions I was feeling. The last thing I wanted was for Shay to get scared from what she read on my face. She was comfortable for now, and I wanted to keep it that way for as long as possible.

Jade and Elsa were quick to make themselves useful, fetching blankets and pillows for Shay. I was grateful for their efforts, but I couldn't help feeling restless. I needed to do something, anything, to make sure Shay would be okay.

My ankle throbbed as I lowered myself into an armchair, and my head felt like it was about to explode. I closed my eyes and took a deep breath, trying to calm myself down. I had to stay strong for Shay. This wasn't about me. It was about her and removing the damn curse once and for all.

A few minutes later, Polly marched into the apartment, holding a small vial filled with a dark liquid. "Is she ready?" she asked, her eyes fixed on Shay sitting on the couch with Valen beside her.

I nodded, leaning forward. "What do we need to do?"

Polly joined Shay next to the couch. "We need to get some of the vampiress's blood into her system," she explained. "It's the only way to counteract the curse. The vampire blood will act as an antitoxin, destroying the curse from the inside out." Polly looked at Shay. "I'm going to inject this into your arm. It should work within a few minutes."

"*Should* work?" I couldn't help the sound of alarm and disappointment in my voice. "Olin said it *would* work." I looked at Shay, and I didn't like the fear that danced in her eyes. I'd promised her it would work.

"Olin?" asked Polly. "Who's Olin?"

"The other healer," said Valen, just as Jade and Elsa returned. "He's the one who told us about Freida and how we could use her blood to remove the curse."

Polly's face creased in thought, and for a second, I thought she was about to bad-mouth the other healer. "Ah. Yes. Well, I say *should* because *I've* never tried it before, and I've never heard of using the blood of a vampiress to remove a curse. After you called, I've been doing a lot of research, and I've made a few phone calls to some of my healer colleagues. And they all agree it should work."

It wasn't really the answer I was going for, but I was putting my faith in that little healer back at the compound. Maybe I should have rubbed his hair for luck.

"It'll be fine," said Elsa. "Polly can do this."

The healer flicked her eyes at me. "That bald head is distracting."

"I can get a wig," said Jade, beaming.

I cringed on the inside. "Maybe later."

A smirk formed on Polly's mouth as she plunked out a syringe from her coat pocket and inserted it into the vial of dark liquid. She carefully drew some of it up into the syringe and then turned to Shay. "This might sting a little," she warned.

Shay stiffened, her eyes on the syringe. I pushed myself up, shuffled over to her, and sat next to her on the couch. I took her hand and squeezed. "It'll only be for a second." But I wondered if the effect of this antidote would hurt her. It could.

Shay didn't squeeze my hand back, but she didn't pull away either. "Okay," she mumbled. She blinked a few times, and then she slumped in her seat. I reached out and caught her before she fell forward. Her skin felt clammy to the touch, and her breathing was shallow. Panic started to bubble up inside me, but before I could say anything, Polly put a hand on my shoulder. "We need to act quickly. The fever is bad. The curse is killing her."

"Hurry. Do it."

"Here we go," said Polly, eyeing Shay from under her brows as she injected the substance into Shay's arm.

Shay winced at the needle's sting, her eyes opening and then closing again. But she didn't cry out. She was stoic, brave, just like me.

Jade and Elsa crowded around us, their faces etched with worry. I glanced at Valen, but his face was a blank canvas, giving away nothing.

After Polly removed the syringe, she raised her hands and moved them around Shay. Her lips moved in what I could only imagine was a spell. The air crackled with the sudden inflow of magic. A healer's magic. I felt a mist-like haze fall around Shay. Though I couldn't see it, I felt it. The swirling mist swayed and wavered. The air shifted, and then the haze lifted.

"Did it work?" I stared at Shay, not seeing any changes. My gaze flicked to Valen, but he was staring at Shay with an intensity like he was afraid this treatment had only made her worse.

"Only time will tell," answered the healer, stepping back.

I glared at her. "Then how long till we know?"

"I'm not sure. Could be an hour, could be two," said Polly, stuffing the syringe and the now empty vial into her pockets. "It depends on how strong this vampire blood is and how long the curse has been inside her. Many variables to consider. But it could also take less time. It could work in a matter of minutes, and it could just as easily have worked right away. I'm not accustomed to this type of treatment. But… if your friend is correct, I predict it should work fast."

I let out a shaky breath, and as we all watched, Shay slumped against the couch.

Then, just as I was about to lose hope, Shay opened her eyes, her features twisting.

"What is it?" I asked, alarmed. Valen tensed on her other side.

"I feel... different," she said, her voice barely above a whisper. She hunched over like she was about to be sick.

"*Good* different? Or *bad* different?" I asked, my heart racing and feeling like *I* might throw up.

Shay nodded. "Good, I think. It doesn't hurt, but it feels... weird."

"That's the curse being removed," Polly said, a smile stretching across her face. "The vampiress's blood is working. It's eating away at the curse."

Elsa let out a loud whimper, clutching her locket as big, fat tears rolled down her flushed cheeks.

"Here," said Jade, her eyes wet, and she handed the older witch a tissue before proceeding to blow her own nose with another.

Shay looked up at us, her eyes wide in wonder. "I think I'm better."

I breathed a sigh of relief, feeling the tension in the room dissipate. "Thank god," I murmured, feeling tears prick at the corners of my eyes. "So, it's over. She's cured?" I dipped my head to get a better look at my sister's face. Her skin was a nice healthy pink with no traces of dark circles under her eyes or any signs of a fever or a curse. It was finally over. Shay was going to be okay.

Valen sighed and raked his fingers through his hair like he was trying to release the tension that had clamped his body tightly since we'd left Freida's garish abode.

"It appears to be," said Polly. "Now we wait. The curse will take some time to remove itself from

Shay's system fully. But I'll keep a close eye on her. I'll be back in a few hours to check up on her. But yes. It seems the worst has passed." She looked at Shay and said, "You're going to be fine."

We all breathed another sigh of relief.

Polly smiled, visibly relieved. "I'll leave you all to rest. Call me if anything changes."

"I will. Thanks, Polly."

The healer beamed, straightened the front of her jacket, and said, "My pleasure." And with that, Polly walked out of the apartment and disappeared down the hall.

"I need a drink." Elsa sniffed, and she blew her nose.

"Make that a bottle." Jade walked into the kitchen, Elsa behind her, in search of a bottle of wine.

I watched them go and then turned to Shay. "How are you *really* feeling?" Not that I didn't believe her when she said she was feeling better. I just thought without everyone hunkering around her, she might feel more comfortable now. Maybe she'd been holding back.

Shay pulled herself upright, looking more alert. The change was evident in her eyes, which now had a bright spark in them. She looked as healthy and attentive as the first time I'd seen her right here in this room with our father.

"Better." She blinked and said, "The headache is gone, and I don't feel sick anymore."

I smiled. "I never thought I'd say this, but I'm

glad we ran into Freida. Without her... without her blood... you wouldn't be cured."

Shay's face wrinkled in disgust. "I don't like her. And her house was ugly."

Valen let out a laugh, sounding very much like his old, post-grumpy self. "I don't like her either, kiddo."

"Is she dead?" asked Shay.

I glanced at Valen before I answered. "Not dead. But she won't be bothering anyone anymore. Not ever." No, because apparently, she was on her way to get lobotomized. I was still disturbed about that. But it wasn't the time to let my thoughts wander off to that evil vampiress.

As I looked at Shay, all glowing and radiant in her newfound health, it occurred to me that she could go back to school, back to Fantasia Academy. I knew Shay would be absolutely thrilled about going back to that school.

I let out a sigh and rubbed my thighs. "And that's it? That's all? You don't feel anything else?"

Shay looked at me and said, "I'm hungry."

I laughed. "Of course you are."

"I'll make us a pizza," said the giant, smiling as he stood. But when he turned his gaze on me, his smile turned devilish, seductive, and his eyes gleamed with a desire that sent my heart and lady bits pounding like a bass drum in a marching band.

It appeared as though I was getting my dessert later.

Oh, yeah.

CHAPTER 26

Of course, after Freida's defeat, we had to celebrate. Meaning the entire thirteenth floor was a party.

The voices of several tenants had already begun to reverberate throughout the hallway, rising and falling with the energy of a celebration. Among them, I noticed the unmistakable voice of Barb, the matriarch of the thirteenth floor, scolding the ten-year-old twins for some offense as she pointed at them in a grandmotherly manner. Her long, white hair billowed behind her as she hurried after the twins. She was tall and fit for someone in her seventies, with piercing blue eyes that held the wisdom of decades.

The twins, dressed like *The Addams Family*'s Wednesday, in a black dress with a white collar, along with dark braids, let out peals of laughter and darted into a neighboring apartment, the sound of things crashing echoing in their wake.

Cassandra, the twins' mother, watched the scene unfold with a proud smile, her arms wrapped around Julian as she leaned into him gently. He turned around and kissed her on the lips. It was quick, but even I could feel that spark of desire between them. He had that *honeymoon* look about him, like nothing Cassandra did was bad and he was on his best behavior.

I smiled. I was happy for my friend. He deserved to be happy and in love. Julian had proven to be a great ally in battle with his potions. And Elsa with her magical headbands that saved me from Freida's compulsion, which I believed Jade was now selling like hotcakes on her new witch website, WITCHES R US.

The news of Freida's defeat and Shay's recovery, more like her being cured of the curse, had obviously spread quickly. The thirteenth floor was now just as vibrant and noisy as it had been the first time I'd set foot on it.

Every tenant had come out of their residence, congregating around the large tables filled with food and various alcoholic drinks. They were all enjoying each other's company, exchanging pleasantries, and having a good time.

With every step I took, I could feel a palpable sense of joy and excitement in the air. It was as if everyone in the hotel was preparing for a new beginning and wanted to be a part of it.

I breathed in the comforting scent of familiarity, a

reminder that I had come full circle and that there was still hope even in the most uncertain of times.

Valen had gone to pick up Shay from school today. I'd never seen a kid so happy to go to school when she'd only slept three hours. She had practically galloped the entire way to Fantasia Academy, me trying to keep up behind her.

Kids were surprisingly resilient—something I was learning quickly. And seeing the smile on Shay's face this morning at the prospect of going to that paranormal school, you'd never guess she'd been at death's door only hours before. Or that she'd been used as a weapon to try to kill me, her sister, by a wicked vampiress.

"Let me see."

I turned to see Polly marching my way, appraising me in one glance. "It's grown back a bit since this morning," I said as I touched my scalp with relief at feeling the strands through my fingers.

Polly had returned a few minutes after she'd injected Shay with the so-called antidote while we were all munching on Valen's excellent pizza to give me a jar of rotten-onion-smelling ointment for my scalp.

The healer grabbed my head between her hands and inclined it forward. "Yes, definitely new growth," she remarked, her warm breath fanning my scalp. She tilted my head backward and gave me a quick assessing look. "Your eyebrows have returned too; although, if you don't want a unibrow, you'd better get some tweezers."

"What?" I knocked her hands from my face. "Are you kidding me?" I'd just checked them an hour ago, and they looked just as they did before Shay burned them off.

Polly let out a chuckle. "Healer humor."

I glared at her. "Not funny."

"The good news is, is that there is new growth," said the healer. "Bad news is that it might take a few months to get to the same length you had before."

"It's fine." I pulled at the strands near my chin. "I can tie most of it back. Valen likes it. Says I look young." I was just glad that I didn't have to wear one of Jade's wigs. Even if my hair was much shorter than before, I preferred to wear my own. Thank you very much.

"All right, then." Polly tapped my head like I was a well-behaved cocker spaniel, spun around, and shuffled toward one of the buffet tables. She began describing all the delectable dishes she had worked so hard to prepare for everyone, to those gathered around.

I chuckled, and as I turned around, Shay bounced my way, Valen walking behind her, his broad shoulders swaying. He looked at me, his dark eyes glistening with amusement.

Shay stopped in her tracks, her green eyes widening as she took in all the food and people congregating about. Her glance traveled around the hallway before settling on me with a questioning expression. "Is this a party?"

Valen laughed and rubbed Shay on the head, much like Polly had done to me a moment ago.

"In a way, yes." I stared at Shay. She looked perfectly healthy. She had an added bounce in her step, and she was smiling more than usual. "How was school today?"

Shay shrugged. "Okay. Is that pizza?" Her eyes were glued to one of the buffet tables, where Valen had set up an array of mini pizzas for everyone to enjoy.

"Yes. Mini pizzas."

She looked up at me. "Can I have some?"

"Of course you can. You can have as much as you like."

"Awesome!" Without another word, she hurried over to the pizza table and began piling her plate high with the mini pizzas. I watched her devour two in record time before heading back for thirds.

Seeing how happy and healthy she was filled me with relief—and gratitude toward Polly and Valen for coming together and helping us out in our time of need. The thought made me realize I should call Olin and thank him. If it weren't for him, we'd never have known that Freida's blood would remove the curse. Maybe I should get him a gift? What does one gift a healer? A tiny good-luck troll, that's what.

"She looks happy," I said to Valen as he neared. "I take it school went well."

"The little squirt showed off her magic in class today," said the giant, smiling proudly.

My lips parted. "You're kidding. And? Was this

her showing off, or was this prompted by her teachers?"

"Teachers. It was a 'show and tell your magic' kind of class today. I think it went well."

I smiled, staring at Shay, who was trying to shove three mini pizzas into her mouth simultaneously. "Guess she missed out on Manners 101."

"Yeah." Valen's expression pulled into a whole smile, radiating warmth and making him look downright gorgeous. I breathed in his irresistible scent—a mix of musk and aftershave—and my skin tingled. Yum.

His eyes sparkled with amusement as Shay continued to devour the mini pizzas like a starving street kid. But despite the lightness of his mood, I could still see a hint of sadness in him, as if he were thinking about something painful from his past.

"I heard After Dark reopened this afternoon."

"It did."

"Must be nice to have your restaurant back. I know the gang is excited."

Valen's shoulders bounced as he chuckled. "Yeah. They were our first customers this morning."

I leaned against him. "You know, I feel like there's something you're not telling me. Something from your past. Something that makes you incredibly sad when you look at Shay. Is it your wife?" I realized this was most probably none of my business, and he wouldn't tell me. But I cared about him. And I could see that something had him upset.

Sensing his reluctance, I blurted. "Sorry. None of my business."

Valen tensed at my words. His eyes flashed with sadness. "Remember when I told you that giant offspring are rare?"

"I do. I remember."

"Well, my wife and I tried for years. She wanted a family. And I desperately wanted to give her one," he said softly. "We tried everything. And then, by a miracle, she got pregnant."

"Oh." I waited, knowing there was more to this story. Valen had never told me he had a child.

He let out a long breath through his nose. "She had a miscarriage."

My breath caught, and it was like I was being stabbed in the gut repeatedly. "I'm so sorry," I said, placing a hand on his arm. I knew all too well the hurt that came along with not being able to get pregnant, but I'd never lost a child. And I couldn't even imagine that pain.

Valen had lost his wife *and* his child.

My eyes filled with water as I blinked the tears that fell down my cheeks. "I know now why this thing with Shay had you all worked up. I'm sorry." It explained a lot. Everything. His shutting down, his overprotectiveness toward Shay, and his despair at seeing her so sick, nearly dying.

Valen shook his head, a small smile playing on his lips. "It's okay. It was a long time ago, and I've made my peace with it. But sometimes it feels like just yesterday."

"I can't imagine how difficult that must be," I said, my heart aching for him.

"It's been tough, but Shay makes it easier," he said, his eyes drifting toward our little squirt. "She's a lot like you. Only smaller."

I snorted, and it came out with some snot tears. Yeah. Not pretty. But Valen didn't even notice, his eyes still on Shay. Clever as I was, I did a covert wipe with the tissue I had in my pocket.

"Hey, man." Arther came forward and clasped Valen's hand in a handshake, aiding in my covert snot-tear removal.

"Good to see ya," said Valen, patting the other beast of a man on the shoulder. "So, how long you staying?"

"Couple days," answered the alpha male. "They're releasing Catelyn's parents from the morgue tomorrow. She wants to have a small funeral."

"Sorry, man," said Valen. "How she doing?"

Arther didn't answer. Instead, he just looked at me like somehow I had the answer.

I looked away, and my eyes found Catelyn. She was leaning on a wall away from everyone, like she felt as though she wasn't welcome. She'd obviously come with Arther. And although she had been part of the thirteenth-floor gang, she looked lost. Like the first time she'd come here.

Leaving the two males, I grabbed two glasses of red wine and made my way across to her.

"Here," I said to Catelyn, holding up a glass.

"Thanks," she said, surprise in her voice and her expression.

"You don't have to stay so far away from everyone, you know." I sipped my wine, seeing the hallway cramped with tenants. The party was definitely in the hallway.

Catelyn stared at the floor. "Didn't think I'd be welcome... after... you know..."

"Anyone who saves my ass is welcome here," I told her with a smile.

Catelyn eyed me with uncertainty. "Are you sure?"

"I am. You saved me from Freida. And because of you, I was able to get that bitch's blood." I'd always be grateful for that. Always.

Catelyn blinked and turned away. She shook her head. "What I did to you... I'm sorry. I'll never forgive myself."

"Well, you should. Because I have."

Catelyn's bottom lip shook as she took control of her emotions. "I shouldn't have done what I did. I was horrible to you. After all you did for me... after those *experiments*."

"But I know why you did," I said, sipping my wine. Now came the hard part. "I'm sorry about your parents, Catelyn. I never meant for them to get hurt. You have to believe me."

Catelyn sniffed. "I know. Wasn't your fault."

In a way, it was, but I didn't want to bring that up again. We'd said our peace.

I felt eyes on me, and when I turned my head,

Arther and Valen were watching me, watching us, and I could see the relief on Arther's face that we were having a normal conversation and not throwing around fists.

"He's hot," I said and looked at Catelyn. "Very sexy. Good choice, by the way. Does he look that good naked?"

Catelyn burst out laughing. "Better."

"Damn."

"Damn."

We both laughed like idiots.

So, I was right. Arther and Catelyn *were* a thing. Come to think of it, they did make a really nice couple, a very *pretty* couple.

"What are you guys laughing about?" Jade came our way, with what looked like a chicken-salad sandwich in one hand and a glass of wine in the other.

"I was just admiring Catelyn's new guy." I nodded in the direction of the alpha male talking with Valen.

Jade's face lit up, eyes wide, as she glanced from Catelyn to Arther. "Yeah. He reminds me of a young Billy Idol," she added dreamily. "It's hot." Not sure that's how I would have described the alpha, but whatever.

"What's hot?" Elsa appeared with Barb next to her.

"Catelyn's boyfriend," said Jade, angling her head toward the alpha male who had just realized that we females were all ogling him like a piece of meat. He looked embarrassed.

He was certainly a striking alpha with a formidable presence and a way of holding himself that gave the impression of a more experienced man.

"Ah, yes," said Barb, running her fingers through her long, white hair as she surveyed the alpha male. "Wonderful specimen. And look at the size of his feet. We all know what they say about the size of a man's feet."

I spat some wine out of my mouth. "You did *not* just say that?" I glanced at Catelyn who had a strange smile on her face, her eyes on her male. Guess that answered the question.

"You're something else, Barb. Who knew you had a sharp eye for men's feet," I quipped, chuckling again as the white-haired witch lifted her chin with pride.

It felt nice, more than nice, to have Catelyn with us once again. Turned out, after I'd told my tale of how she'd saved me from Freida to the gang, the group slowly warmed up to her again: at least the idea of her.

"Leana," said a generous-sized woman, walking out of my apartment and joining us in the hallway.

"What's up, Louise?"

Louise hooked a thumb over her shoulder. "A guy in there wants to speak to you."

"A guy? Who?" My first thought was Clive. The bastard must have heard that we'd vanquished his mistress, and now she was out of business. Was he here for revenge? That would be dumb. I was surrounded by friends, family. Was he that stupid? I was about to find out.

Louise shook her head. "Never seen him before. Asked to see you."

"Thanks," I answered as I made my way inside the apartment. I was in a fantastic mood. Even Clive couldn't put a damper on it. Hell, the fact that he was here actually made me all giddy inside. I'd put him out of business too.

I glanced around, but the apartment was deserted except for the mountain of dishes that I wasn't going to do.

But a man stood in my living room, and it wasn't Clive.

"Matiel?" I scowled at the figure standing in front of the couch.

He'd just materialized as he'd done before. No warning.

"Leana," came Shay's voice behind me. "Valen says—"

My kid sister brushed up against me, and her body went rigid. Then, seeing her father, she let out a squeal. "Dad!" She shot forward.

I whipped out my hand, grabbed her by the arm, and pulled her against me.

"What are you doing?" Shay struggled in my grasp. "It's Dad. Let me go!"

But I wouldn't. I stared at my father while Shay continued to fight me, her little fists hitting my hand as she tried to break free of my hold. But I wouldn't let her go.

Matiel, our *angel* father, looked the same since I'd last seen him. His grizzled hair ended just beneath his chin and had probably been dark once. He had a short beard of the same color, which accompanied his green eyes, framed by thick black eyebrows. A heavy black cloak hit the shins of his dark boots.

But something was different. He looked… dare I say… nervous?

"Tell me what's going on," I said, keeping my voice calm despite a storm of emotions brewing. "Something's going on. I can see it in your face. Tell me."

At that, Shay stopped fighting me, and she straightened. "Dad? What's she talking about?"

Matiel sighed through his nose. He stood there, jaw clenched, his expression clouded, and thoughts flashed behind those green eyes, Shay's eyes. He looked like he was trying to come up with something to say. A lie?

At his silence, I pressed, "Where have you been? You promised you'd come by." My voice was rough. I expected an answer from the father who'd sworn to his eleven-year-old child that he'd be visiting every week. That didn't happen. Even though Shay said it hadn't bothered her, I knew she was lying. Kids always wanted to see their parents.

Matiel pursed his lips as he considered my words. His eyes, far older than his face, seemed to search for and find an answer that evaded me. "Away."

"No shit. I tried to contact you," I said, feeling the heat rising in my cheeks as I saw Shay looking up at me. "And you know what happened? My ritual went up in flames. Burned. Like someone didn't want me to talk to you. Or you didn't."

Matiel's gaze was steady and unblinking. He seemed to be assessing me, trying to make a decision on what to tell me, but said nothing.

I felt the air move behind me and then saw Valen move to the kitchen. He leaned on the wall, crossing his arms over his chiseled chest as he observed my angel father.

My father's gaze flicked to Valen, and I saw interest spark in his eyes. Something that was different from when I noticed people meeting Valen for the first time. Usually, they cowered away, wanting to put as much space between them and the giant. But Matiel was an angel. Guess not much scared him.

"I—*Shay* needed you," I corrected. "She was sick. Deathly sick. Cursed with something foul. And I know you angels have the power to heal. We could have avoided all of this," I added, knowing he probably had no idea what I was talking about. "You could have healed her."

The angel just nodded, looking both defeated and agitated. "I'm sorry. I had no idea."

"Not good enough. I don't care about your excuses," I seethed through gritted teeth. Yeah, I was pissed. "I want answers, and I want them now. Why didn't you show up? What's going on?"

"I wanted to. Many times. But I couldn't. Not if I

didn't want to put you in danger." Matiel glanced at Valen and then back at me.

I frowned. "But you're here now. What's changed?"

Matiel kept his face blank. "There's something you need to know. Remember our conversation about the Legion of Angels? Something's happened—*is* happening with the Legion of Angels."

I wrapped my arms tightly around Shay. "No. They're not getting her. No fucking way. I'll kill every last one of them. I don't care what you are. They're not taking Shay. You hear me?" I was absolutely livid, my anger coursing through me and ready to explode at any moment. My body tensed with the readiness to lash out.

"That's just it," said my father, horror etched on his face. "They don't want Shay." He looked at me. "They want *you*."

Well, crap.

Don't miss the next book in the Witches of New York series.

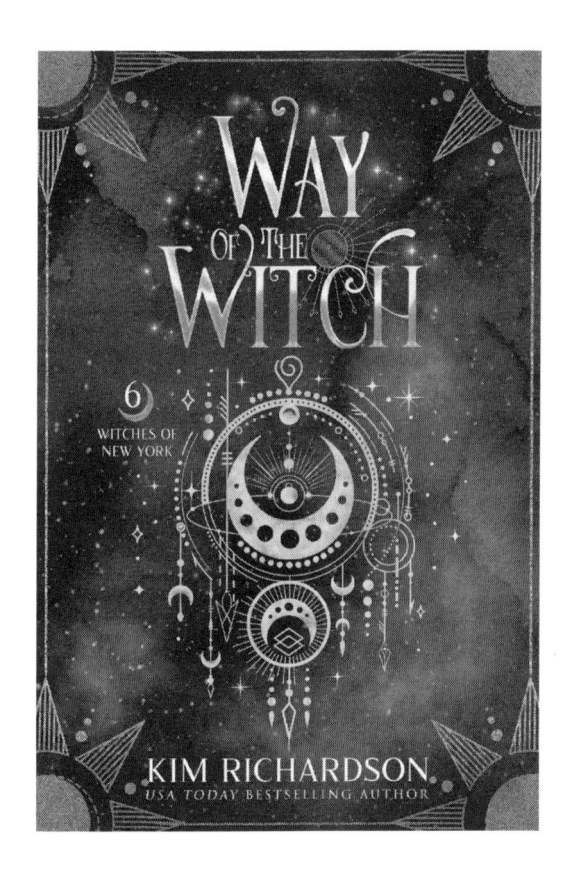

BOOKS BY KIM RICHARDSON

THE WITCHES OF HOLLOW COVE

Shadow Witch

Midnight Spells

Charmed Nights

Magical Mojo

Practical Hexes

Wicked Ways

Witching Whispers

Mystic Madness

Rebel Magic

Cosmic Jinx

Brewing Crazy

WITCHES OF NEW YORK

The Starlight Witch

Game of Witches

Tales of a Witch

THE DARK FILES

Spells & Ashes

Charms & Demons

Hexes & Flames

Curses & Blood

SHADOW AND LIGHT

Dark Hunt

Dark Bound

Dark Rise

Dark Gift

Dark Curse

Dark Angel

About the Author

Kim Richardson is a *USA Today* bestselling and award-winning author of urban fantasy, fantasy, and young adult books. She lives in the eastern part of Canada with her husband, two dogs, and a very old cat. Kim's books are available in print editions, and translations are available in over seven languages.

To learn more about the author, please visit:

www.kimrichardsonbooks.com

Printed in Great Britain
by Amazon